DOCTOR WHO

VANDERDEKEN'S CHILDREN

CHRISTOPHER BULIS

BBC BOOKS

Published by BBC Worldwide Ltd,
Woodlands, 80 Wood Lane
London W12 0TT

First published 1998
Copyright © Christopher Bulis 1998
The moral right of the author has been asserted

Original series broadcast on the BBC
Format © BBC 1963
Doctor Who and TARDIS are trademarks of the BBC

ISBN 0 563 40590 2
Imaging by Black Sheep, copyright © BBC 1998
Cover illustration by Colin Howard.

Printed and bound in Great Britain by Mackays of Chatham
Cover printed by Belmont Press Ltd, Northampton

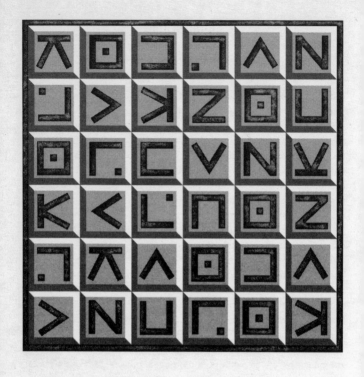

Keypad mechanism on derelict space vessel
See page 65

Chapter One
The Derelict

The steady tolling of the bell brought Samantha Jones back to the TARDIS's console room at a breathless sprint.

She'd been exploring a dark, twisting, flagstoned corridor, which she was reasonably certain had not been there the day before, when the first sonorous warning notes reverberated through the ship. Other vessels might have employed buzzers or sirens to alert their crews; the TARDIS had bells that would have graced any church tower. They communicated a sense of alarm far better than many more raucous alarms Sam had heard.

Completing a two-hundred-metre dash, Sam burst into the unlikely expanse of the console chamber.

'Vortex discontinuity,' the Doctor said in answer to her unspoken question, without looking up from the central console.

'Victorian ironwork gothic' had been one phrase that had come to Sam's mind shortly after she'd seen the improbable chamber for the first time. 'Jules Verne meets Canterbury Cathedral' had been another – once she had recovered from her initial shock.

The chamber's edges were dimly lit by assorted candelabra, torches and oil lamps, which Sam noted did not seem to burn down or need refilling quite as often as they should. In their soft pools of light were gathered an eclectic collection of easy chairs, side tables, statues, clocks and curios. Towering bookshelves and stacks of dark wooden drawers almost obscured the walls. Carelessly scattered rugs softened the flagstone floor, which gave way to parquet only in the chamber's very centre. Here was set the TARDIS's main control console, arched over by six massive lattice girders which met above it to support the upper half of the device the Doctor called the time rotor. This was a transparent cylinder in which two sets of glowing blue rods, like matching clusters of stalactites and stalagmites, rhythmically intermeshed and drew apart.

The lower half of the mechanism was enclosed by a hexagonal control board, and it was around this that the Doctor bustled. A Christmas-tree selection of multicoloured lights flickered and pulsed as he threw switches and levers, tapped brass-rimmed dials and consulted the kind of tumbler displays Sam had only ever seen elsewhere on an antique fruit machine.

It was absurd and improbable and yet, somehow, it worked.

As Sam crossed the floor to the console she felt a tremor run through the ship and grabbed one of the girders.

'Should I start getting worried about now?' she asked mildly above the throb of the console and the still tolling bell.

Even as the Doctor flashed her a quick reassuring grin the ringing ceased, leaving only an echo in her ears. The frantic pulsing of the control lights slowly settled.

'We're not about to be sucked into oblivion, if that's what you mean,' he said. Then he added disconcertingly, 'At least, not in the foreseeable future.'

Unfortunately, as Sam knew only too well, when you travelled with the Doctor the future often arrived earlier than you thought.

'So what's the panic about, then?'

'Any discontinuity in the space-time vortex is always a potential hazard,' the Doctor explained as he pulled the main monitor down on its heavy spring-loaded lazy-tong mount over the console. An image grew on its screen.

It was a flickering, coiling, writhing thing: as though a rainbow-hued snake was on fire and shedding its burning skins, each of which formed other snakes that coiled back on themselves to merge with the first snake again. Sam felt a knot forming between her eyes as she tried to make sense of what she was seeing. After a few seconds she gave up.

'Of course, this is only a four-dimensional approximation of a fifth-dimensional cross section of a multidimensional phenomenon,' the Doctor explained helpfully, continuing to stare at the apparition without apparent discomfort.

'So it's a psychedelic artist's nightmare,' Sam agreed, squinting at the object again through splayed fingers and frowning in disapproval.'But what does it do?'

'Well, it can disrupt the TARDIS's flight path as a storm at sea would a sailing ship. It could, for want of a better word, sink us if we got too close. So, like any hazard to shipping, it must be charted. If it's a natural phenomenon its magnitude and drift must be plotted...' He paused to tap a dial. 'If it's artificial, it must be investigated.'

'And this one's artificial?' Sam said.

The Doctor smiled broadly. 'I rather think so.'

It was a beguiling and dangerous smile. It spoke of a passionate delight in discovery, of intense curiosity coupled with boundless energy, of old knowledge and new horizons. Nobody else could wear it quite the way the Doctor did.

'Unfortunately I can't plot its parameters properly,' he admitted. 'But it seems to have at least one extension into normal space. We'll have to establish its co-ordinates there to fix a station point.'

The console lights reflected in blue eyes set in a lean face, with something of the look Sam had once seen in a character in a Pre-Raphaelite Brotherhood painting. His wild, shoulder length, curling, light-brown hair accentuated the impression, as did his frock coat and wing-collared shirt, pinned grey cravat, brightly patterned waistcoat and narrow trousers. He fitted his surroundings as well as any surroundings could fit him. A man out of time and yet of all times.

A steadily deepening mechanical pulsation reverberated through the console room. They were descending from the complex of higher dimensions, which enfolded all space and time, to those mundane four in which Sam had spent most of her life. The pulsation fell to a bass tone, there was a dull booming thud, then silence.

'Where are we?' Sam asked.

'Temporally in the year 3123 by your calendar. Physically we're several hundred light years from Earth in deep space. Somewhere close by should be the interface between the hyperspatial aspect of the vortex discontinuity and real space.'

She stared at the monitor. For a moment it displayed only a scattering of stars shining hard and untwinkling in the void. Then, as the external camera panned, an object came into view.

It was a cylindrical form with a curious projection rising from its mid-section, like a segment of some vast machine. There was a scale grid along the bottom of the monitor screen and Sam made a quick calculation.

'It's big – over four thousand metres long.'

'At least that,' the Doctor agreed.

Sam frowned and adjusted the monitor controls so that the image of the strange vessel swelled and overflowed the edges of the screen as she zoomed in. There was no sign of any interior illumination from portholes, or of navigation lights. In the pale starglow its hull appeared overall to be a dull green and was formed of numerous raised plates, scale-like slabs, nodules and branching pipes. Here and there she saw tints of maroon, brown and occasionally silver. Flared rings or flanges encircled both ends of the central shaft like monstrous bracelets. Eight tall spires or horns radiated perpendicularly from each of them into space. The conning tower, or whatever it actually was, that rose from the middle of the shaft resembled a conical stack of variously sized plates, pierced through by several vertical pipes rising from the main body of the craft. The not altogether agreeable image came to her of a tree stump smothered in bracket fungi.

Either the TARDIS or the alien craft must have been drifting, for, as Sam watched, the end of the massive hull slowly turned towards them and she saw it was hollow. The interior was a tunnel large enough to drive a supertanker through. But apparently it did not run the length of the craft, for there were no stars at the other end, only a fathomless blackness.

The whole aspect of the craft was unfamiliar and deeply alien.

'That's funny,' Sam said. 'The near end of that ship, or whatever it is, looks like it's out of focus...' She peered closer and caught her breath. 'Doctor, do you know, I can see stars through the fuzzy half of it?'

'No, but if you'll sing it I'll hum along.' His expression became momentarily apologetic under Sam's withering glare. 'It appears to be translucent because part of the craft is extending into hyperspace,' he explained more soberly. 'That's the source of the discontinuity we detected.'

'Have you ever seen anything like it before?'

'No. But then even I am not familiar with every vessel ever put into space.'

'Isn't there some sort of data file you can check? Jane's *All the Galaxy's Spaceships*, sort of thing?'

'There is, and I consulted it while you were gawping at our find. Nothing like it is listed – but then not every ship gets registered.'

Sam felt the great hulk looming intimidatingly at them. She took a deep breath and tried to sound offhand: 'Then I guess we'll just have to check it out for ourselves.'

'Unfortunately, that might not be possible,' the Doctor said, frowning at the console displays. 'The craft's emanating an unstable and very powerful energy field in real space as well as the higher dimensions. It means I can't materialise the TARDIS much closer to it than this. However, as you may have noticed, we're moving towards it at a steadily increasing velocity. The craft must have considerable mass to influence us at this distance.'

'Will we hit it?' Sam asked, her voice betraying nothing of the alarm she felt.

'Fortunately no. Due to the interference we materialised with some intrinsic motion. That, combined with the attraction of the alien ship, has put us on a hyperbolic trajectory. We'll make our closest approach in half an hour or so, then pull away again.'

'Well, have you got any spacesuits with flight packs on board? We could buzz over and take a closer look while we pass it.'

'Possibly… somewhere,' the Doctor said absently, running his lean quick fingers over the controls like some maestro pianist. 'But I'd like to filter out some of this interference first. It might affect the flight pack circuitry at close range, and it wouldn't do to get ourselves marooned over there, would it?'

As he worked, Sam idly tracked the monitor image about, examining the alien craft curiously. What was its purpose? That huge central shaft couldn't possibly be a drive tube, could it? Perhaps the whole thing was some form of spacegoing dry dock.

Then a twinkle of light beyond the edge of the craft caught her eye. The image on the monitor shrank as she zoomed the camera out to encompass a wider angle of space. Two other ships appeared, standing off on opposite sides of the alien vessel. And even on this long view she could see internal lights sparkling on them.

'Doctor, we've got company.'

The Doctor looked up, his eyes narrowing. 'So we have. Apparently somebody else detected the same energy disturbance we did. How long have they been here? I wonder.'

'Perhaps that thing belongs to them.'

'I don't think so. Those ships are of quite different designs.'

Sam enlarged the picture and saw immediately what he meant.

The ship on the left of the alien craft had a slender, gleaming white hull decorated with green and red livery stripes. Several rows of large observation windows glowed along its sides. At least three domes rose over its upper decks and within them she could see what looked like greenery and the sparkle of water. Everything about it suggested luxury, grace and, improbably in airless space, streamlined speed. Clearly a passenger liner.

The ship opposite it and nearer to them was, by contrast, an unprepossessing, dull, grey, compact bullet. Pods mounted on short outriggers ringed its tail section while unidentifiable teardrop blisters broke the smooth curve of its nose. Lights showed from a mere handful of portholes. There was nothing graceful about its lines, merely functional efficiency. It looked nastily like a warship, Sam thought uneasily.

Even as she watched, the warship – if that was what it was – rolled slightly towards the alien craft. One of the hull blisters split apart to reveal a point of blue-white light within it.

'Force-beam projector,' the Doctor said.

A faint path of sparkling radiance sprang into being between it and the larger ship, like dust motes caught in a beam of sunlight. It flickered about the strangely textured hull, but did not seem to quite touch it. After half a minute the beam was cut off.

'No luck,' the Doctor observed. 'The interference is preventing them locking on. They'll have to rig an actual tow line if they want to move her. Ah, the liner's trying it now.'

A beam, projected from a hatch in the liner's hull, also scattered across the alien ship without apparently finding any purchase. After a few seconds it too was extinguished.

'I think they're as puzzled about that ship as we are,' the Doctor mused, his hands dancing across the controls. 'I wonder if they're discussing the matter...'

A crackle of static issued from a speaker grille, then a distorted voice. 'Ship-to-ship channel,' said the Doctor, making some fine adjustments. The speaker's words became clearer.

'... a mistake on your part to think we have given up just yet, Commander,' said a woman's voice firmly. 'We are not relinquishing our claim.'

'There's a visual signal as well,' said the Doctor. The external view on the monitor faded into an indistinct blur for a moment and then resolved itself into the head and shoulders of a strong-featured woman of about fifty, wearing a merchant navy captain's uniform and a determined expression.

'May I remind you,' she continued, 'that we discovered this derelict within the borders of our protectorate zone, and under interstellar convention we have first rights to salvage.'

'Leaving aside the fact that we also have claims on this sector of space,' a man's voice responded scathingly, 'may I in turn remind you, Captain Lanchard, that discovering a vessel first does not, legally, grant you exclusive rights to it.'

The Doctor flashed a bright grin at Sam. 'Let's see if I can conjure up a split screen.'

The screen image divided into two to show a man's head and shoulders. Sam smiled weakly. 'State-of-the-art. Impressive.'

The man on the screen was also in uniform, but one of a darker and more severe cut than the woman's. He continued: 'Until you have succeeded in landing a boarding party or making a secure tow, we too may attempt salvage as long as our activities do not hazard

7

your ship.'

'Commander Vega,' Lanchard said stoutly, 'I am pleased to hear you are so familiar with Federation law, even though you are not a signatory to its statutes. I trust you will abide by its rulings in this matter. I'm sure you wouldn't want any word of any infringements of that law to reach the Federation council.'

'As I'm sure neither would you,' Vega replied smoothly, 'in the current circumstances.'

'Then you will allow us to continue with the salvage unhindered?'

Vega smiled coldly. 'You don't seem to have had much success so far, despite your so-called superior technology. Perhaps we shall have better luck. Meanwhile we shall be observing your actions closely – just in case you should suffer some mishap, for instance.'

'Is that a threat?' Lanchard snapped back.

'Not at all,' Vega replied unabashed. 'But in uncertain situations such as this, dealing with alien technology, accidents do happen.'

'Oh dear,' sighed the Doctor, and voiced his concern at the same time as Lanchard.

'That sounds like a threat to me.'

'But why should I feel the need to threaten you? After all, what threat does a mere liner pose to a fully armed front line Nimosian warship?'

Lanchard smiled coldly. 'Commander Vega, as we are not actually at war, I trust that the relative strengths of our vessels will remain academic. Please remember there are over two thousand civilians on the *Cirrandaria*, some of them Federation citizens.'

Vega smiled. 'I might point out that the Federation will not look kindly upon someone who risks the safety of their citizens by attempting to salvage an alien vessel which, in all probability, will prove quite worthless –'

A voice interrupted him, speaking softly from off-screen. He turned back to face Lanchard with a scowl further darkening his stern features. 'It seems I underestimated you, Captain. Were you keeping me talking as a distraction?'

'What do you mean?'

'There is a small object approaching us. A one-man shuttle or a spying device, perhaps?'

'I don't know what you're talking about…' She glanced aside for a moment and spoke to somebody out of shot, then turned back to the camera. 'Apparently we have it on our screens as well now, but I've no idea what it is.'

'Its trajectory will take it between ourselves and the derelict,' Vega said. 'Have you modified a probe to overcome the interference?'

'We're working on the interference problem – just as you are, I imagine,' Lanchard admitted. 'But none of our shuttles or probes have been deployed.'

Vega was receiving more whispered information. 'It appears to be unmanned, with an unfamiliar energy signature.' He frowned. 'It will pass close by us. As it is not displaying a standard navigation beacon I could consider that a hostile act.'

'Perhaps it came from the alien craft,' Lanchard suggested.

'Impossible. We would have observed anything leaving the craft. And we detect no other vessel in the vicinity but your own. What are you trying to do, Captain?'

Lanchard sighed. 'Nothing! You're acting like a typical paranoid Nimosian.'

'And perhaps you are being a typically devious Emindian. Recall the probe.'

'How can I? It's not ours.'

'Then you will not object to its destruction – since it is clearly a hazard to navigation.'

'Go ahead. But if you think a show of force is going to make me abandon my position, you're sadly mistaken.'

'We shall see, Captain.' Vega turned aside: 'Main battery, target unidentified object…'

The Doctor frowned. 'What are they talking about? There's no other ship around here.'

'Besides us,' Sam remarked idly.

Nodding solemnly, the Doctor cut the visual element of the intercepted conversation and an image of the Nimosian warship filled the screen. Sam saw that another of the teardrop blisters on the forward section had opened to reveal a turret bearing a complex-looking coiled barrel. It lifted and swung about to point directly at them.

'Fire!' said Vega over the sound channel.

'Doctor!' Sam shouted.

The screen filled with searing light as an incandescent plasma pulse enveloped the TARDIS.

Chapter Two
The Diplomat

A curious sound echoed along the narrow, dimly lit aisles between the stacks of cargo containers.

It was a rasping sigh, rising and falling rhythmically and steadily deepening in pitch. A flashing light appeared, hovering in midair like a will-o'-the-wisp. Then a ghostly object materialised under it and took on a solid form. The sound became a harsh throaty whir, then ceased abruptly with a final dull reverberating thud. Externally the new arrival resembled a battered British police public call box – a device made obsolete by advances in communications technology over a thousand years before the current time.

The lantern on its roof ceased to flash. A narrow door in its side opened and the Doctor and Sam stepped out. For a moment the console room was visible behind them, its spaciousness somehow contained within an object no more than two metres wide and three high. Then the Doctor closed the door on the pocket universe of folded time and space, leaving only its incongruous exterior on show.

'What do you know,' said Sam. 'A narrow escape. Haven't had one of those for hours.'

The Doctor was looking about him with satisfaction. 'Right on target: the liner's cargo hold. The TARDIS seems to have an affinity for such places. I feel quite at home. Many's the eventful hour I've spent in them hiding, being arrested as a stowaway or evading the clutches of some shambling monstrosity with bad breath. Actually, cargo holds are the ideal spot for a clandestine arrival. Nobody about to ask you awkward questions. At least not usually...'

'You should write a book on them,' said Sam. 'Bestseller material, cargo holds.' The Doctor looked at her sharply for traces of sarcasm, but her blue eyes were wide and innocent. 'So now we're free again with a single bound,' she continued, 'what do we do next?'

'First, find out what course of action these people intend to take regarding the alien ship. I don't want them interfering with it until I've had a chance to examine it more closely myself. There's obviously no love lost between them and the crew of the warship. They mustn't goad each other into acting rashly.' He looked about him again. 'We might as well work from here; clearly drifting in free space close to the derelict will only incite more misunderstandings.'

'And you think they'll take kindly to stowaways?'

'They won't have to,' the Doctor said mildly. 'We'll establish ourselves legitimately to prevent awkward questions being asked. We might have to stay for a while and somebody would inevitably notice if we kept popping down here. Yes. Let us be upwardly mobile and acquire some conventional lodgings more suited to our status.'

'You mean find some cabins. And just what status do you have in mind?'

'Something appropriate to the circumstances which we may turn to our advantage should the need arise.' He narrowed his eyes thoughtfully. 'Can we take advantage of our relative isolation? I wonder. What were Vega and Lanchard saying about the Federation? Ah, yes. Just a minute.'

And he slipped back inside the TARDIS again, leaving Sam alone to contemplate the limited attractions of the cargo hold. She kicked a shelf bracket moodily. 'Real bestseller material.'

Being the Doctor, he actually did rejoin her one minute later.

He was carrying a coil of cargo binding tape identical to that securing the cartons around them. With Sam's help he wrapped several bands around the TARDIS, still allowing room for them to duck between them to use the inward-opening door, and tied a replica cargo label in place. It bore only their names – their room numbers and destination were blank.

'We'll fill in the details later,' he explained. 'Now you'd better take this.'

He fished out a couple of thin rectangles of plastic card from his pocket and handed one to Sam.

'Ever thought of going into forgery in a big way, Doctor?' she said, as she examined the impressive identity card bearing her face, coded retina pattern and thumbprint. 'If this is me, who are you?'

He showed her his card. She whistled.

'Can even *you* carry that off?'

'Naturally,' he assured her airily. 'If one is going to be an impostor, one might as well impost in a big way. Now, shall we see if we can find a lift?'

The hold's crew door was locked, but a few seconds' work with the Doctor's sonic screwdriver persuaded it to open for them. At the end of the utilitarian corridor beyond was a lift. Several deck levels were listed beside the control panel, together with their amenities. Sam thought the Hydrosolaria and Games Courts sounded interesting, but the Doctor chose Passenger Deck 2: Library. The lift ascended silently, and in a few seconds the doors had opened on to a wide, thickly carpeted corridor. The Doctor held Sam back for a moment until a couple of people, casually dressed in shorts and brightly patterned, loose shirts, walked past. Then they slipped out. As the lift doors closed behind them Sam saw they were labelled CREW ONLY.

Following the signs, they found the library with its banks of book disks, reader screens and computer stations. The room contained only a handful of people and the Doctor rapidly found a free terminal. He selected 'keyboard function only', cutting the audio responses.

'Just make sure nobody looks over my shoulder for a couple of minutes,' he said quietly.

As Sam kept watch his fingers flew across the keyboard faster than any human hands could move. His own eyes were wide, intense and unblinking, a slight smile turning up the corner of his mouth. A few times the screen flashed in protest at his delving into files he should not have accessed, but evidently whatever passwords and security locks the system possessed were no match for his hacking skills. He really looks like some wild musician, Sam thought, playing a symphony of deception.

The Doctor tapped the last key with a flourish and sat back, flexing his fingers.

'You can relax now. We are officially passengers of the G&C Lines Star Cruiser *Cirrandaria*, registered on Emindar. We only boarded the ship at its third port of call, Renaris 5, two days ago, which explains why our faces will be unfamiliar to the other passengers and crew. We have two adjoining first-class cabins. Note their numbers and deck levels in case anybody asks. We'll probably be invited to sit at the Captain's table when the computer, belatedly, alerts the steward to our eminence.'

Sam shook her head in amused disbelief, and the Doctor beamed and flicked an imaginary speck of dust from his coat collar. 'A little luxury once in a while never hurt anyone,' he observed. Then with a sudden rush of energy he sprang to his feet. 'But that's for later. First we must find out exactly what's going on here.'

There was a folded pamphlet lying on a side table bearing the legend, 'Guide to the SC *Cirrandaria*'. The Doctor opened it to reveal a plan of the ship. Scanning it intently, he strode out of the library, turned sharply left and disappeared down the corridor. A moment later he reappeared heading in the opposite direction, followed by Sam, who was trying to keep a straight face.

Captain Coryn Lanchard glared across at the distinguished personage sitting opposite, and wished once again that J. Kale Rexton, HC, had chosen another ship to grace with his presence; preferably one belonging to another shipping line. There was still a military edge to his manner, though he'd been a Councillor for ten years and on the High Council for three. He was tipped as the next First Councillor when Kapour stepped aside, which didn't make the task of facing him down any easier. That was why she'd invited him to join her in her day cabin, where they could speak in private. There was a possibility she would have to use language unsuitable for the ears of junior officers, and of which G&C Lines' board of directors might not approve.

'I'm as much a patriot as you are, Councillor,' she assured him, as soon as they were seated. 'But I have a duty to my passengers and crew which must take priority. I have been as firm as I can with Vega, but at the first sign of any physical threat either from him or that alien ship, I will have to give way.'

Rexton leaned forward, chin thrust out intimidatingly even as his clear blue eyes transfixed her.

'I don't doubt your patriotism, Captain, just your inexperience in situations like this. If you stand fast the Nimosians will not dare to use force against us. The offworlders aboard are a guarantee of that.'

'And you heard me point that very thing out to Vega. But suppose he decides to call my bluff?'

Rexton made a dismissive gesture, as though brushing aside the lives of almost three thousand people as inconsequential.

'It is a calculated risk. All that matters is that the Nimosians must not be allowed to take possession of that craft out there.'

Lanchard slammed the arm of her chair with her clenched fist. 'But why? What's so special about it? Give me some reason for all this.'

Rexton did not rise to her show of anger and his face merely became stonier. 'I'm afraid I cannot tell you anything more at this time. Just be assured it is a matter of the highest priority. The security of Emindar itself may be at stake here. You must hold this position until a relief force arrives.'

'But when will that be? We're a long way from the nearest naval base.'

'They'll come at maximum speed, I assure you. Meanwhile you will remain on station and make every effort to board the craft before the Nimosians.'

'You are aware,' she pointed out carefully, 'that this may be a first-contact situation – if there are any crew left on that ship. We are neither equipped nor trained for this sort of operation. Presumably the relief force will be. There are rules about handling such situations which –'

'There are *guidelines*,' Rexton corrected her. 'And they are subject to change depending on circumstance. You can be sure the Nimosians won't let themselves be hindered by them in the least, so we cannot afford to be either. The evidence suggests the vessel is abandoned, but should it prove otherwise I know all ships' captains are briefed on the correct procedure. If you feel unequal to the task I will take full responsibility for the consequences and you may complain to the proper authorities in due course. But meanwhile you will do as I tell you.'

He didn't raise his voice particularly, but then there was no need. She noted that Rexton's hands as they rested on his knees were clenched so that the corded tendons showed across their backs. His greying hair still bristled in a severe military cut, reminding her that he was still a general in the spacefleet reserve. His eyes were steady, implacable and determined. Lanchard knew then that he was absolutely set on his course of action and that no arguments, reasoned or otherwise, were going to sway him. She could call in her master-at-arms and have him confined to his quarters, of course, but then her career would be over as soon as they reached home port. It would be she who would have to compromise.

'At least let me have the lifeboats readied in case some sort of emergency arises. That can't do any harm.'

Rexton considered for a moment. 'Very well. But it must be done unobtrusively.'

'Naturally,' Lanchard said. 'We don't want to alarm the passengers.'

'Not them,' Rexton corrected her, 'the Nimosians. They mustn't detect any change in our situation or they might interpret it as a sign of weakness.' Before Lanchard could respond he continued, 'Now, how are the modifications to that shuttle proceeding? Your engineer said she thought she could shield its systems from the interference. Then you must call for volunteers to take possession of the alien vessel. The crew will understand when you tell them the future of Emindar may be at stake.'

The *Cirrandaria*'s port-side upper promenade deck was thronged with passengers looking through its multilaminated and screened observation windows at the alien vessel. Most were human, or at least humanoid, with only a sprinkling of more exotic species. All were too intent to recognise Sam and the Doctor as newcomers as they mingled with them.

Some sixty degrees to the left of the derelict, and also receiving its share of the passengers' attention, was the irregular speck of light that

16

marked the position of the Nimosian warship. Sam saw that the stars appeared to be turning slowly past the other two ships, even though both were maintaining their relative positions.

'Are we in orbit about that thing?' Sam wondered, staring at the derelict.

The Doctor had drawn out a gold hunter pocket watch and was timing their motion.

'Apparently,' he concluded after a minute, snapping the lid of his watch shut again. 'It must mass at least as much as a small asteroid, which suggests it contains degenerate matter. Stabilised neutronium, perhaps. That might go some way to explain the distortion it's causing in hyperspace.'

'But why would anybody want to stack a ship full of neutronium?' Sam wondered.

'Ah, now that's a question for later. Meanwhile, mouth shut and ears open...'

The air was full of the usual mixture of gossip and rumour – ten per cent reasonable, ninety per cent wildly ill-informed – that permeated all such gatherings, dominated by the voices of those self-opinionated few who always thought they could run things better than the professionals. But gradually, from a score of eavesdropped conversations, they assembled a picture of recent events.

The *Cirrandaria* had detected an energy discharge of unknown origins some eight hours earlier. The Captain had announced they were dropping out of hyperspace to investigate, as they were obliged to do by interstellar convention in case a vessel was in distress. They discovered the alien ship, but aborted a close approach when the erratic energy field it radiated began to disrupt the *Cirrandaria*'s systems. At about this time one of the VIP passengers had been seen making his way to the bridge, and it was assumed he was now advising the Captain. Why the alien ship should be worth such attention nobody knew, but there was no shortage of speculation on the possibilities.

There had been no reply to multichannel friendship messages or even the emergency signal lamp, so the nature of its crew, if any, was still a mystery. The arrival of the Nimosian ship just two hours ago, which had apparently intercepted their report of the discovery of the derelict, had rapidly polarised opinion on board. Apparently Emindar and Nimos had a long history of border skirmishes and minor wars going back over a century, and there was clearly no love lost between them. The Emindian nationals, who made up the bulk of the passenger list, were almost unanimous in their approval of the Captain's firm stand against them, while the smaller percentage of offworld tourists were less happy. They could see no point in risking a violent confrontation over a piece of space flotsam, however large and mysterious it might be, and several had already made representations to the Captain. Reportedly they were less than satisfied with the assurances they had received in return.

The evident fact that the Nimosians could get no closer to the derelict than they could was viewed with a mixture of relief and surprise. The recent Nimosian gunfire had created a wave of alarm that was only just now dissipating. Few seemed to have any idea what the Nimosians had been firing at, but the die-hards continued to proclaim that if it was intended as an act of intimidation, it was wasted on them.

Finding they had a section of window to themselves for a moment, Sam said quietly to the Doctor, 'It looks as though it's a standoff. No need for us to charge in to save the day if nobody can get any closer than this.'

'I hope that eventuality will not arise,' the Doctor said. 'But unfortunately your species are amazingly stubborn creatures. It's the Everest syndrome: it has to be climbed because it's there. An unknown force prevents them from indulging their curiosity, therefore it must be overcome.' He smiled slightly. 'Perhaps that's why I like them so much.'

Sam considered the alien vessel in its slowly drifting frame of stars. 'But is it really dangerous? Maybe it's just an old wreck with degenerating power cells inside shorting out and creating the disturbance.'

'And how do you account for the blurring of half the ship?'

18

'Some sort of hyperdrive motor accident? Maybe that's why the crew abandoned it.'

The Doctor's eyes followed the direction of her own, as though trying to penetrate the hull of the vessel by the sheer intensity of his gaze. 'Possibly. But I have a... boding about it.'

'Pardon?'

'An ominous presentiment. I feel I've seen it before somewhere, yet I know I haven't.'

Sam gasped theatrically. 'You mean you've got a premonition of impending doom? *Déjà vu* and stuff like that?'

'If you like.'

A shiver ran through Sam, despite her jovial air. 'Well, maybe they'll get bored and give up after a few days. We can have a bit of a holiday here until they leave, then tackle it at our own speed.' She looked around her with approval at the long broad sweep of the promenade. 'I could enjoy myself in a place like this. What do you think?'

The Doctor did not reply, apparently lost in thought.

There was a denser swirl of onlookers halfway along the promenade. As the Doctor and Sam drew closer it became evident that a man and woman, clearly celebrities of some sort, were at the centre of it. Some of the crowd were asking for their autographs.

The man, Sam acknowledged as she caught her first proper sight of him past other people's heads, really was tall, dark and handsome. He had a strong jaw, deep, brown eyes, a wide sensuous mouth and boldly drawn eyebrows. He was smiling and chatting to those around him in a very easy manner, suggesting familiarity with being the centre of attention.

He knows exactly how impressive he looks, Sam thought, *and carries himself accordingly.*

His companion was blonde and equally attractive, if less self-consciously so. She seemed intent on using the complex and expensive-looking camera slung around her neck, and was busy taking pictures of both the alien ship and occasionally the crowd around her. They'd already seen several other passengers doing the same thing, but there was something more fluent and assured in her

19

actions that distinguished the professional from the amateur.

'Now there is a true artist,' the Doctor commented, as they joined the fringe of the crowd.

'Why?'

'Because she's recording not only the obvious focus of interest but also those witnessing the scene. She's searching for the response in others that will put the spectacle into context.'

The photographer caught sight of the Doctor and gave him a look of searching interest. He hooked his thumbs into his lapels, lifted his chin and struck a pose. She grinned and snapped a couple of rapid shots of him. The Doctor smiled back at her and made a slight bow.

Sam felt a pang of jealousy, which she tried with only partial success to smother. Chiding herself for raking over old bones, she looked away.

There was a shorter, older man orbiting round the couple, who seemed to be attempting to marshal the crowd.

'Now Mr Delray and Ms Wynter just want to take a look like the rest of you,' he was saying loudly. 'Please give them a little room!'

'What do you think of the alien ship, Mr Delray?' somebody called out.

'Must be quite a problem to park,' he replied lightly, causing a ripple of laughter.

His voice exactly matched his appearance: deep and resonant with a hint of gravel. The man's a classic cliché film star, Sam thought dismissively, finding herself staring at him nevertheless.

'Why do you think the Nimosians are interested in it?' somebody else asked.

'Even a burned-out hunk of scrap would interest them – it would still be an improvement on their own ships. But we found it first, and if they don't like it that's too bad. They've got to learn that's the way civilised people behave.'

That reply brought forth a general murmur of approval.

'What do you think of the alien ship, Ms Wynter?'

'I wish we could get closer,' the blonde woman said. 'It's got a wonderful textural quality to it, almost as though it was sculpted.

20

Whoever built it must be very different from us. This might be the first contact with a new race. Even if it's abandoned we could learn a lot about them.'

'Would you like to take a look inside it?'

'Of course.'

Sam saw Delray glance disapprovingly at his companion, then quickly change the expression to a resigned smile.

'Lyset's always ready to go anywhere for a picture,' he commented. 'Even when it might be dangerous and she should know better,' he added meaningfully.

Before Lyset Wynter could respond to this, somebody called out loudly, 'The warship's moving!'

They all flowed to the rails again.

The angle between the Nimosian craft and the derelict had begun to narrow. Clearly it was edging towards the alien vessel. Then the slow drift of stars caused by the *Cirrandaria*'s own orbit about the derelict changed as the liner activated its own manoeuvring thrusters.

The public-address system came to life.

'We are making a minor adjustment to our orbit to maintain our relative position to the Nimosian ship,' said a reassuring voice. 'There is no cause for alarm.'

A fresh babble of voices broke out as they strained their eyes to see what was happening. Sam looked around for somewhere to get a better view. There were several large pairs of binoculars mounted on pedestals along the rails rather like those found at seaside resorts, presumably so the passengers could observe the sights directly rather than over the ship's screens. But they were all occupied. The Doctor reached around the large man in a floral shirt who was monopolising the nearest of them and tapped him urgently on the shoulder. As he turned about, surprised to find nobody there, the Doctor slipped nimbly between him and the instrument and pressed his face to the eyepieces.

'What's happening?' Sam demanded, ignoring the large man's angry glare.

'They're holding a stationary position with the thrusters,' the Doctor said. 'A hatch has opened… a small craft's coming out… It's moving very slowly towards the alien ship.' He pulled back from the eyepieces and looked resignedly at Sam. 'Sometimes your kind are too ingenious for their own good. I was hoping they hadn't thought of that.'

Chapter Three
Pendulum

The service pod hung between the *Indomitable* and the alien vessel, being lowered like a cautious spider on the end of an almost invisible, woven, single-molecule line. Within the pod, Technician Arvel Kerven mentally reminded himself, once again, that the line's breaking strain was ten thousand kilos. It was not that he seriously expected it to fail, he merely wanted nothing to distract him from the task in hand.

Kerven did not consider himself a particularly brave man; indeed his colleagues, if asked, would probably say he was too cautious and unimaginative to be courageous. He had volunteered because he was the best-qualified person to carry out the mission. But it would provide a useful talking point. Next year, when he retired from active service and took up his tutorship at the space engineering sciences college, he would use the incident as an illustration of how the job of maintenance and EVA pod operative could have its unusual moments.

'Twenty-five hundred metres run out,' came the voice of his commander, First Tech Reng, over the comlink. 'Anything to report?'

'No, Chief,' Kerven replied. 'Internal systems still functioning normally. Your signal's breaking up a little, though.'

The transmission was conducted via a comm laser feeding into the small receptor dish on the dome of the pod. This system should have been immune to all normal interference, yet already there was a distinct background crackle and wavering of tone. By the time he reached the alien craft conventional communications might be impossible. However, that eventuality, and all other foreseeable contingencies, had been provided for.

Of course, that still left the unforeseeable.

The already cramped interior of the pod also contained chemical heater packs, spare oxygen cylinders and a catalytic carbon dioxide scrubber unit. These, together with Kerven's pressure suit – which he was wearing with the visor up – would substitute for the pod's own systems should they fail due to the interference from the alien vessel. That same interference made remote operation of the pod impossible and necessitated Kerven's presence. Despite everything, Kerven felt a certain satisfaction in knowing there were some situations that still required direct human presence.

As he passed the twenty-seven-hundred-metre mark he began to notice a faint but distinct sensation of weight within the tiny cabin. That was almost unknown inside a pod except for the acceleration forces generated when its small drive motor was operating. Kerven checked the direct-reading mechanical-strain gauge on the line: it was creeping up to a little over twenty kilos.

The bulk of the alien ship, visible through the direct-vision ports that ringed the top of the pod, was filling a quarter of the sky. As he examined its dimly lit form he was assailed by a most unexpected sense of *déjà vu*, which momentarily disconcerted him until he identified its source. It was a historical vid he had seen showing the descent of a primitive miniature submarine into the sunless depths of the ocean to salvage a sunken surface vessel. Yes, the parallel was a good one. Even he could easily imagine that the stars around him were flecks of plankton caught in the lights of his submersible, and that the craft below was really a familiar vessel with its outlines strangely distorted by marine growths, silt and decay. How often did life repeat itself, albeit on a grander scale? Here he was descending through the depths of space towards a derelict many thousand times larger than that ancient lost ship, and certainly of far stranger origins.

At twenty-nine hundred metres' deployment, the soft whir of the air pump, normally almost inaudible, rose to a shrill whine, stuttered, then recovered again. But he could hear its tone deepening raggedly. He cut its power, opened an oxygen cylinder and activated one of the chemical replenisher packs clipped to the wall beside his head. He watched the sensitised patches on the outside of the pack until they changed colour, then reported his actions.

'Have shut down air system due to interference. Backup operating normally.'

He felt a slight jerk as his descent ceased.

'Are any other systems affected?' Reng asked, his words fading and intermittently drowned by the wash of static.

'Not yet, Chief…'

The gyro motor began to falter and Kerven cut its power.

'Correction,' he said. 'Gyro motor has just malfunctioned. Letting it freewheel. Should be enough inertia stored to stabilise me for touchdown. Continue lowering.'

'Understood,' Reng replied, and Kerven's descent resumed.

At thirty-one hundred metres the lights on the control panel began to flicker. The atmospheric-integrity alarm gave a half-hearted wail, then was silent. Calmly Kerven disabled it in turn. His suit would protect him if there was a genuine loss of pressure.

After another hundred metres the controls of the pod's thruster pack flickered and one gave a brief pop of expelled gas. He hurriedly cut their circuit along with the rest of the operating controls. It was better to travel inert than with systems he could not rely upon. Now the only illumination in the pod's interior was the soft green glow emanating from the bioluminescent tube he had stuck to the wall at the beginning of his descent. He reported back again. Reng's reply was almost unintelligible but Kerven thought he could detect a note of concern behind the words. Who'd have thought it of the old man?

At thirty-three hundred metres the comlink finally failed and Reng's voice vanished into a howl of static.

Kerven cut its power and uncoiled the bypass optical fibre that linked directly with the external dish, fitted a cup over the end and placed the lens of his powerful hand torch to it. The simple chemical cell and filament bulb functioned normally as he tapped out the pulses. The light should be clearly visible through the telescope the *Indomitable* had constantly trained on him. He withdrew the torch and applied his eye to the cup.

The slowly pulsing comm laser flickered back the reply, RECEIVED: CONTINUE LOWERING.

When he was a thousand metres above the derelict, spotlights from the *Indomitable* blazed into life, their invisible beams illuminating the vast hull in two-hundred-metre-wide circles with the cold starkness of bright moonlight. Suddenly Kerven found the alien ship had become an artificial landscape under a coal-black sky, with all but the brightest stars washed from sight. The *Indomitable* was a tiny brilliant point directly above him, the Emindian liner a dimmer irregular speck two-thirds the way down towards the derelict's lateral horizon. He was descending equidistant from the ringed ends and just below the derelict's tower-like superstructure – hopefully as near to the centre of gravity as they could estimate it. The line load showed he and the pod now had a combined weight of almost fifty kilos in the derelict's unnaturally steep gravitational gradient.

Kerven studied the vast hull the best he could through binoculars without their normal electronic augmentation.

It seemed to be a single mass of pipework, of all sizes and cross sections. Some, raised on short pylons, ran straight and unbroken from one end of the vessel to the other like monotrain tubes, while others wriggled like snakes: curling, branching and merging with each other. Some of them had to be twenty metres across. If they were conduits of some kind, what could they possibly carry? Briefly he turned his attention to the blurred end of the ship, but could make out no more details than he had from further out. Radar pulses had come back oddly distorted from that section, and until they understood its nature he had been briefed to keep well clear. His immediate task was to find some spot where he could set down safely.

At a hundred metres up he signalled a halt while he surveyed the surface beneath him closely. The pod bobbed slightly as, four kilometres above him, Chief Reng was playing the line in an attempt to steady him against the intermittent action of *Indomitable*'s thrusters, which were holding the ship stationary. The increasing weight of his pod must have been causing the *Indomitable* to drift and Kerven knew Commander Vega could not risk the ship getting any closer to the derelict. The motion was unsettling. Kerven gulped dangerously for a moment and hurriedly cut in the gyro to impart what remaining stabilisation it could, and then forced himself to concentrate on the topography of his potential landing site. A pod was no place to be motion sick.

A little to one side of his current position was a node where a dozen conduits converged, feeding into a structure resembling a flat-topped drum some thirty metres across. Close by was one of the 'monotube' support pylons, arching over like a flying buttress on an ancient cathedral, to bury itself amid the bundles of pipes and tubes. It was of solid latticework construction, probably connected to the craft's main structural frame, and looked sound enough for his purpose.

He signalled, LEFT 150. By the convention he had agreed with Reng before he started, the tower-like structure was up, the opposite down, and the two long arms of the vessel left and right.

After a few seconds he felt the line tighten and he began to drift along the length of the alien craft. Using direct linkage he extended the pod's external manipulator arms, flexed them experimentally, then left them locked spread wide.

Just before he reached the pipework node he signalled: STOP. The line tightened, swinging him up in a long lazy arc over the target area, then back again. The pendulum-like motion faded surprisingly after only a couple of minutes. It must have been damped by interaction with the alien ship's energy field. At least the interference effect had some benefits.

When he was still again, he signalled, DOWN 50.

He felt the drop this time as the drum surface spread to meet him. He hoped the *Indomitable* would hold still for the next few seconds. He halted, swaying and bobbing. He estimated his distance again and sent, DOWN 30.

Another drop. He was now ten metres clear but drifting towards one edge of the drum top. Quickly he sent, FREE.

The line ran out on a friction clutch. The multiple shadows of the pod cast by the *Indomitable*'s searchlights merged into one. Kerven braced himself. There was a thud and bounce, then the pod fell forward on to its outstretched arms, making a tripod with its base. Twenty metres of slack line fell behind him, then stopped. He was down.

Kerven found he had been holding his breath and exhaled shakily. He sent, DOWN SAFE.

With the normal monitors nonfunctional, he checked for external radiation by observing a simple gold-leaf electroscope and self-developing film strip mounted on the pod's outer shell. After five minutes the levels still showed normal for open space. He signalled, COMMENCING EVA, then closed and sealed his visor and activated his suit's simple chemical life-support pack. It was good for only two hours but he had replacement sets. Hopefully his task would not take that long. He shut down the pod's improvised air system and cautiously opened the purge valve. His suit tightened about him slightly as the air hissed away. He unlatched the access hatch set in the back of the pod and climbed slowly out on to the surface of the alien ship.

The ground under his boots glowed a dull crimson under the vertical light from the *Indomitable*. But the colour was not constant, and he could see swirls of deeper purple mingled with the occasional streak of surprisingly brilliant green. The marbled pattern suggested half-mixed paint allowed to dry. He could even make out a faint ridged pattern matching the swirling colours. The surface felt hard and unyielding, and he could not determine whether it was metal, ceramic or some unknown composite. At least the texture gave good traction in the local gravity field, which, he estimated, was about one-half standard.

Kerven looked about and, for a moment, was overwhelmed by the sheer intimidating artificiality of the structure. Behind his back the massive cylinder of the hull curved away sharply. Before him was the base of the encrusted tower, which by his orientation was tilted almost horizontally, its plated growths and stanchions forming a veritable forest that faded into the shadows beyond the reach of the *Indomitable*'s lights. To either side the twisted mat of pipework flowed towards the far ends of the ship where, two kilometres distant, the flaring spire rings appeared like horned moons rising over the edge of the world, the one to the right made even more mysterious by virtue of its eerie translucency.

Suddenly he felt very alone, without even the usual open comlink for company, and he found his hand sliding to his holstered regulation pistol as though seeking reassurance from its presence. With an effort he drew his hand back, reminding himself that he was a practical engineer and he had a job to do.

He unclipped the line from the pod and fastened it to his suit harness. Its drag would be negligible over a short distance and it meant he could be hauled back up to the ship in an emergency. It would also serve, once he fixed it to the support pylon, as a guide down which they would lower the heavier tow cable.

They had used all their store of single-molecule mooring line, emergency repair filament and tape to fashion the tow cable. Reng had estimated maximum working load would only be two hundred and fifty tonnes. Even if it had been greater, the *Indomitable*'s engines were incapable of accelerating the huge mass of the derelict to any useful velocity. But a token gesture was all that was required. Simply having it under controlled tow would give them legal possession and so deny the Emindians any claim.

Kerven could send and receive signals directly, now he was clear of the pod, so he clipped the torch to his belt. Then he walked over to the edge of the drum and stared out across the humps and valleys of the pipes.

Seeing them closer to, he became less certain they were necessarily all conduits. Apart from their mottled colouring, they were of very organic appearance, some tapering distinctly along their length and dividing in a dendritic fashion like the branches of a tree. Or vines, perhaps. He had a sudden impression of the true hull many metres below smothered by a growth of huge, clinging creepers. Or perhaps it was intentional. Did they form part of the craft's external structure, providing support and bracing to the skin of the hull? Crystals 'grew'; could you grow a vessel this size?

Almost under his feet a broad pipe emerged from the drum and passed close to the nearest 'monotube' support, which was about fifty metres away. From there he would only have to traverse a couple of smaller conduits to reach it.

He dropped the couple of metres on to the top of the pipe and began to make his way cautiously along its upper curve, drawing the line after him. As he moved, one of the spots from the *Indomitable* shifted as well, keeping him in the centre of its reassuring disc of light.

There were fanlike blooms in the substance of the pipe, aligned along its length, forming matching ridges. Frost patterns, he thought; more growth. Why did he keep feeling that this desolate machine was grown?

Then the hairs on the back of his neck rose. He halted and looked about him, certain for a moment that he was being watched.

He wished he was truly as unimaginative as his shipmates thought him. He knew anything could be hiding out there in the shadowy valleys between the pipes, or up on the tower. But why should anybody hide from one man? he rationalised desperately. Besides, any crew had had several hours to make their presence known. The craft had to be abandoned and dead.

He wished he hadn't thought that last word.

Would he be able to pass this incident off with a light laugh to his trainees at the college as an example of emotion clouding commonsense judgment? Or perhaps his subconscious had noted something amiss and was trying to warn him. Even a practical engineer could not afford to ignore his instincts, and right now his instinct was telling him to leave this alien place immediately.

But he still had a job to do.

Kerven had taken ten more resolute paces when he felt the vibration through the soles of his boots.

It was a slow heavy beat, gradually picking up in tempo, telling of sleeping forces slowly stirring. The whole pipework plain seemed to shimmer and a sparkling haze rose up about him. He blinked, thinking his eyes were playing tricks, until he realised it was simply dust caught in the spaces between the pipes being displaced by the vibration. But his relief was short lived. A wave of sickness passed over him and he shakily sank forward on to his hands and knees, swallowing hard, unsure whether the nausea was all in his mind or the product of external forces. The vibration was drumming up through him now. Perhaps it was liquid thundering through one of the massive conduits.

The ground suddenly shimmered with unexpected highlights and brief shadows, as though illuminated by a flash of distant lightning. Lightning in space? He twisted about.

Blue-white electrical discharges were arcing between the bases of the spires that ringed the more substantial end of the derelict. Jagged bridges of fire climbed up the huge tapering shafts and flared into space, as though sparking between the electrodes of some primitive electrical machine. Again and again the lightning bows rose and vanished, even as the pounding under him grew stronger. He sensed that somewhere within the derelict vast energies were being marshalled, and he was witnessing merely the secondary effects of their actions.

Was it a chance power surge from an unattended system – or the deliberate act of the vessel's crew?

Suddenly the vibration under him grew distant and he felt curiously light-headed. The pipe was moving. No, he was falling. Scrabbling futilely, he slid across the curve of the pipe and dropped into the V-shaped valley between it and the next.

Dazed, he found himself wedged between vibrating walls looking up into the black sky and the dazzling point of light that marked the position of the *Indomitable*. But it was no longer directly above him. Then the red eye of the comm laser began to pulse rapidly, C OF G SHIFT. ABORTING. PREPARE FOR RECOV–

Another wave of sickness knotted Kerven's stomach and the ground seemed to heave. How could the alien craft's centre of gravity shift? The *Indomitable*'s spotlights blinked out, leaving him in sudden shocking darkness. He began to roll out of the pipe valley, the line tangling round his legs. He slithered ungainly over the top of the pipe and fell on to the side of the next. Now he understood what was happening. Down was no longer where it had been when he had landed. In effect the derelict was tilting up under him, and what had been level ground was becoming a wall. Down was now the ringed end of the hull over two thousand metres below.

A grotesque shadowy form seemed to lunge out of the darkness towards him, its skeletal arms spread unnaturally wide. His cry of fear was cut short as he realised belatedly that it was just his pod, displaced as he was by the gravity shift. It fell past him, tumbling and bouncing away in the starlight across the ribbed field of pipes. Then it was gone.

Kerven tried to halt his progress but the surfaces around him offered no handholds. He fumbled with his thick gloves for the line tangled about his feet, even as he tumbled into the next channel. It curved with the branching pipes, turning ever downwards, and he slid helplessly along it like an unseated tobogganist – towards the distant ring of still arcing spires.

Then there was constriction about his legs and he was jerked out of the valley and into space, twisting upside down, blood rushing to his head in pounding waves. The slack of the line had run out. With a desperate convulsion he managed to free his legs from the entangling line so that he hung, twisting and bobbing but at least upright once more. He glimpsed the *Indomitable* high above him cartwheeling slowly against the stars. Of course, her own stabilisation must have been thrown off by the gravity shift. As soon as she was steady they would winch him in, he told himself.

As suddenly as it had begun, the lightning ceased to play about the spires, and the derelict became cold and apparently lifeless once more.

Kerven reached the top of his long arc and slowly began to swing back down again, still trapped by the derelict's local gravity. Had the *Indomitable* pulled him far enough away to take up the slack he'd had on the surface? Otherwise he'd hit the hull as fast as he'd left it. He tried to haul himself up the line, but it slid through his thick gloves. The dimly starlit bulk of the derelict was filling the sky again and it seemed as though the gaping maw of its black tunnel mouth was waiting to swallow him. For a moment he thought he saw something moving within that blackness: blue white sparks stretching and falling into a dull red glow lurking infinitely far in its depths.

The monstrous cathedral spires of the tunnel rim appeared to stab up at him. What if they discharged again while he was this close to them? But then he was past them and swinging over the curving plain of the main hull. He was slowing – the new mass centre was now behind him, residing somewhere about the tunnel mouth. But even so he was still travelling dangerously fast. If he hit at this speed he would tear his suit open, even if he didn't break half the bones in his body. The snaking pipes were only metres away now. Instinctively, he pulled up his legs as far as he could, trying to get out of the way. He almost succeeded.

His left foot struck the side of a conduit with sickening force, sending him spinning obliquely towards one of the 'monotubes', which now seemed to run down the hull like a monstrous guttering pipe. He missed the tube itself but passed underneath a support pylon and his line wrapped about it. Abruptly, he was pulled up into an ever-tightening curve, flipped over and jerked to a sudden halt, dangling free in the space between hull and tube.

Before he could recover his breath the line started to run back around the pylon, hauled upward by the still uncontrolled motion of the *Indomitable*, dragging him with it until his harness jammed against its flanged edge. He heard the pylon groan as the tension increased and he twisted desperately about, trying to find a hold so that he could release himself.

'Slack! Give me slack!' he shouted by reflex into his useless helmet microphone.

As he clasped the flange there was a sharp metallic click. He felt the tension vanish and the line whipped away into space.

His harness clip had snapped.

Weakly he drew himself up and clung to the pylon, wrapping his arms and legs through its lattice. Now all he could do was hold on, he told himself. As soon as the *Indomitable* was stabilised and they realised what had happened they would recover him somehow. He still had an hour and a half of life support left. They would find him in time and drop a fresh line. They would do something. Commander Vega would never abandon one of his crew.

Another wave of sickness passed though him and he felt the vibration returning, throbbing through the structure and setting the pylon shivering. The tingle of some massive static charge soaked through his suit and set his hair on end, though he saw no lightning discharge. He felt the centre of attraction shift slightly, as though settling into its new location, and he tightened his grip. He didn't try to analyse what was happening; his future trainees would have to do without an explanation. Life had become a simple matter of holding on and waiting. Nothing else mattered.

Only when all was still again did he realise his left leg was hurting like hell. He didn't dare examine it. He closed his eyes and tried to ignore the pain.

And then, for the second time, he felt their presence.

Even unimaginative children have nightmares. He remembered as a child being terrified to look at the fearful things that had invaded his bedroom in the dead of night, and hoping the covers he had pulled over his head would protect him until morning. But there was no morning out here and he knew that this time they wouldn't go away. He was utterly alone and they were stealing closer and closer…

With a whimper he opened his eyes.

They stood under the pylon looking up at him. Impossible things reaching out with what served them as hands, wanting to enfold him in their horrible embrace.

Kerven cried out in utter terror – shocked beyond any thought of consequences or reason. All he knew was that he had to get away from them.

He let go of the pylon.

He was still screaming when he smashed into the flared ring of the tunnel mouth two thousand metres below.

34

Chapter Four
Executive Pressure

Sam felt a sombre mood descend over the *Cirrandaria* in the hours following the Nimosians' disastrous attempt to secure a foothold on the alien ship.

At first there had been mild alarm and not a little excitement when the gravity waves generated by the derelict had struck and Captain Lanchard had hastily put them into a higher orbit. The *Indomitable*, being closer to the derelict, had evidently been more seriously affected. But as soon as she was stabilised they saw several shuttlecraft leave her bays and begin quartering an expanding volume of space about the huge craft. It was obvious they were searching for survivors of the mission. From the reluctant manner in which they were recalled after several hours, it was equally obvious they had been unsuccessful. Captain Lanchard announced, in the spirit of the common bond between spacefarers, that she had sent a message to her opposite number on the *Indomitable* expressing sympathy for the loss of their crew. It had been acknowledged with grave formality.

There was a slight but noticeable shift in feeling towards the Nimosians. A sneaking admiration for their ingenuity and boldness, coupled with a secret sense of relief that they had failed.

'Perhaps this'll frighten both sides off,' Sam suggested to the Doctor in his cabin, as he finished dressing for dinner.

A surreptitious trip to the TARDIS an hour earlier had allowed them to pack some bags, which had then been dispatched by internal cargo tube to their rooms, both of which were adjacent to the promenade deck and sumptuously furnished. Sam could happily have spent longer in her bathroom merely experimenting with the accessories provided, but there was just time for a quick shower, choosing a few pieces of jewellery, and slipping on a sheer floor-length dress of deep metallic blue she had been wanting to try out for some while. The

Doctor, of course, had freshened up but not changed his costume. Style and fashion, beyond the ensemble he was comfortable with, apparently held little interest for him. But he had deferred to the occasion sufficiently to put a fresh red rose in his buttonhole.

Examining his new floral display critically in a mirror, the Doctor shook his head in answer to her suggestion.

'No, Sam. If anything this will only strengthen the resolve on both sides: the Emindians to succeed where their rivals have failed, and the Nimosians as expiation for their initial failure. I just hope they don't attempt anything foolish. Meanwhile, we have a few hours' grace to establish ourselves as bona fide passengers, just in case we need to bring ourselves to the attention of the command staff later. Until I can overcome the interference problem we'll have to use the *Cirrandaria* as a base to monitor the alien ship. This is one occasion where the TARDIS's normal mode of translocation is a distinct disadvantage.'

'How do you mean?'

'Well, if I don't exactly negate the interference of the energy field we might materialise not just inside the ship, but occupying the same space as some part of its solid structure.'

'Ugh, nasty.'

'That's one way of putting it. I made a few tests while you were sorting through your wardrobe in the TARDIS, but I can't negate the field sufficiently to allow materialisation safely in, or even on, the derelict. Unless we steal a shuttle, we'll need the Emindians' co-operation to visit it. And I feel certain we shall have to do just that, sooner rather than later. I sense tremendous potential power contained within that vessel, a power that neither Emindar nor Nimos can be allowed to possess at this delicate stage in their relationship.'

Sam tried to sound offhand: 'Soon be time for us to make a move then.'

He smiled brightly and offered her his arm. 'But not before we dine.'

The *Cirrandaria*'s main dining saloon was furnished somewhat after the manner of the great Earth liners of the past, which in turn reflected the style of grand restaurants of the period. A forest of marble-faced columns reached up to a six-metre-high ceiling, while a lush undergrowth of exotic plants bordered the walls. A small holographic orchestra played convincingly in one corner. A hundred large round tables, each decked with a brilliant white linen cloth and glittering table service, filled the floor space.

The Doctor's earlier prediction had almost been fulfilled. Thanks to their newly assumed status they had been seated at a table adjacent to the Captain's own. Looking across, Sam thought the Captain looked distracted, and suspected she was putting in an appearance only to reassure the passengers. Seated beside her was a greying but hard-looking middle-aged man, with whom she conducted several brief and apparently terse exchanges during the course of the meal.

Their own table seated eight. As it happened, due to the rotation of places to ensure an interesting social balance at dinner and their integration into the complement, they shared it with Lyset Wynter and Don Delray. The small man they had seen marshalling the crowd on the promenade was also there and introduced himself as Evan Arcovian, Delray and Wynter's agent. As Sam had suspected, Wynter was a professional photographer while Delray was a famous Emindian vid star – a fact Arcovian had made clear to everybody within two minutes of taking their places, by recounting the details of his client's latest epic with bubbling and apparently genuine enthusiasm.

Eventually Delray said, 'I think they've got the message now, Evan.'

Arcovian blinked, looking a little like a snubbed puppy. 'Sorry, Don.'

The last three seats were taken up by the Engers family, comprising Daniel, his wife Jeni and Dan Junior, aged about ten. They were senior environmental engineers from a Federation colony world. Dan Junior was looking in awe at Don Delray, who responded by giving him a wink and good-natured smile with practised suavity, which made the boy blush and squirm with embarrassed delight.

'You're his favourite actor, Mr Delray,' his father admitted.

'Glad to know my work gets seen outside Emindar,' Delray said.

Menu pads appeared, hovering over the middle of their place

settings, and they keyed in their orders. In a minute the floral display in the centre of their table, which Sam had assumed was real, melted away. Glasses of wine and then their food appeared, rising up through irising hatches to be placed before the respective diner by disembodied, white-gloved, robotic arms. Sam almost caught herself saying 'thank you' to them before the arms and hatches vanished to be replaced by the holographic bowl of flowers once more.

As they ate, Sam could not help admitting that Lyset looked extremely attractive. Sam felt distinctly dowdy in her presence and was still wary of her interest in the Doctor. However, Lyset turned out to be disarmingly straightforward about it all.

'And what do you and Ms Jones do, Doctor?' she asked.

'Oh, we're mere Federation functionaries,' he said lightly. 'Civil servants, you know.'

'Odd that I didn't notice you before.'

'We only joined the cruise at the last stop,' Sam said quickly.

'And we've been dining in our cabins up to now,' the Doctor continued smoothly. 'Hyperspace lag, you know.'

'You have an interesting face,' Lyset declared simply, 'and I like interesting faces. If you've the time I'd be pleased if you could sit for me for a proper study.'

'Now you won't get an offer like that very often, Doctor,' said Delray. 'You know how much people have to pay to get their portrait taken by Lyset Wynter?'

'You've seen Lyset's work of course,' Arcovian added.

'I regret we have not,' the Doctor admitted. 'Our own work tends to take us to obscure corners of the galaxy.'

'Places you've never heard of,' Sam said.

'We're out of touch for quite long periods,' the Doctor continued, adding gallantly, 'Our loss, I'm sure.'

Inevitably, as the meal progressed, the discussion turned to the alien ship.

'What do you think about it, Dan?' Delray asked Engers Junior over dessert.

The boy blushed at being included in the adult conversation. 'I think it's really weird, Mr Delray,' he blurted out. Then added, 'If there are aliens on board, will you fight them like you did in *The Black Star Squadron*?'

Delray chuckled. 'I'm on holiday, Dan. I don't plan on fighting anybody. Besides, I didn't bring my battlesuit along.'

'Bet you could beat them even so!' the boy said loyally.

'And what do you think about the alien ship, Doctor?' Lyset Wynter asked.

The Doctor sipped his wine meditatively for a moment. 'I think there are times to leave well alone. At least until you fully understand what you're dealing with.'

'There may be something in that,' Evan Arcovian said, adding quickly, 'Don't get me wrong. I'm as much a patriot as the next Emindian: I don't care for the Nimosians in any way. But we're not soldiers or scientists or explorers. I mean, what's so important about that hulk anyway, eh? And there are some pretty important people on board here too, like Don and Lyset.' He glanced at Dan Engers Junior. 'And children, of course. They should think of that.'

Sam thought he was hiding more anxiety than he was letting on. Delray shook his head.

'We can't do that, Evan. Sometimes you've got to take risks for what's right.'

'But we're not part of your dispute with the Nimosians,' Daniel Engers pointed out forcefully. 'They shouldn't involve foreign nationals in this.'

His voice rose over the last words and Sam was aware that diners at the adjacent tables were looking at them. Don Delray spoke up clearly: 'You're worried about your family, Mr Engers, and I respect that. And I hope you get off this ship as soon as possible if that's what you want. But the rest of us will stay, if our being here stops the Nimosians from getting something they're not entitled to. We've been fighting them on and off for the best part of a century and sometimes you've got to draw the line and stand firm on a principle. And right now we're on that line. Maybe there's nothing worthwhile in that ship over there, but if we give in, what comes next? The Nimosians taking one of our ships just because they take a fancy to it? No. It's our space and we don't move until we're good and ready.'

There was a scattering of applause from the other diners, which Delray acknowledged with a grave smile.

The Doctor nudged Sam. A junior officer had come to the Captain's table and was whispering in her ear. After a moment she quickly made her excuses to her guests and walked briskly out, followed by the stern grey man.

'I think something might be happening,' the Doctor said. 'Who's the man going out with the Captain?'

'High Councillor Rexton,' said Lyset Wynter.

'Is he somebody important?' Sam asked.

'Most people seem to think so,' Lyset said drily. 'He's certainly been taking a close interest in the alien ship.'

'Then I think I will be making his acquaintance very shortly,' said the Doctor. He glanced at Sam, who nodded fractionally. 'After we've finished dinner, perhaps.'

'Well, they won't let you in,' Delray said. 'Even I couldn't swing it. Rexton's had them put guards on the entrances to the command deck after some of the passengers started turning up to complain. I tried to talk him into letting Lyset in there but he wasn't taking any calls, even when I sent a note reminding him that I made some pretty big donations to Stability Party funds before the last election.'

'Ah, a telling argument,' said the Doctor. 'It usually works with politicians. Perhaps it's a measure of the seriousness of the situation that the councillor hasn't been paying you due consideration. Nevertheless, I think they'll see us.'

'Do you really think so, Doctor?' Daniel Engers asked. 'Will you remind them they've got quite a few Federation citizens on board?'

'I shall certainly do that,' he promised.

'But why should you get special treatment?' Delray demanded.

'You might say I have an ace up my sleeve,' the Doctor said.

'And a card in his pocket,' Sam added, thinking of the document the Doctor had provided for her and hoping he'd got all the details right.

'Then do you think you could get me in on this too?' Lyset asked. 'I want to record everything as it happens, especially if there's a chance to visit that ship.'

Evan Arcovian gaped at Lyset Wynter in obvious alarm. 'You aren't seriously thinking of going over to that thing? Not after what happened to the Nimosians.'

'But it's what I do, Evan,' she replied simply.

'You may not thank me,' the Doctor said gravely. 'You know it could be dangerous.'

'I know,' Lyset said. 'But I'd kick myself for passing up the chance.'

'Well if Lyset's set on going, you'd better put me down as well,' Delray sighed in good-natured resignation. 'If you can swing it, that is.'

'Not you too, Don,' Arcovian exclaimed. 'You should be talking her *out* of this.' Delray simply grinned and shrugged.

'Promise you'll try?' Lyset added, gazing intently at the Doctor.

Sam saw the mercurial mix of concern and irreverence within the Doctor briefly compete for dominance, and she thought she understood why. How very quintessentially human, he was thinking, to risk danger for the sake of a few pictures. Slowly a wistful smile spread across his face, encompassing them all in its warmth and softening for a moment even Delray's impatient self-assurance.

'We shall see,' he said.

Captain Lanchard read the message slip twice after it came out of the decoder before handing it to Rexton. He scanned it rapidly without displaying any sign of special satisfaction, as though it was merely what he had expected.

From: *G&C Lines Co. HQ, New Renberg, Talasia, Emindar.*

To: *Capt. Lanchard, C., Commanding CIRRANDARIA.*

Subject: *Salvage of unidentified alien derelict space vessel.*

Under government emergency powers directive 351, you are hereby ordered to remain in the immediate vicinity of the alien vessel, protecting the Emindian claim to salvage rights, until a suitable relief force arrives. You are further ordered to give every assistance to J.K. Rexton, HC, in pursuance of the above, so long as such action does not place the Cirrandaria or its complement in imminent, repeat imminent, danger. The Federation Central Assembly on Mizar has been informed of the situation and is rerouting a ship to evacuate their citizens. Such a transfer will be expedited with all haste as soon as it becomes feasible, without prejudicing the situation relative to the alien vessel and Nimosian warship.

Meanwhile you are authorised to inform the passengers that they will be fully compensated for any inconvenience or delay caused by the current special circumstances. The crew will also be eligible for hardship and special-duty bonuses.

You are further notified that Councillor Rexton's military rank (General in the Space Reserve) has been reactivated, and he should be given all considerations pursuant to such status.

Signed: Palverly, A.C., President.

pp: Board of Directors, G&C Lines.

'Well, you have your orders, Captain,' said Rexton, looking up from the document. 'I trust you now appreciate the vital importance of our situation.'

'I see how it is perceived back home,' Lanchard corrected him. 'But unless you tell me what all this is really about, I don't yet "appreciate" anything. However, I shall follow my orders *to the letter*, General,' she assured him pointedly. 'The moment *I* judge the ship to be in "imminent" danger, we shall leave without argument. I trust that is clear.'

'Quite clear.'

Lanchard glanced at Lorron Bendix, her first officer, who had been waiting patiently in the corner of her day cabin ever since he had brought her encrypted message. He need not have carried the message personally, but perhaps, guessing what it contained, he wanted to see the expression on her face. Bendix was a competent officer, but keen and perhaps a little too ambitious. She worked with him well enough, but his attitude made it all too plain that he regarded his position merely as a stepping stone in his career. He had no real love for the ship.

'Progress report on the modifications to the launch, Mr Bendix?' she asked.

'Chief Manders says the work will be completed on schedule, Captain,' he replied smoothly. 'Request permission to lead the boarding party.'

'Even after what happened to the Nimosians?' Lanchard asked.

'We'll be better prepared, Captain,' Bendix replied calmly. 'We won't make the same mistakes.'

'I will be leading the mission,' Rexton said. Then he smiled at Bendix. 'But I'd like Mr Bendix to accompany me.'

'An honour, sir,' Bendix replied.

'Your request is noted, Mr Bendix,' Lanchard said curtly.

She knew Bendix admired Rexton, while Lanchard herself had never quite accepted the distinguished soldier turned politician at face value. Perhaps she saw too many similarities in the two men's characters. Or perhaps she was getting old and set in her ways. Should she let Bendix go? He was fully capable. From the tone of her instructions, perhaps he was just the sort of man the undertaking required. But others among the crew might volunteer out of loyalty because she asked them. She might be sending them to their deaths – and for what?

Meanwhile, she'd better relay a suitable version of this latest communication to the rest of the ship. Keep them informed about developments to prevent wild rumours spreading. For a moment she found herself envying Vega. At least he didn't have irate passengers to mollify.

Thom Vega sat before the desk screen of his tiny private cabin and contemplated once again the orders from Fleet Command that had caused him to send a good man to his death.

'... the involvement of Kale Rexton, as revealed in intercepted transmission I/NFC/739X, indicates situation to be of highest priority. You will use every means to secure the alien vessel for the sole use of the Nimosian people at the soonest opportunity.'

And he had done just that, not waiting for the alternative arrangements to be completed for fear that the Emindians would beat them to their common goal. He knew command would agree it had been an acceptable risk in the circumstances. But he could not escape the feeling that he had allowed himself to be pressured into taking it. As a consequence they had delayed the other work and lost face before the enemy.

Damn the Emindians! What was so important about the derelict that was making them risk a civilian vessel anyway? Was it mere chance that Rexton was on board, or part of some clandestine deception? Well, he wasn't going to make the same mistake again. Nobody would approach the alien ship within the critical boundary in any craft that was not completely reliable and fully controllable. If they were caught in any more of those gravity shifts they had to be able to hold their station. The brief image the telescope monitor had managed to catch of Kerven's fall would haunt him for years. He wished they could have found his body, but all they'd recovered had been his mangled pod drifting in space. Presumably he was still lying in some cranny on the alien ship. That was another reason for taking possession of the craft for Nimos. At least he would see Kerven got a proper funeral.

He blanked the message from the screen and called up the engineering bay. First Tech Reng's face appeared. Vega could hear drilling in the background as heavy cables were run through the superstructure of a Class Two shuttle.

'How's it going, Lio?' Vega asked.

'About as expected, Commander. The new emitter circuit will generate a counter-field to neutralise the interference. We'll run the system off a sensor and inverter so that it's always in opposite phase. That should blanket at least ninety-five per cent of the emissions. The additional passive shielding we've put in will handle the rest.'

'Very good. When will the modifications be finished?'

Reng scratched his chin, unconsciously smearing it with a streak of grime. Vega thought he looked more than just tired, but then that was understandable. Kerven had been one of his longest-serving technicians.

'Three hours to finish the installation and hook it up to the secondary power cells. Then I'd like a test run to calibrate the system and establish performance tolerances. I'd say that'll take another hour.'

'All right. But make your tests close to the ship. We don't want to give anything away to the Emindians.'

Vega broke the connection.

So, he could set the mission go time for zero nine hundred. What time would that be by the *Cirrandaria*'s clock? Zero two hundred: virtually the middle of their night. Good. With any luck the whole business would be concluded before their passengers woke up.

Chapter Five
Moderator

'You're actually going to hit them with your real name?' Sam said, a mischievous glint in her eyes, as they stepped into the lift. The Doctor occasionally went under the transparent pseudonym of John Smith, but Sam had discovered that his real name was something quite alien and virtually unpronounceable.

'It's what I registered under,' the Doctor replied, as he played his sonic screwdriver over the lift's control panel, causing it to take them to the bridge deck against its programming. 'With the greatest respect to the Smiths and Joneses of the galaxy –' he paused while she curtsied graciously – 'there are times when a more individual cognomen has its advantages when one wants to impress.'

Sam smiled, then asked, 'I thought you'd go all out to put Lyset Wynter off going. You think that derelict's dangerous.'

He shrugged. 'The choice is hers. She fully understands the potential danger. At some point every species must allow its members to behave as adults. It's the innocent and those forced to follow orders that need protection. But also –' for a moment a faraway look crossed his face – 'I had a feeling it was... destined, somehow ...'

'Well, at least she's got Don Delray, man of action, to look out for her,' Sam pointed out.

'So she has,' the Doctor agreed, brightening again. 'But I don't think Mr Delray is enjoying the responsibility as much as he might. What tensions are hidden within that outwardly amicable relationship? You humans do lead such complex lives.'

Sam saw he was beaming now, pleased to enter the fray despite his misgivings. Just like a big kid, she thought.

The lift door slid back to reveal a corridor less plushly finished than those on the passenger decks, with a solitary guard at the far end. Sam straightened up and tried to appear suitably self-assured.

'OK, to the bridge. Lead on, Macduff!' Sam said.

'A common misquotation,' the Doctor corrected her as they strode forward. 'The phrase is actually "Lay on, Macduff". Macbeth was inviting his opponent to heft his sword and continue combat. I told Will people would get it wrong in the future, but he wouldn't listen...'

Sam tutted. 'Fancy someone else thinking they know better,' she teased.

The guard, Sam noticed as they approached, looked tired and irritable. Clearly he had been forced to deal with too many irate passengers in the last few hours. He frowned at them. 'You shouldn't be on this level. No passengers allowed in here.'

The Doctor smiled at him beatifically as though he had just been given a hearty welcome.

'We wish to talk to the Captain,' he said mildly, holding up his identity card for inspection. As the guard's eyes flicked across it a new image flashed into being over the standard information bars. 'Tell her Federation Moderator Doctor — wants to see her concerning the alien vessel.'

The name, if it had been a name, spoken in the middle of the sentence had obviously been quite incomprehensible to the guard. But he certainly seemed to recognise the Federation shield readily enough, accompanied by the scarlet-and-black band of the Moderator's office. Almost everywhere, the Doctor had told Sam, those symbols were known and respected. A Moderator was an independent troubleshooter with virtually unlimited plenipotentiary powers, backed by the forces of the Federation. Even on non-Federation worlds a Moderator's opinion was valued, and they might be called upon to act as an impartial judge and jury in the most serious of disputes.

The guard swallowed nervously.

'Yes, Moderator Doctor... er, I'll tell her you're here. If you'd just wait a moment.' And he spoke urgently into his wristcom.

The Doctor beamed benignly at him and Sam tried to copy his nonchalant stance.

In half a minute the door was opened by a junior officer who ushered them deferentially inside. 'Captain Lanchard will see you in her day cabin,' he informed them.

Sam thought the bridge looked almost deserted with only three crew present. Most of the liner's functions were evidently handled automatically by the tiered sweep of consoles with their shimmering displays that ran along the rear wall. There was, however, a single deep chair set before the main forward viewport, which served as a reminder that the ship still had a sole captain in whom ultimate responsibility resided.

They were escorted to a smaller compartment leading off the bridge, which was comfortably furnished like a lounge-cum-office. Captain Lanchard and Councillor Rexton were waiting for them. Sam read perplexed interest in the Captain's face and barely concealed annoyance in Rexton's. Once again the Doctor presented his impressive identity card and Sam followed suit, hoping her features displayed the right expression of serious high-minded professionalism. Without a word Rexton took their cards and fed them into a tabletop scanner. Sam felt the expression freeze on her face, while the Doctor exhibited a tolerant smile. After what seemed an eternity a green light flashed on the machine. Rexton handed back the cards. From his grimace Sam suspected he would have been happier if he had discovered they were impostors. Now he had to spare them a little time and respect.

'My assistant, Ms Jones,' the Doctor said, introducing her formally. Rexton nodded curtly while the Captain shook their hands.

'Ms Jones, Doctor... er...' She hesitated.

The Doctor waved a negligent hand. 'Don't trouble yourself. "Doctor" will suffice. I'm quite used to it.'

'I didn't know we had Moderators on board,' Rexton said as they seated themselves, with more than a trace of suspicion in his voice.

'We don't normally advertise our presence when not on official business, Councillor,' the Doctor explained. 'We are simply on holiday. However, as the situation remains unresolved, I thought it best to make ourselves known to you and formally offer our services.'

'In what capacity?' Lanchard asked.

'In the interests of peace and goodwill between planets, naturally,' the Doctor said.

Sam felt Rexton's intense scrutiny pass over them. He's a politician, she thought. He knows he can't ignore a Moderator, so he's trying to make the best of it.

'Then you should talk to the Nimosians first,' he suggested. 'They're obviously more in need of your services than we are. Remind them they're infringing our territorial space, and that we have prior claim on the derelict.'

'Oh I will, if it becomes necessary,' the Doctor assured him, leaning forward to emphasise his words, his eyes glittering intensely. 'In fact I will do anything to avoid unnecessary harm coming to any occupant of the *Cirrandaria* or the *Indomitable* – or even the crew of the alien vessel, if it has one. I hope you will bear that in mind.'

Rexton bristled, taking the words as a thinly veiled warning. He glowered at the Doctor, as though trying to cow him with the force of his will. Sam saw their eyes lock and realised Rexton assumed the Doctor was as mild and youthful as he looked. But after just a few seconds it was Rexton who turned aside, as though he had seen unexpected depths in those cool blue eyes opposite him.

Lanchard tried to lower the tension. 'We're very grateful for your offer, Doctor. Of course we hope that the situation can be resolved peacefully.'

'Then you will stay well clear of the derelict?'

'We cannot weaken our claim to salvage,' Rexton said.

'You have over two thousand civilians on board,' the Doctor reminded him. 'You cannot involve them in your dispute with Nimos.'

'We don't intend to,' Lanchard said. 'A Federation evacuation ship is on its way. By the way, do you wish to contact the Assembly yourself to confirm the arrangements? You are welcome to use our priority channel.'

'That won't be necessary,' the Doctor said quickly. 'I'm sure it's coming as fast as possible.'

'As long as the proper measures have been taken,' Sam explained, 'we like to keep a low profile. Our main concern is the alien vessel.'

She saw Rexton frown suspiciously but continued, 'Obviously if it *is* the property of a previously unknown alien race then the Federation must be fully briefed. For all we know their sphere of influence may border on Federation territory. I trust we can count on your co-operation in this matter, which I'm sure you will appreciate is clearly in the best interests of both the Federation and Emindar.'

That sounded pretty smooth, Sam thought. Out of the corner of her eye she caught the Doctor's tiny approving smile and felt a warm glow of pleasure.

'Naturally,' Rexton assured her. 'We want to maintain amicable relations with the Federation.'

'That being the case,' the Doctor said brightly, 'how soon will your modified shuttle be ready to attempt a landing on the derelict?'

Rexton looked taken aback.

'Oh, it's inevitable you'll make the attempt,' the Doctor said. 'As will the Nimosians, I should think. But don't turn this into a race, Councillor. You might all lose in the end.'

'You can't stop us landing on the derelict and claiming salvage rights,' Rexton said.

'Even after what happened to the Nimosians?' Sam pointed out. Rexton didn't trouble to reply.

'No, I can't stop you,' the Doctor admitted, 'though I do most strongly advise against it.' He looked hopefully into Rexton's face but saw only stubborn defiance. 'No, I thought you wouldn't change your mind. In that case I request places be set aside for us to accompany the mission.'

'I'm not sure that will be possible,' Rexton said quickly. 'The capacity of a shuttle is limited. We will need to send a full team over. Technical experts and suitably qualified personnel, you understand.'

'But we *are* experts,' Sam insisted.

'And supposing there are members of the alien crew still on board the ship,' the Doctor pointed out. 'Having Federation representatives with you would be an advantage – one the Nimosians would not have should they land before you. We do have considerable practical experience in similar situations which you would benefit from. Post-

51

spaceflight industrial archaeology is a hobby of mine. I once wrote an article on it for the *Interstellar Pangraphic*. Have you read it? No? Remind me to send you a copy.'

Sam saw Rexton's expression change subtly. 'Very well, Doctor. I accept your arguments have some merit. You and Ms Jones may accompany the boarding party.'

'Ah, and I promised to ask, on behalf of Lyset Wynter and Don Delray, if they could also join the exploratory party,' the Doctor added. 'Ms Wynter would like to record events for posterity and take a closer look at the derelict.'

'The photographer and the actor?' Rexton scowled. 'Ridiculous!'

'Foolhardy on their part, perhaps,' the Doctor said, 'but not necessarily ridiculous. I would have thought a professional photographer would be quite useful to help document the interior of the craft.' A fresh thought appeared to strike him. 'Unless you think there's something about it that should be kept secret?' he mused guilelessly.

'I will not speculate on the matter,' Rexton replied stiffly. He frowned. 'I suppose Wynter may come as long as she submits her pictures for official vetting before they are published.'

The Doctor beamed at him. 'I'm sure she'd agree to that.'

'And Don Delray?' Sam asked.

'No. This is not some juvenile adventure vid,' Rexton said firmly.

'No, it's merely the investigation of a derelict spacecraft which you're turning into an interstellar incident,' Captain Lanchard interjected. 'And it's making the passengers and crew uneasy. Delray is a popular figure people can identify with. If he and Wynter want to go along – and they'll sign waivers absolving the company of any responsibility – then it might help reassure them. Remember, you need this ship to remain calm for another couple of days until relief forces arrive. Think about it.'

'The Captain may be right,' the Doctor said.

Rexton sighed. 'Very well,' he conceded with bad grace.

'We'll let you know when the shuttle modifications are complete,' Lanchard said to Sam and the Doctor. 'About two hours from now was the last estimate.'

'Good,' said the Doctor, rising from his chair. 'We have preparations of our own to make.'

When they were back in the lift descending towards the hold, Sam looked at the Doctor curiously. 'Looks like Lyset Wynter's going to have her destiny fulfilled like you said. Did you think out the argument for taking her along as soon as she asked? And were you ready to speak up for Delray as well?'

'It did occur to me that their proposed participation might influence matters somewhat,' the Doctor admitted. 'Captain Lanchard was obviously thinking along the same lines, so I think it was inevitable. Anyway, Rexton's response suggests he knows more than he's letting on about the derelict. He's acting on more than mere speculation.'

'Yeah, he knows something all right,' Sam agreed. 'Actually I'm surprised he let us tag along so easily.'

'Probably because he realised our presence, as Moderators, might dissuade the Nimosians from taking drastic action against the boarding party,' the Doctor explained matter-of-factly.

Sam found that her mouth had gone curiously dry. 'So we're a sort of insurance policy?'

'Something like that. I hope our premiums are fully paid.'

Vega had the boarding party – except Reng, who was still working on the shuttle modifications – assemble in the briefing room. On the big screen covering most of one wall were pictures of the alien ship taken from every angle. For an hour they had analysed its every detail and plotted likely points of access, referring to the enlarged views showing what they tentatively assumed were hatchways, almost hidden amid the complex topography of its hull.

As they conferred Vega examined the team with a critical eye.

Lieutenant Matt Tane, third in command and the *Indomitable*'s armaments specialist, would lead the party. Exhibiting his usual external coolness, he was making careful notes on his personal datapad. First Pilot Del Argen was half smiling, his eyes flicking across the images as though it was a new land he was about to conquer. In contrast Second Tech Kender, Reng's assistant for the mission, looked quietly resigned to his duty. Seated behind them were the six marines who would provide their escort, appearing professionally alert and easily concealing any anxiety they might be feeling. After all, this was what they were trained for. A little apart from them was the solid form of Squadleader Harren Sho. As always his face was unreadable. If he had ever exhibited any sign of the slightest outward anxiety in any situation, Vega had never heard of it. He was not a comfortable person to have around. His men respected but did not like him, and as far as Vega knew he had no close friends. But if you needed somebody to rely on absolutely to get a job done, no matter what the cost, he was your man.

When the briefing was concluded, Vega addressed them.

'Although we still believe the vessel is empty, after what happened to Kerven we can't take any chances. The energy discharge and gravity shift may have been a routine function or some defence mechanism. Be extremely cautious before committing yourself. Remember this may be a first contact situation. Make it peaceful if you can – we're not looking to make any new enemies. But don't hesitate to defend yourselves if it becomes necessary. Aliens must learn to treat Nimosians with respect.

'We've no idea why the Emindians are so interested in the alien craft, but if they're willing to risk facing us down with a civilian ship carrying Federation passengers then, in the opinion of the Intelligence analysts back home, it must be something important. A task force will be dispatched from the Fourth Fleet to reinforce us, but even at top speed they're over a day away. Meanwhile the Emindians may try to land a party on the alien craft with a view to occupying it. Hopefully we will board first, in which case your mission is to discover whatever the Emindians are after and recover it for our use. This is your prime objective. If that is not possible and, in your judgement, the item or knowledge could pose any possible threat to Nimos, then at the very least you will deny it to the

Emindians. That'll be your decision, Matt, if there's no opportunity to confer with me.'

Tane nodded slightly. 'Understood, sir.'

'If the Emindians effect entry and establish a bridgehead on the craft before we do, then they must be removed, peacefully if possible. But if it becomes necessary, you are authorised to use whatever force necessary to achieve your objective.'

The brief message, relayed via ship phone to their suite, stating that Councillor Rexton would be honoured if Ms Lyset Wynter and Mr Don Delray would accompany the craft soon to be dispatched to explore the derelict, was greeted with unalloyed delight by Lyset.

'The Doctor came through!' she exclaimed. 'He must have some pull.'

'So he must,' Delray admitted.

Lyset had already turned out her camera case and was sorting its contents. 'What did he say he was again?'

'Just a functionary,' Delray said glumly. 'Apparently civil servants stick together.'

Lyset paused in her work to reach out a hand to brush his cheek. 'Don't feel bad about it, Don. Just because this time you couldn't swing it for me.' She turned back to her case again before he could take her hand, half talking to herself: 'Better use film with that interference… no fancy circuitry. Wish I'd had the Hamnex vacuum-proofed. Have to take the Scintar with the booster tube… and the mini-floods. Maybe an infrared converter as well…'

Delray watched in silence for a minute as she checked over the equipment with her quick, practised hands, then asked, 'Are you sure you want to go through with this? It could be dangerous.'

She looked up at him with frank puzzlement showing plainly across her face. 'That's never stopped me before, you know that. What's different about this time?'

'Because I'm actually here and I couldn't stand seeing anything…' He fumbled for words. 'Trite as it sounds, meeting you was the best thing that ever happened to me.'

'That romantic encounter in Evan's waiting room,' she said with a reminiscent smile. 'I always wondered if he planned that.'

Delray managed a weak smile. 'A good agent can arrange anything.'

'True. Hey, hadn't you better let him know what's happened, and get ready yourself?' She turned to her wardrobe. 'Now, where's my field kit?'

'The insurers will never stand for it, Don!' Evan Arcovian said five minutes later as they stood in the lounge of his own cabin. 'They were sticky enough over you doing that dive for real in your last picture.' He threw his hands up in the air. 'This'll kill 'em, I swear it will.'

'Well they're going to have to live with it, Evan. I'll sign a waiver or something if necessary, but if Lyset's going then I've got to as well. No choice. Can you imagine what the news slots would say if I didn't? Anyway, think of the bonus side: publicity. I'll be part of a real adventure for once in my life…' He saw the little man's face fall and added hastily, 'There's probably nothing to worry about. The thing's just an old hulk with some bad power cells.'

'Don – you felt the kick that thing gave us earlier. What if it does it again while you're on board?'

'Look, Rexton's leading this jaunt. War hero or not, I don't think he'd risk his skin unless he thought he had a pretty fair chance of making it through safely. He wants the top job, remember? Anyway, Evan, just fix it. Earn that ten per cent.'

'Don't I always, Don?'

Delray smiled. 'Fine. Now I've got to get ready.'

He turned about and left the cabin quickly. He didn't see the expression on Arcovian's face as he went, or hear the quiet: 'Take care, Don', spoken to his retreating back.

Chapter Six
A Meeting at the Rail

Lester Plecht was woken by his wife's elbow digging into the small of his back. Years of habit caused the words, 'What's wrong, dear?' to issue from his lips even before he was fully awake.

'Do you hear that?' Rhonda Plecht said indignantly.

Lester raised his head from the pillow and listened. The distant shuffle of feet and raised voices were filtering through from the corridor side of the cabin.

'Just some people outside, dear,' he said drowsily. 'They're not very loud and I'm sure they'll go away soon.'

'What's the time?'

He squinted at the illuminated bedside display.

'Uh, half past one, dear.'

Rhonda sniffed. 'I thought so: the middle of the night. Some wild party, no doubt. I assumed we would only have people on this voyage who showed proper consideration for others. Find out who they are and tell them to stop.'

'Right now, dear?'

'Of course.'

'Can't we just call the steward –'

'They never do anything. Remember how unhelpful they were last time I complained. Now go out there and stop them.'

'Yes dear,' Lester said resignedly, throwing back the covers and searching for his slippers.

Lester did not find the drunken merrymaking his wife had assumed was taking place, when he cautiously emerged from his compartment. Instead, a steady stream of people, many still in their nightclothes, as he was, were making their way to the promenade deck. Most were carrying cameras and several had children with them; some were being dragged along by their offspring.

Puzzled, Lester joined the flow. On reaching the promenade he found the rails already well crowded. Pushing forward as vigorously as his nature allowed, he managed to squeeze himself into a narrow gap and peer out into space. There was the rather sinister-looking bulk of the alien vessel, and to one side of it the smaller form of the Nimosian warship. Nothing seemed to have changed. Yet all around him people were talking and pointing and holding their cameras ready. What was going on? There was a bulky blue-skinned Yevron male to his left, but he was always nervous about talking to aliens for fear he might unwittingly say something rude.

'Excuse me, but what's happening?' he asked the person on his left, realising only as he did so that it was a young and rather attractive woman. She turned a bright face to him and gave a carefree smile.

'Any minute now they're sending a shuttle over to explore the derelict. Lyset Wynter and Don Delray are going with them.'

She was tall and lithe, rising half a head over his small and slightly portly figure. He realised she was quite unselfconsciously dressed in a very brief nightshift which, he couldn't help noticing, was her only garment. The crush of bodies pressed them together, but it didn't seem to bother her. He was suddenly acutely aware of her warmth and the scent of her body.

'Really,' he said, grasping for words. 'How… exciting.'

She favoured him with another smile and he basked in its innocent warmth. 'Delray must be doing it for the publicity, of course, but I wonder what sort of pictures Wynter will bring back? Have you seen much of her work?'

Before he could reply an all-too-familiar voice cut through the babble about him.

'Lester! Where have you been?'

He spun about guiltily. Rhonda, wearing her full length dressing gown pulled tightly across her front, was glaring at him. A space rapidly opened up between them, as it tended to before the force of her glare, leaving him feeling terribly isolated.

'Just trying to find out what was going on as you asked, dear,' he explained rapidly. 'It wasn't a party after all. They're sending a shuttle over to the alien ship.'

Rhonda was eyeing his companion. 'Well, if we are going to be woken in the middle of the night by hordes of curiosity seekers marching past our door, they might at least dress correctly. There are certain standards of decency, you know.'

The young woman glanced down at her costume in mild surprise, then at her accuser. 'You're lucky I stopped to put it on,' she replied simply. 'Sorry if it bothers you.'

In a desperate attempt to divert Rhonda's scorn, Lester said, 'Apparently that actor, Don Delray, and Lyset Wynter will be on the shuttle, dear.'

'Lyset who?'

'The photographer, dear. Remember those striking pictures of the Tor-zak war –'

'Those pictures were quite revolting,' Rhonda said.

Lester seemed to shrink a little. 'Yes, dear. But I only meant that... they brought home the reality of the suffering.'

He felt himself begin to sweat. Out of the corner of his eye he saw that the young woman was still watching him. Why should somebody so attractive have to start paying attention to him now of all times?

'We do not need to be exposed to the nauseating details,' Rhonda Plecht said flatly. 'Everybody knows wars are unpleasant.'

'Yes, dear,' Lester agreed meekly.

'But perhaps some people need to be reminded from time to time?' the girl said, unexpectedly standing her ground against Rhonda in a way Lester hadn't done for twenty years.

Rhonda Plecht sniffed again, as though to indicate that respectable people knew what should be seen and what should be left well alone.

'I must say it is a little inconsiderate of the company to send a party over there after what happened to the Nimosians,' Lester continued, trying desperately to divert Rhonda's attention from the girl, who was still standing really too close to him. 'It might be dangerous.'

'Might it?' came an excited voice.

Dan Engers had joined the growing crowd at the rail with his slightly embarrassed father in tow.

'That child ought to be in bed,' Rhonda Plecht told Engers Senior.

'Let him have his fun,' the young woman said before the man could respond. Lester cringed and took a surreptitious step away from her. She was actually going to argue with Rhonda!

However, Dan spoke up for himself. 'I'm allowed to stay up when we're on holiday if there's something special. Don Delray might be chasing aliens out of there any minute now.' He had clearly come prepared to do battle in support of his hero, armed as he was with a toy raygun.

'They won't be doing anything of the sort, young man,' Rhonda Plecht said censoriously. 'Really! All this fuss about an old wreck. Still, anything to prevent those dreadful Nimosians from getting their hands on it, I suppose.'

'Yes, dear,' Lester Plecht said with relief.

'Well, if you've satisfied your curiosity, we shall return to our compartment and try to get a little sleep.'

With a last disapproving glance that took in the gathering crowd on the promenade, she swept away, Lester trailing meekly behind her. As he rounded the corner he glanced back wistfully at the sight of people innocently enjoying themselves. He caught the eye of the young woman again, and she gave him another of those wonderful smiles, tinged with sympathy. He was sure she understood his situation and felt sorry for him. He felt his hand begin to lift in an acknowledging wave, but then came a shout of, 'There they are!' and she turned her attention back to the stars.

Chapter Seven
Out of the Shadows?

Kale Rexton stared intently at the image of the derelict as it filled the monitor screen that extended from the arm of his seat.

He felt that familiar heightening of the senses he associated with going out on patrol in the days when he'd been flying from the good old *Griffon*, bless her creaking launch ramps. It made everyday existence seem pallid by comparison, merely a prelude to the real purpose of life. It was a feeling he thought he had lost for ever. But now fate had dealt him one more hand. At last, after all these years, they might have the answers they wanted. By our resolve we shall prevail, he reminded himself silently.

He glanced around him at the crew of the shuttle *Doria*.

The Doctor and his assistant were currently examining the image of the derelict on their own screens and exchanging murmured words. He'd have to keep an eye on them, especially the Doctor. He was harder than he looked. Rexton resented their presence, of course, but military training had taught him to turn circumstances to his advantage. The pair might yet have other uses before the mission was over.

The same could probably not be said about Delray and Wynter. He could just about tolerate the photographer, but an actor! Still, their presence had undeniably improved morale on the *Cirrandaria*. The rails had been lined by waving passengers when they set off. He just hoped the pair would stay out of his way.

The professional shuttle personnel, he decided, probably represented the best that could be assembled in the time from what there was available.

Bendix he already knew was keen enough. Perhaps a little brash and overconfident, but that was not necessarily a fault if one had the nerve to back it, as he judged Bendix did. He'd been the same himself once.

Manders, the chief engineer, and her two assistants were presently nursing the counter-interference system, which had been hastily retrofitted to the shuttle. They were an unknown quantity, but Lanchard had assured him of their competence.

The pilot navigator, Lieutenant Jenez, appeared ridiculously young and had apparently graduated only a year ago. From the expression on his face it was clear the whole business was an adventure to him. But his hands were steady on the controls and he flew the small craft with precision and assurance. Rexton hoped the reflexes of youth would not be put to the test in the next few minutes.

Rexton leaned forward from his seat immediately behind Jenez and pointed.

'There, Lieutenant. Under the overhanging shelf to the right. There should be an airlock hatch large enough for us.'

'I see it, sir,' Jenez replied.

Bendix, in the right-hand seat, glanced across at him curiously. But if he wondered how Rexton knew where to direct them, then he had the sense not to ask. The Doctor, however, had no such inhibitions.

'You seem very familiar with the layout of the alien ship, Councillor,' he observed mildly.

'I've been studying it carefully,' Rexton replied. The Doctor raised his eyebrows but said nothing more.

The derelict became a wall of intricate complexity gliding against the ports. Rexton waited for the first sign of instability, but their trajectory remained smooth.

'Engineer, what is the status of the counter-interference generator?'

'If it wasn't functioning properly you'd already know it, Councillor,' Mander replied simply. 'As long as we keep below five hundred k.p.h. we should manage.'

Rexton sat back in his seat with a slight smile. He could accept a straight reply as long as the speaker knew their business.

The last of the key crew members Rexton was less concerned about. Dessel, the *Cirrandaria*'s master-at-arms, was an ex-soldier. Only he looked at ease with the pistol strapped to the waist of his suit. He was also cradling a heavier riot-control gun in his arms.

Nothing like the firepower the Nimosians could muster, of course, but Rexton realised he should be grateful regulations demanded interstellar liners carry basic armaments at all – a hangover from the last skirmish with the Nimosians. He reminded himself to see that provisions were strengthened when this was all over.

Of course, if all went well, perhaps there would be no need for Emindian civilian ships to carry weapons ever again.

'Pulse signal coming in from *Cirrandaria*,' Bendix said from the forward console. 'The Nimosians have acknowledged our message informing them we would be landing a party… and they say they're about to do the same!'

'So it will be a race after all,' the Doctor said.

Matt Tane hunched forward, staring out of the viewport of the shuttle *Resolve* at the slowly swelling bulk of the derelict. He wished they could travel faster but cautioned himself against impatience. The counterphase generator that Reng was monitoring in the compartment behind him put a strict upper limit on their safe speed. He consoled himself with the knowledge that it was probably the same for the Emindian shuttle.

It was an interesting irony that both sides had overcome the interference to allow them to land on the derelict within minutes of each other. And the Emindians had taken such trouble to ensure they knew they had a Moderator with them. Trying to win favour with the Federation, no doubt. Well that would not prevent him carrying out his orders. The Emindians would soon discover that merely landing on the derelict was one thing, taking control of it quite another.

The entrance hatch, which Sam saw was segmented like a camera shutter, nestled in the valley between two of the huge projecting fins that grew out of the base of the derelict's central tower. At Rexton's direction, Jenez set the *Doria* down beside the fifteen-metre-wide ring. The hiss of the underjets died away as the craft settled on its landing skids.

'Down and secure, sir,' Jenez reported.

'There should be a manual control point close by,' Rexton said briskly, fastening his suit.

'You'll not go outside without an escort, General,' said Dessel firmly.

Rexton smiled. 'Thank you, Mr Dessel.'

'Perhaps we should stretch our legs as well,' the Doctor suggested, as he and Sam locked down their visors.

'As you will,' Rexton said.

Wynter and Delray were also preparing to exit the craft. Sam saw a look of disdain pass over Rexton's face.

'You understand I take no responsibility for your safety out there,' he told them.

Lyset nodded impatiently while Delray said lightly, 'Message received, Councillor.'

They squeezed into the *Doria*'s small airlock and waited as the air was exhausted. After half a minute the outer hatch slid open and a small flight of steps unfolded. Before descending they fastened inertia-reel tethers to their belts and clipped the ends to eyelets beside the airlock. If there was a gravity shift Jenez could hold the shuttle steady with the thrusters and gyrostabiliser until they could pull themselves back inside. They stepped down on to the hull of the derelict, moving easily in the half-gravity field. As Rexton flashed his torch about him Lyset Wynter began snapping pictures eagerly.

Sam noted that 'down' was now almost directly below them, indicating that the derelict's centre of gravity must have shifted away from its far end. They hadn't detected the change from space so it must have been less spectacular than before. Sam hoped the derelict was settling into some state of equilibrium.

The artificial valley, which was about thirty metres across, curved smoothly up into the great fins that enclosed it on either side, reducing the sky to a strip of speckled blackness that arched over their heads. The dancing circles of their torches picked out muddy rainbows of colour that rippled across the floor and into the walls, reminding her of folded rock sediments. At either end of the valley two more of the fins cut the sky. They were pierced at right angles by two of the slender columns rising from the main hull of the derelict.

'Over there,' Rexton said, his beam picking out a scalloped alcove in the base of one of the fins. Even over a few metres the interference crackle threatened to drown the signal of his suit transmitter. They loped across the green-bronze-rippled floor in long strides. A raised black disc or wheel some half-metre across was set at head height in the wall at the back of the alcove. Mounted on opposite sides of its rim were two short projecting pegs. Its function was obvious.

Rexton grasped the pegs and twisted the wheel in a clockwise direction.

It didn't move. Rexton tried again, exerting more force. Sam heard his grunt of effort.

'Needs a spot of oil, perhaps?' the Doctor suggested.

'Let me take one side, sir,' Dessel said.

But their combined strength could not budge the wheel.

The Doctor examined their surroundings as they strained. His torch beam came to rest on a panel a little to one side of the disc. It was patterned with a six-by-six grid of fist-sized raised squares, each of which had a distinctive geometric character embossed upon it. Sam saw squares with a dot in the centre, zigzags, right angles, a channel, arrow heads with a dot in the corner opposite the arrow point and what might have been a pi symbol. After a moment she realised there were only six symbols in different combinations and orientations on the panel.

'A code lock?' Sam wondered aloud, as Rexton and Dessel ceased their futile efforts. 'Base-six numerology?'

'Perhaps,' the Doctor said, tilting his head from side to side as he examined the array. 'I don't suppose you know the solution?' he asked Rexton.

'Would I be wasting my time here if I did?' Rexton said sharply. Wynter and Delray had walked across to join them and the flash of her camera was obviously not improving his temper.

'No, I don't suppose you would,' the Doctor agreed, continuing to scrutinise the panel. 'You just expected it to be unlocked.'

'What I expected is of no concern of yours, Doctor,' Rexton said. 'If you have any useful suggestions to offer I am prepared to listen to them. Otherwise we will find another hatchway and try that.'

'And if that's also locked?'

'Then I will send back to the ship for cutting equipment.'

'You don't think this might be a sign that your presence is not welcome?' the Doctor suggested. 'Locked doors often are.'

'Any crew have had ample opportunity to communicate with us before now. It is a derelict and, one way or another, I am going to take possession of it.'

'Yes, you are determined, aren't you?' the Doctor agreed after a moment's silence. 'I suppose I can at least prevent unnecessary damage.'

And he turned to the panel and depressed six of the keys with his palm in quick succession. 'Now try the wheel.'

With evident incredulity Rexton grasped the manual-release wheel and twisted. This time it turned smoothly. Sam swung her torch about to see the segments of the hatchway set in the floor of the valley begin to slide open, revealing darkness beneath. Lyset loped quickly over to it.

Delray said, 'Careful Lys. Don't fall in!'

'It's just a landing bay,' she said, taking another picture. 'About twenty metres deep. Seems to be empty. Plenty big enough for the shuttle.'

Rexton stared at the Doctor. 'How did you know the correct code?' he demanded.

'I simply worked it out,' the Doctor replied. 'You could have done the same if you'd thought about it.'

Rexton looked baffled but apparently decided not to press the matter further. 'Back to the shuttle,' he ordered.

Sam turned off her radio for a moment and touched her helmet against the Doctor's so only he could hear her. 'How did you do that?'

'It was very simple. Too simple. Quite absurd in the circumstances.'

'How do you mean absurd?'

'Tell you later.' He sounded more concerned than he had before.

Dessel took over at the wheel and slowly the hatch aperture widened. In a minute it was fully open. They made their way back to the *Doria*'s airlock, reeling in their safety lines as they went. As they climbed the steps Sam took one last glance around – and halted abruptly.

'What's that?' she said, pointing down the valley.

'Where?' Lyset asked, swinging her camera about eagerly.

'Something moved,' Sam said. 'Around the far corner of the right-hand fin, or hill or whatever it is. It was dark – man-sized, I think. It was just there for a moment, then it slipped aside.'

The others strained their eyes but could see nothing.

Sam shivered. From being a place of wonder the bleak, starlit, improbably artificial landscape suddenly seemed full of shadows and menace. 'I think we're being watched,' she said quietly.

'I wouldn't be at all surprised,' the Doctor agreed.

'It may be a Nimosian scout,' Rexton declared. 'We know they were heading for the other side of the ship, but they may have sent somebody round. The sooner we get inside and close the hatch the better. Pilot, signal the *Cirrandaria* that we're about to enter the alien ship.'

Over five hundred metres away on the other side of the tower, Tane shielded his eyes against the glare of the primitive but functional gas cutting beam. So far they had found two small hatches, but both had been locked. Tane had decided not to spend time puzzling out their opening codes. Now they were employing more direct methods against the third and larger hatchway they had come across.

The *Resolve* rested on the narrow strip of level surface between the edge of the pipework tangle and the base of the tower. While the technicians were working on the hatch the marines were spaced in a ring around them, looking out alertly along the long furrowed hill that was the main hull of the derelict. Sho was moving between his men, following the safety lines they had strung across the derelict's surface. Tane could see his helmet turning from side to side as he ceaselessly scanned their surroundings. He had to admit he found his presence reassuring, for there was an uneasy atmosphere about this vast silent hulk. This was the place Technician Kerven had died, and his body was probably no more than a couple of kilometres away. When they secured the craft for Nimos a proper search would have to be mounted for him. He hoped he would not get that detail.

The blue-white brilliance of the cutter faded, leaving a glowing cherry-red groove in the material of the hatch. Reng pushed up his tinted visor and examined it.

'Well?' Tane asked impatiently.

'It'll be a long job,' Reng said. 'This stuff's highly conductive and the heat dissipates too quickly.'

'Then we'll have to punch a hole. How thick is it?'

'At least ten centimetres – that's the deepest I've got, anyway.'

Tane scowled. Standard demolition packs wouldn't do. They'd need Type Seven shaped-ring charges. More than he'd bargained for.

'I'll send the *Resolve* back for heavier charges. Meanwhile try another spot. See if you can find somewhere thinner.'

Tane trudged back towards the *Resolve* until he stood at the foot of its extended ramp within its counter-interference field. To his relief, the persistent crackle over his earphones faded and he could speak normally.

'Argen, go back to the ship and collect some extra explosive packs. I'll send and tell them what I need so it'll be ready for you –'

He saw a flicker out of the corner of his eye, and felt a momentary sensation of dizziness. He took a step aside to steady himself and looked around him. Was this the prelude to another gravity shift? Nobody else seemed to notice anything amiss. Reng's team were still crouched by the surface hatch and the marines appeared as vigilant as ever. Was this place getting to him?

'Sir?' Argen's voice came to him.

'Nothing. Be as quick as you can.'

He stepped back and watched the ramp retract and close up. The *Resolve*'s lift jets flared and it rose smoothly into the sky and in a moment it was gone. Tane made his way over to the tripod- mounted emergency communications reflector and picked up the sending key. The battery-powered bulb began to pulse.

HATCHWAY HEAVIER THAN ANTICIPATED, he sent in code.

PREPARE MUNITIONS PACKS 7 AND 10B FOR TRANSFER TO RESOLVE.

Vega ensured the explosives Tane had requested were ready and waiting when the *Resolve* glided through the faintly glowing pressure curtain of the hangar bay five minutes later. On the bay monitors he watched it set down and open up to receive its cargo. As the packs were loaded he conversed over the command circuit to the *Indomitable*'s first pilot and temporary shuttle jockey.

'How are the modifications holding up, Del?'

'Fine, sir,' Argen reported. 'Handles well as long as we keep her top V down.' There was a pause and Vega saw him frown. 'But I'll be glad when Hentle takes his spell.'

'Why? You said the flying was easy.'

'It's not that, sir… it's that place. It makes you jumpy. The engineer and I both noticed it on the way back up. You want to keep looking over your shoulder, even when you've left it. And the cold stays with you.'

It wasn't like Argen to talk like that, Vega thought. Conditions on the derelict must be stranger than they had anticipated. Perhaps he should –

'Commander!' the landing-party observer said urgently, looking up from the scope relay screen. 'Multiple energy discharges on surface of derelict in the vicinity of Mr Tane's team. I think it's gunfire, sir.'

The communications monitor said, 'Partial signal from surface, sir. Emergency code followed by SHADOWS OUT OF – That's all, sir.'

'Marine second squad, to hangar deck at the double!' Vega ordered, the words spilling out quickly but clearly even as ice gripped his heart. 'Flight Control, hold launch of *Resolve* until they are on board. Helm, take us in to four kilometres over target. Observers, report immediately any activity in landing zone.'

He felt the *Indomitable* begin to drop down towards the derelict.

'Sir,' Val Fayle, his second in command, spoke up, his face stony and set. 'Shall I activate main batteries and target the Emindian vessel?'

'What?'

'Their party must be responsible for this attack, sir.'

Fayle had personal reasons for disliking the Emindians more than most, Vega recalled. Occasionally it coloured his thinking.

'Not until we have more information, Mr Fayle.'

'But who else could it be, sir?'

Who indeed? 'Shadows out of' – what? Had the sender, presumably Tane, meant something was coming out of the shadows? What was happening down there? If only they had two modified shuttles operational...

He reopened the channel to the *Resolve*.

'Del, as soon as the marines are loaded get down there at maximum safe speed. We'll have the area illuminated with the main beams again. Make one low pass over the landing area to assess the situation, then pull up out of the interference zone so you can report to me. Do not make a landing until ordered, understood?'

Argen nodded. 'Understood, sir.'

The scope observer said, 'Gunfire has ceased, sir.'

'Anything else?'

There was a pause. 'I think there are two bodies, sir.'

Vega transferred the scope image to his own command-chair screen. The image was less distinct than it should have been at this distance due to the interference effect distorting the light waves, but he could see the dark strip of flat ground beside the tower. And two blurred smudges that might indeed have been bodies.

'Shuttle *Resolve* loaded and away,' came the announcement from the hangar.

The external screen showed the shuttle dart out of the hangar bay and bank sharply towards the derelict. As it powered away Vega was once again assailed by those doubts that all commanders lived with. Should he have waited until they had two modified shuttles in operation? If one had remained on the derelict then perhaps the landing party could have been evacuated when they came under attack. But then the Emindians would have reached the derelict hours before them. His eyes fixed on the image of the alien ship. Its secrets had better be worth all this.

On the screen he watched the *Resolve* make its low pass, then climb back up towards them. With the decreasing distance the comlink cleared sufficiently for Argen to make his report.

'I can confirm there are two bodies down there, Commander. No sign of the rest of the party nor any hostiles. Request permission to land and make ground search.'

There was no choice and Vega knew it, but he hated giving the order.

'Request approved, Del. But take all possible precautions. At the slightest sign of danger you are to lift off at once, understand?'

'Understood, sir. Argen out.'

Argen set the *Resolve* down less than thirty metres from the bodies, now lit by the stark illumination of the *Indomitable*'s searchlights. He could see the toppled tripod of the emergency sender and the cutting equipment still lying by the hatchway, but apart from the two twisted bodies they had seen on their first pass nothing else seemed out of place. He felt the familiar taste of fear, but oddly none of that crawling of the skin on the back of his neck he had sensed on the first trip back from the derelict.

As they touched ground the *Resolve*'s rear ramp dropped flat, disgorging the reserve squad of marines that had been packed into the airlock with weapons powered and ready. Above them the turret gun whirred as it swung round to cover the looming mass of the derelict's tower. In seconds the soldiers had fanned out in a broad arc, running in a half-crouch. As soon as their line had encompassed the bodies the leaders dropped flat, facing out into the darkness beyond the spotlights' glare, while a medic and his assistant knelt by the fallen. Argen saw them make a rapid examination, then the voice of the corporal commanding the squad came over the cracking link.

'It's Detter, from Sho's squad.' he said quickly. 'Leastways, what's left of him.'

'Was he shot?' Argen asked.

There was a long pause, then, 'No. There are no blast marks. It looks… it looks like he was torn to pieces by some kind of animal.'

Chapter Eight
Family

The *Cirrandaria*'s chief purser, social hostess and manager of entertainments were all unnecessary to the mechanical operation or safety of the ship, but they were indispensable to the contentment and wellbeing of its passengers and crew. Therefore Lanchard had arranged additional meetings with them until the emergency was over. For the moment the liner's complement were bearing up reasonably well, but she wanted to be ready for any eventuality. Extra diversions were being planned should they be needed.

'We'll keep them busy for you, Captain,' Oscar Castillo, the chief purser, promised.

'If need be, revive that gambling club of yours that I'm not supposed to know about, Oscar,' she told him.

'Gambling club, Captain?' he replied with perfect innocence.

The conference over, Lanchard returned to the bridge. Evan Arcovian was still there.

The little man had talked his way on to the bridge using his famous clients' names as leverage, and now there seemed no way of removing him except by force. At least he kept out of the way, however, and, apart from a few whispered calls on his pocket phone to Emindar relayed through the ship's transmitter and an almost absent-minded request for a cup of coffee, he remained largely silent. He spent his time staring at the screens showing the alien ship and, beyond it, the *Indomitable*, which had moved round to hold station over the area the Nimosian landing party had set down upon.

At first Lanchard had thought Arcovian was merely troubled by the possibility of losing two valuable clients, and was putting on a show of concern. Then she suggested he wait in the officers' lounge, which was only a little way down the corridor, and promised to inform him as soon as anything happened. His response caused her to modify her opinion.

'No thanks, Captain,' he said with a slight smile. 'I've gotta be here. This is the nerve centre, right? Anything that happens, you'll know it here first. I promised I'd watch out for them, you see. They're two really great people...'

And Lanchard found herself listening, half mesmerised by his enthusiasm, to the story of how he met them, of Delray's rise to vid stardom, of Lyset's exhibitions, of how Don had said this really funny thing, and the fact that Lyset had once been so determined to record a certain story she had shaved her head to pass for a Kleckt native trader. There was something touching and a little sad about his evident concern for them, his watching the screens intently for any sign of movement even as he spoke to her, nervously chewing his lower lip.

The sudden approach of the *Indomitable* to the derelict caught them all by surprise. Without interrupting the monitoring of their own party's landing site, Lanchard had the *Cirrandaria* manoeuvre to keep the *Indomitable* in view. They saw it take up a new station point only four kilometres from the derelict and watched as its shuttle dropped down to the surface for a second time.

'Are they up to something?' Arcovian asked anxiously.

'I don't know,' Lanchard admitted.

For almost ten minutes nothing further appeared to happen. Then a call came through from Vega.

'Yes, Commander,' Lanchard acknowledged, noticing as she did so that Vega looked drawn and hollow-eyed.

'Some unidentified force attacked my landing party within the last half-hour,' he said bluntly. 'At least two have been killed and the rest are missing. Could your people have been responsible?'

The accusation was delivered so flatly that she found herself responding in the same controlled manner. 'No. They are armed, but they'd have no reason to attack your people unless they were provoked.'

Vega studied her face intently for a moment, then nodded fractionally. 'No, I didn't really think they would be stupid enough. In that case there's something very dangerous down on that ship. That's all the warning I'll give you, take it or leave it. If you can, I suggest you remove your party for their own safety. Vega out.'

The screen went blank.

'We must get them out right now!' Arcovian said, his eyes wide.

'It's not as simple as that, Mr Arcovian.' It was easy to forget that, though the *Cirrandaria* carried a transmitter capable of signalling across several light years, they were not in direct contact with a group of people only a few kilometres away. 'We arranged that they should call us every hour from the time they entered the alien ship,' she reminded him. 'We can't tell them anything until then.' She consulted her watch. 'And they won't be calling us again for another twenty minutes at least.'

'Well, haven't you got another shuttle you can use?'

'The engineers worked for almost fourteen hours straight to modify the one they're using. They need a rest before starting on another.'

Arcovian looked despairing and clutched at a slender reed of comfort. 'Maybe Vega's message was just a bluff to get us to leave the alien ship to the Nimosians. Perhaps it's all a trick,' he suggested hopefully.

'Perhaps,' Lanchard said. But privately she thought the look on Vega's face had been very convincing.

Watching the small man's troubled expression she was reminded just how much Arcovian genuinely cared for Delray and Wynter. Despite her own preoccupations she found herself wondering if he treated all his clients like his family. Suddenly it occurred to her that he might have no close relations of his own. People like Delray and Wynter could be all the family he had.

Chapter Nine
The Experiment

The chamber beneath the surface hatch was clearly a shuttle bay of some sort, though Sam could detect no indication as to what type of craft normally used it. Jenez set them down in its centre and they examined their surroundings.

The bay was circular, perhaps a hundred metres across, illuminated by a score of large softly glowing, pale-blue discs set in the ceiling. About its perimeter the floor curved smoothly upward to become the wall, with several recessed doorways spaced along it. Beside one of these were a wheel and a key panel identical to the ones they had seen on the surface.

On seeing this Rexton said, 'Our first priority is to close the external hatch before the Nimosians follow us in here. Jenez, stay with the shuttle and keep it locked and tight. If the Nimosians get in use the jets to keep them clear. If we don't return in three hours, use your own initiative. Otherwise stay put. I'm relying on you to be ready to lift us out of here if we need to make a rapid withdrawal.'

'Yes, sir,' Jenez said solemnly.

They sealed their suits and disembarked.

Sam noticed, when they got beyond the shuttle's stabilising field, that the interference on the suit radios was less pronounced than it had been on the outside of the hull. That, at least, was reassuring.

With Dessel and Bendix beside him, Rexton crossed the marbled floor to the wall panel and tried the wheel. It moved freely. He spun it vigorously and Sam watched the circle of stardusted sky contract and disappear. Had they shut the enemy out, she wondered, or trapped themselves inside with something worse? She shivered and tried to get a grip on herself. Why should an innocent bare chamber suddenly fill her with such a sense of disquiet?

Rexton was looking at the hatch with a frown. 'Can we stop it being opened again from outside? It would cover our line of escape and prevent the Nimosians following us in.'

'If you must,' the Doctor said. 'I suspect this will do the trick.' And he pressed four keys in quick succession. Rexton's frown deepened and he tried the wheel. It would not budge.

'How did you do that?' Rexton demanded.

'It's obvious,' the Doctor said gravely, 'as long as you look without preconceptions. I could explain it, but then you'd probably think it was a joke, which would be dangerous because that's the last thing I think it is.'

They were all looking at him in puzzlement. Sam was as baffled as the rest but tried not show it.

'I don't have any time for riddles, Doctor,' Rexton said. 'As long as something functions reliably I don't care why.'

'That's what I'm afraid of,' the Doctor said.

Rexton ignored him. 'Show me the release sequence again.'

The Doctor pressed the same keys he had used on the surface panel. The manual wheel turned freely once again. Sam could still not see what had caused the Doctor to choose the keys he had.

'Jenez,' Rexton said, alerting the shuttle pilot, 'take a note of this in case you need to use it. To release the bay hatch press the keys on the panel in this order, working down the rows and counting in from the left: three, four, two, five, three and six. To seal it press four, five, four and one.'

'Got that, sir,' Jenez said.

The doorway beside the key panel was another smaller version of the irising surface hatch, but this time mounted vertically. There must have been a simple sensor built into the floor because it opened as Rexton stepped up to it. At the end of the small chamber beyond was an identical hatch. Rexton stepped inside confidently and the others followed. The hatch closed automatically behind them and a moment later the one in front opened. There was another identical chamber beyond that. As they passed through Manders looked at the gauge on the arm of her suit.

'Pressure's building up,' she observed.

Again the door ahead opened a few seconds after the one behind had shut. They stepped through this to find themselves in the ship proper. Sam saw Rexton looking about him with eager, hungry eyes.

They were at the junction of three corridors, each circular in section, about four metres across and dimly lit by more of the blue ceiling discs. The curving lower halves of the corridors were floored with some dark rubber-like material moulded with a heavy transverse rippling tread. A pair of handrails carried by close-set stanchions ran continuously along them, dividing the floor into three lanes and breaking only at the junction itself. To the left and right the corridors appeared perfectly level, but the corridor in front of them arched slightly, following the curve of the hull, so that the ceiling lights seemed to dip towards the floor in the distance.

'Corridors with abundant railings and a high-traction floor,' observed the Doctor. 'No doubt provision for shifts in the centre of gravity when the ship's functioning.'

'Of course,' Sam heard Rexton mutter to himself under his breath.

'They're rather high,' Sam pointed out.

'Yes,' the Doctor agreed. 'Perhaps the users are taller than the humanoid average. The diameter of the rail is also rather large, suggesting –'

'That they had big hands,' Sam concluded with a smile.

Manders had been using a direct-reading radiation counter on their surroundings. Now she was holding up a chemical sampler. She examined the reagent patches carefully, then said, 'The air is OK. Oxygen low but within the limits. No particulate or biohazard indicators showing.' She checked the thermostrip on the back of her glove. 'Temperature four degrees above zero. Fine for suit work. If we can breathe in here that'll extend our EVA endurance by hours. I'm going to test it.'

'I think I should do that first,' the Doctor said quickly. 'I have a nose for subtle toxins.'

He released his visor, raised it cautiously and sniffed. Apparently satisfied, he took a deeper breath, then another.

'A little musty and rather thin,' he declared, 'but otherwise quite acceptable.' He opened his visor fully, and the others followed his example.

Sam thought she could taste dust and a tang of ozone, combined with faint chemical odours she could not identify. But as the Doctor had said, it was breathable.

'Now, where shall we go from here?' the Doctor mused, facing the radiating corridors in turn.'Eeny, meeny, miny, mo –'

'This way,' Rexton said, pointing down the middle corridor.

'As you wish,' the Doctor said easily.

Simmons, one of Manders's assistants, unclipped a small can from his belt and sprayed a luminous orange arrow on the corridor wall pointing in the direction they were taking.

'I thought we'd better not get lost,' Manders explained.

'I didn't think of that,' the Doctor admitted. 'Of course I was intending to rely on my own sense of direction.' He turned suddenly to Rexton.'But what were you going to use?'

Rexton simply strode away down the corridor, Bendix beside him. Dessel motioned the others on, then took up the rear, carrying his shoulder-slung rifle at the ready, turning every few paces to check behind them.

The corridor ran on for over a hundred metres, giving the illusion they were crossing a very long hump-backed bridge. Halfway along it a large plaque was mounted on the wall, covered with more of the shapes they had seen on the hatch keypads, plus an array of additional geometric symbols. Lyset photographed it.

'Well, Doctor?' Rexton asked expectantly.

'Sorry?' said the Doctor, who had been tilting his head and squinting at the jumble of symbols.

'What does it say?'

'I don't know. I can't read it.'

'Not even the numbers?'

'They're not numbers.'

'But they're the same symbols as on the keypads.We assumed –'

'It can be dangerous to assume anything.They're all letters.'

'But then if you deciphered the keypads, why not this?'

'Because it's gibberish.'And he smiled, as though inviting Rexton to join in his appreciation of the joke the universe was playing on them. Rexton merely glowered and stomped away.

As they continued along the corridor Sam whispered to the Doctor, 'I thought you could read almost any language.'

'Not if it contains no intelligence. That display really was nonsense.'

'Then why put it up there?'

The Doctor didn't answer.

Sam became aware of a deep, slow, throbbing pulse that reverberated through the thin air and along the floor from somewhere ahead of them. The end of the tunnel came into view and they approached cautiously. The space beyond widened and suddenly they were standing on a gallery encircling an open shaft as wide as the landing bay. Above were more galleries linked by long spiral ramps. The centre of the shaft was half filled with massive conduits made of glass or plastic which glowed with multicoloured inner light. Between them were glittering metal grids, lenses and mirrors, all set at angles as though to deflect energy out of the vertical shaft and off to the sides.

'Hell of a setup,' Delray exclaimed, as Lyset began snapping away at the scene.

'If this is a power plant, then it's like nothing I've ever seen before,' Manders admitted.

Rexton looked about him in silent awe and satisfaction.

Sam stepped over to the gallery rail and peered upward. The jumble of pipes and lenses seemed to blur into a haze high above her.

'It must run right up the centre of the tower,' she said.

She looked down. The strange array of conduits ran into darkness, like pipes disappearing into a well. In fact, she could almost imagine she could see reflections of water in the distance. She narrowed her eyes. There really were sparkles of light down there – blurred streaks of softly scintillating colour that seemed to drift at some indeterminate level. She realised the Doctor was by her side following her gaze.

'Is that the main tunnel that runs through the ship?' Sam wondered.

'I think so.'

'But it's open to space at either end. I suppose there must be a pressure curtain or something keeping the air in here.'

'Or something,' the Doctor agreed. He sounded distracted and was staring intently into the inky blackness.

'And what are those coloured lights?' she asked.

'I rather think they're stars.'

'What?'

The others had heard him too, and suddenly he was the focus of attention for several incredulous faces.

'You'll see,' he said. 'Come on!'

And before she could ask any more, he was bounding up the nearest ramp to the next level. The others followed after him in confusion.

The gallery above was crossed by one of the conduit arrays running off the central shaft. The core of this was a tube of silvery wire mesh, surrounded by a framework of supporting struts. The Doctor followed it along a radial corridor and into a large semicircular room. The open end of the tube faced an array of angled mesh panels mounted on a solid-looking black plinth. These seemed to serve as prisms and mirrors to whatever energy was being guided down the conduit, for smaller conduits radiated out from it into half a dozen large banks of twisted green, bronze and silver machinery which were ranged in an arc about the walls of the room.

Sam walked over to one of them. Its control panel was patterned with large, round, multicoloured buttons arranged in short arcs, together with circular glass display screens, all labelled with embossed lines of the unreadable alien script.

The floor between the freestanding equipment was laid out with grids and track lines, presumably indicating the paths of reflected or refracted beams. Set along these lines were mounted blocks and panels of various materials, as though they might be test targets for exposure to the beams.

Manders was examining one of these curiously. 'It seems fibrous, like dried moss and plant stems. What would anybody want with that?'

Then Sam realised where the chamber was situated.

'This is the inside of one of those projecting fins higher up the tower,' she said. 'I wondered what they were for.'

'Laboratories or control rooms, I should think,' said the Doctor. 'They're probably arranged like this so they can be tilted to compensate for gravity shifts – did you notice the overlapping segmentations along the entrance corridor?' He ducked nimbly under the mesh tubes so that he could examine the strange machinery more closely. 'They tap the central core for energy to run experiments, and probably also feed modulated power or matter back into it to control the shaft potentials.'

'But why? What's its function?' Manders demanded. 'What's this whole ship meant to do?'

The Doctor blinked at them in genuine surprise. *He really forgets how different he is sometimes,* Sam thought. *I really forget.*

The Doctor looked at Rexton. 'You know, don't you?' he said.

'What do I know, Doctor?' Rexton replied impassively.

The Doctor sighed. 'Yes, I was afraid you did. Well there's no point in keeping it a secret then. Obviously this whole ship is an experimental hyperspatial bridge.'

They placed the strips of explosive Tane had requested in a large circle inside the rim of the hatchway. Not trusting to electronic detonators or command wires, they were using a simple chemical fuse. From the shuttle cabin, Argen saw Corporal Martel pull the activator toggle. The squad withdrew in close order, eyes always scanning the shadows for the unknown enemy that had killed their comrades. They disappeared from view beneath the curve of the hull and a moment later he felt the thud of their boots on the ramp. As soon as the HATCH SEALED light blinked on, Argen cut in the underjets and they lifted clear. Five hundred metres up he banked into a wide circle so they could watch the hatch site below them. In a few minutes they would have opened a way into the alien ship. If any of their comrades were still alive that was the only place they could have been taken. And they were going after them.

* * *

'You can't be serious,' Delray said incredulously.

'If the Doctor says this is a hyperspatial bridge, then you'd better believe it,' Sam told him.

'I've heard all the usual theories and rumours about such things,' Manders said. 'But as far as I know nobody's ever come up with anything practical.'

'I didn't say this construction was practical,' the Doctor corrected her. 'I said it was experimental. In fact elements of it look ill-conceived and quite unstable.'

'But this is alien technology,' Manders protested. 'How can you possibly understand any of it after two minutes' examination?'

'I travel a lot,' the Doctor said lightly. 'One picks these things up.' His eyes found Rexton's and a new compelling tone entered his voice. 'And based on that knowledge I tell you that this ship is dangerous. There are forces here you cannot comprehend. I would strongly advise you to leave it be.'

They all sensed the conviction behind his words.

Rexton was staring at him intently now, as though weighing every nuance and inflection of his words. 'Then you really claim to know how all this works?'

The Doctor took the room in with an appraising glance. 'I dare say I could reason most of it out.'

'Then you can explain it to me.'

The Doctor shook his head. 'Apart from the matter of technical comprehension, there would be no point. This machine must not be used.'

Rexton's hand moved to rest on the butt of his holstered sidearm and the others lapsed into a shocked silence. Sam's eyes widened in horror.

'Oh, very clever!' she began, taking a step towards him. 'Threaten a Federation Moderator, why don't you?'

'Don't underestimate the lengths I am prepared to go to in the service of my homeworld,' Rexton warned her. 'I cannot risk this ship falling into the Nimosians' hands. If there is power here then I must have it for Emindar.'

'Power,' said the Doctor, almost sardonically. 'This place must be destroyed – that way neither Emindar nor Nimos stands to gain anything at all, apart from the safety of everyone here. Isn't a resumption of the status quo preferable to the risk of going to war once again?'

'When you're a soldier you learn to take risks,' Rexton told him.

'You also learn when to withdraw gracefully,' the Doctor said, his voice hard. 'You see, I've also been a soldier. I have fought in wars you have never even heard of. And I assure you this craft is not a weapon you can use.' His face softened a little. 'Now, we are going to find the main power source and see about shorting it out so that neither you nor the Nimosians will be tempted into making a catastrophic mistake.' He looked at Rexton's gun. 'I don't really believe you will shoot me in the back for doing that.'

Sam stared hard at Rexton. For agonising seconds Rexton's hand hovered over his holster. Finally, it dropped aside.

'I thought not,' said the Doctor, no trace of triumph in his voice. 'Come on, Sam.'

Just then a faint, sharp shudder passed through the frame of the ship.

'That was an explosion,' Rexton snapped. 'Maybe the Nimosians are up to something.' His lips pinched and he appeared to reach a decision. 'Manders, you and your team examine the equipment in here. There may not be much time but anything you find out may be useful. You!' He stabbed a finger at Lyset Wynter. 'Take pictures of everything she tells you to. Cover the shaft outside as well, especially those power linkages, or whatever they are. Then we'll go to the central control complex.'

Lyset nodded, rapidly inserting a fresh film cartridge into the camera. Rexton continued to rap out orders.

'Dessel and Bendix, you're with me. We'll scout the other side to see what the Nimosians are up to.' He eyed Delray, who up until now had been following quietly along beside Lyset, speculatively. 'Want a chance to show that those vid heroics weren't just play-acting, mister?'

Delray stiffened. 'I'm with you, General.'

'Good.' Rexton spared Sam and the Doctor a passing glance. 'It seems that you won't have time to sabotage anything after all, Doctor. Now if you won't help, stay out of our way.'

But the Doctor wasn't paying attention. His head was cocked sideways and his eyes were narrowed.

'Listen,' he hissed.

There was a change in the power hum coming from deep within the bowels of the ship. A new higher-pitched whine so faint as to be on the limits of hearing. But even as Sam strained to make it out it grew steadily stronger.

'Either some automatic system has cut in, or the shock of the explosion has disturbed something,' the Doctor said. 'Perhaps we'd better –'

With a crack of displaced air the mesh conduit leading into the room from the central shaft lit up with a green radiance. It struck the primary deflector array and split into half a dozen secondary beams that stabbed out across the chamber into the hulking machines set about the walls. As though stimulated by this sudden influx of power, lights began to show on their display panels.

'Don't touch the beams!' the Doctor shouted. 'Carefully duck under them and make for the doorway.'

With a slight hum a pair of the intermediate standing grids began to turn, creating new patterns of crossing beams that swept about the room.

'They must be working on a preprogrammed sequence,' the Doctor said. 'Be careful or else – Sam, get down!'

But it was too late. One of the traversing beams struck her in the back as she tried to take cover behind a target panel. She froze rigid even as another beam touched the panel itself. The light exploded in her mind and her consciousness seemed to dissolve away.

Lyset Wynter saw Sam and the target panel haloed in cold green fire. The panel bowed and split, then burst into powdery dust. Sam screamed and her suit seemed to collapse inward, falling to the floor in a shrunken crumpled heap.

Then the power hum died away and the beams vanished, leaving ghostly afterimages floating before their eyes.

In three long strides the Doctor reached Sam's body and knelt beside her, the others gathering about him. Sam's helmet appeared to be empty. With frantic haste the Doctor unlatched the clips and tore it off. There was nothing inside. He let out a stifled groan of anguish.

'Sam. Sam, Sam... Oh, no... I'm so –'

Then the chest of the suit stirred. Slowly a mop of tousled blonde hair appeared above the collar ring. It was followed by the frightened face of a ten-year-old child.

Whose features were unmistakably those of Sam Jones.

Chapter Ten
Brothers

Rask Chen was playing pitch and catch with Talek. As usual Talek was throwing the ball wide and much too hard – he always had been the stronger one even though he was a year younger. Rask sucked his smarting fingers.

'That's too hard. And don't throw so high. We'll lose the ball over the fence, and you'll have to fetch it this time. I'm not knocking on old Parche's door again.'

'But I had to get your attention, Rask,' his brother said. 'It's really important.'

'What d'you mean?' Rask said absently, looking around him. Now he had lost the ball. It must have fallen in one of the felchia beds. He bent down and pushed his way between the stalks, peering into the cool green-tinted world under their broad leaves.

'You've got to get away from here,' he heard Talek say. 'It's dangerous.'

'Don't be stupid. The thorns aren't hard yet.' He still couldn't see the ball. He pressed forward further, trying not to break the stems. His mother had told him off about that before.

'No. Away from the alien ship. That's what's dangerous.'

'What alien ship?'

'You know. Please listen to me.'

Something was very wrong. The felchia bed was not this deep. He felt the mustiness of the earth and the heavy pollen catching in his throat. He tried to edge his way out, but something was holding him back.

'Talek – help me!'

The felchia were closing in on him, suffocating him under their heavy leaves…

'It's all right, Rask,' he heard Talek say. He felt a hand clasp his. 'All right Rask… Rask!'

He jerked himself awake choking, throwing back the bedcovers.

He was not a boy any more but Second Lieutenant Navigator Chen. Around him was the night-lit cabin on the *Indomitable* that he shared with Lieutenant Borix. Automatically he reached for the comm-unit button, thinking there was a message playing on it from his brother Talek. But the unit was inactive.

He sank gratefully back on to his pillow, and realised he was soaked with sweat. He glanced at the glowing time display beside the bedhead. The alarm hadn't sounded yet. He had plenty of time for a proper shower before he was due on watch.

The shower, alternately hot and cold, revived him. He came out of the tiny washroom cubicle towelling his hair and feeling more like his normal self.

'Shower's free,' he said, then bit back his words. It was the same phrase he had spoken a hundred times to Borix – except that Borix was on second watch and the room was quite empty. But he had spoken because the room had somehow *felt* occupied.

He thought about his brother. Rask had received a spacegram from him a month ago but it had been half a year since they had been together. Talek Chen was a marine corporal on the *Starfire* at least thirty light years away somewhere on the other side of Nimosian-controlled space.

Rask dressed uneasily, trying not to keep turning his head in response to the persistent itch between his shoulder blades. He made himself take the time to check that his uniform was all correct in the mirror, just to prove to himself that he was too sophisticated and intelligent to be frightened by stupid dreams.

Moving with deliberate care, he opened the door, turned off the cabin light and stepped outside.

'Rask,' came his brother's voice, whispering from the darkness behind him.

He bolted down the corridor.

Chapter Eleven
A Patriot's Tale

Sam Jones was terrified. She didn't know where she was or how she'd got there. It wasn't her room at home. It was filled with odd shapes and lights in the ceiling. She was dressed in clothes that seemed far too big, which bunched up around her. Strange people in spacesuits, just like she'd seen on the telly, were looming over her and all speaking at once. What was happening? She started to cry.

Then a voice cut through the babble.

'Sam. Sam, listen to me.'

It was a wonderful reassuring voice. The face, what she could see of it within the strange helmet, was full of concern. He had a long proud nose and eyes that seemed to shine from within. As she looked into them her panicky breathing slowed and the tears subsided.

'Sam,' the man continued in the same gentle tone. 'I know you must be feeling very confused and frightened. But you're quite safe and nobody's going to hurt you. There's been an accident. It wasn't your fault. I want you just to lie still for a few minutes while I try to put things right. Can you do that for me?'

Such was the power of this man's words that a great calmness seemed to flow over her. She nodded dumbly and laid her head back, staring up at the ceiling. The people withdrew a little way from her and she heard a strange conversation taking place.

'What's happened to her?'

'She was struck by a negative temporal charge and regressed along her own timeline while retaining the same location in physical space,' the kind man said.

'Through time?'

'Try to twist space and you affect time. It's inevitable – and dangerous.'

'She doesn't seem to know us.'

'The reversal has effectively wiped her memories. She cannot know

91

at ten what she wouldn't learn until she was twenty-one.'

What were they talking about? Sam wondered. It sounded as though she'd been ill. Maybe that was why she wasn't in school. Perhaps this was a hospital. But it didn't look like one. Where were the nurses – where were Mum and Dad? Too busy to find the time for her again? Well, maybe this was outside visiting hours. But Dad was a doctor – he could come any time. And Mum was always finding time to help other people while she was social-working – single mothers, poor people and thieves – everybody! But what about her? Didn't they care? How could they leave her like this?

Sam started to cry, little choking sobs that she tried desperately to stifle.

Suddenly the kind man was bending over her again.

'Be patient, Sam,' he said gently. 'Everything will be all right again soon. It'll all make sense to you. I promise. Do you trust me?'

And she realised she did trust him. His words were the only thing she had to believe in.

'I trust you,' she said quietly.

He smiled and Sam lay back again. He withdrew from her line of sight and the strange distant conversation continued.

'But what happened to that slab beside her?'

'It was irradiated with a positive charge to maintain the chronetic balance,' the kind man said. 'It was organic material of some kind and aged in the opposite direction.'

'But her suit hasn't changed.'

'The beam must have been attuned to affect organic matter only.'

'That's incredible.'

'It was an attempt to manipulate raw temporal flux as though it was electricity, and that can't be done with this sort of equipment.'

'You seem awfully sure of yourself, Doctor,' said a stern accusing voice. 'How can you possibly know all this?'

'It doesn't matter how I know. I've got to reactivate the system and reverse the process.'

'You think you can operate these controls?'

'There should be some logic to their layout…'

Sam heard more rapid footfalls as the man who had been called the Doctor began to move urgently about the room.

Argen barely allowed time for the fine plume of dust and small fragments blasted upward by the ring charge to disperse, before he took the *Resolve* down to land beside the hatchway. A neat hole had been cut out of its centre. Hardly had the wash of the underjets died away before the marines were piling out and running in long strides across the derelict's marbled hull. They had conferred with Commander Vega as they had circled high over the derelict and knew exactly what they had to do.

As soon as they were clear, the engineering tech closed the hatch. Argen wanted to go with them, to find their lost shipmates and, if possible, teach whoever had taken them that Nimosians never abandoned their comrades. But he was the only pilot and had to stay with the shuttle.

He watched intently through the cockpit canopy as they clustered round the newly formed aperture and shone torches into the void beneath. It was apparently clear, for they began rigging lines. One by one they quickly lowered themselves into the darkness, leaving two men on guard at the top of the shaft.

There came a faint whir of motors from the upper hull as the turret gunner tracked his sights across the machinescape around them. Now all they could do was wait.

Don Delray paced about the gallery outside the time laboratory, his eyes flickering about the levels and the dark mouths of the passageways leading off them. From within he could hear the Doctor and Manders debating some technical point. Lyset circled the central shaft, happily snapping away and building up a record of its glittering complexity as Rexton had requested. Rexton, Dessel and Bendix were on the levels above and below them, watching out for any sign of the Nimosians.

He could tell Rexton wanted them to move on, but he couldn't very well insist that they abandon the Jones girl in the state she was in. He was still a politician and he had an image to maintain. That was something Delray understood only too well – except that Rexton seemed so utterly sure of himself. Delray, on the other hand, didn't know how long he could go on acting the part.

On the bridge of the *Cirrandaria* Arcovian looked anxiously at Captain Lanchard.

'Isn't it time they checked in?' he asked for the tenth time.

'Six minutes more,' she replied.

'And you'll tell them what the Nimosians said?'

He was not being rhetorical, Lanchard decided. 'You can be certain I'll do that, Mr Arcovian,' she assured him.

Vega hunched forward, staring intently at the screens, which reproduced the magnified image of the derelict's hull. A light began to pulse on the beetle-like form of the *Resolve*.

'Mr Argen signals, ALL IS WELL, sir,' one of the observers reported.

He'd ordered Argen to make contact every ten minutes. Of course, that told them nothing about the status of the marine rescue party. Shielded by that massive hull and the interference anything could happen to them and they'd never know it.

He opened a channel to the engineering bay.

'How long before the second shuttle is ready?' he asked.

'At least another two hours, sir,' Reng's second replied.

'All right. Continue at your best speed.'

If only Reng himself had been there, Vega thought, the work would have been done by now. But Lio Reng was somewhere down on the derelict, and Vega didn't know whether he was alive or dead.

He made a note to stop thinking of it as a derelict. He'd convinced himself that it was abandoned, as he suspected the Emindians had, because it was simpler that way. But in fact it was an alien vessel of unknown origins and potential.

And something was alive inside it.

The rising hum of power reverberating through the central shaft brought them all racing back to the time laboratory.

Delray saw that Sam Jones, almost enveloped in her suit, was now standing white-faced and wide-eyed with fear on the spot where she had been struck by the beam. A fresh organic panel had been set up beside her to replace the one that had disintegrated. The Doctor was stepping quickly from one control bank to another, making minute adjustments. Manders and her assistants were standing a little way back from him, watching his activity with baffled interest.

'Are you ready now, Doctor?' Rexton asked. 'We can't risk staying here much longer.'

'Any moment now,' the Doctor called back over his shoulder. 'I can't afford to make a mistake… Keep still, Sam. It's going to be all right.'

'Is this going to work?' Rexton asked Manders.

'Maybe. I don't know how he puzzled out the controls. This set-up's beyond me. Even when he tried to explain I didn't understand a tenth of what he said. But I think if anybody can do it, he can.'

With a crack the conduit filled with the green haze of energy.

'This is it,' said the Doctor. 'Everybody stay clear…'

The young Sam whimpered. The refracting grids began to rotate. The split beams flickered about the chamber and suddenly illuminated Sam and the test panel. Green fire enveloped them. They heard Sam give a shrill scream, then the energy flickered and died.

By the time Delray had blinked away the afterimages, the Doctor was supporting Sam Jones in his arms. Her suit fitted properly once again and her face had regained its maturity. But it still held a look of fearful confusion.

'Sam,' the Doctor asked anxiously. 'Do you remember who I am and where you are?'

There was a long pause. Then comprehension seemed to return. She nodded slowly and made a visible effort to pull herself together.

'You're the Doctor. I've just been zapped by this experimental alien gizmo… and Lyset Wynter has just taken my picture.' She forced a lopsided grin. 'Can I have a couple of prints, please?'

'You've got them,' Lyset assured her with a broad smile. 'Nice to have you back.'

Delray saw a look of immense relief light the Doctor's face as he beamed at Sam. They're close, Delray thought, really close.

'Look at that,' Manders said in awe.

The organic test panel that had been set beside Sam was now a swollen, glistening mass of matted plant stems and crumpled half composted leaves.

'Entropy demands that a balance must be kept,' the Doctor said, helping Sam to her feet. 'Sam's years had to come from somewhere.'

'Then... this machine actually can restore youth,' Lyset said, the possibilities obviously only now dawning on her.

'Was I really ten years old again?' Sam asked. The Doctor nodded solemnly. 'Well it's not worth it,' Sam said to Lyset with feeling. 'Believe me.'

'Any gain in youth would be at the expense of all the memories, knowledge and experience that went to make you what you were,' the Doctor warned Lyset. 'The person who emerged would not be the person who made the decision to regress.'

'Never mind all that,' Rexton interjected impatiently. 'Are you fit to proceed, Ms Jones?'

'I'm OK.'

'Then we must move on.'

'Just a moment,' said the Doctor. 'First you are going to explain how you knew so much about this craft before you ever set foot inside it, and why it's so important to you.'

'You seem quite well informed yourself, Doctor,' Rexton countered.

'That was simply the application of general principles and a little improvisation, not foreknowledge. I've never been in a craft like this in my life – but I think you have. And, volunteers or not, these people are running a considerable risk providing you with an exploration team. They're not soldiers blindly following orders and, as we've just discovered, this is a dangerous environment. They deserve to know the truth.'

'If the General wants to keep his reasons secret –' Bendix began, but Rexton silenced him.

'Thank you for your support, Mr Bendix. Perhaps I should explain.

But first we must get to the central control module. If the Nimosians are on board we haven't much time.'

'After you,' the Doctor said, 'and explain as we go. I'm sure you know the way.'

Alen Jenez twisted the wheel beside the key panel until the roof hatch had irised halfway open. He picked up the powerful emergency signal lamp that he had run out on a long cable from the shuttle, and sighted its scope through the roof aperture to the distant spark that was the *Cirrandaria*. He sent, ALL WELL. EXPLORATION CONTINUING.

The *Cirrandaria*'s lights pulsed back, RECEIVED. NIMOSIAN SECOND LANDING PARTY HAS FORCED ACCESS ON OPPOSITE SIDE OF DERELICT AFTER REPORTING FIRST PARTY ATTACKED BY UNKNOWN FORCES. SUGGEST YOU ABANDON EXPLORATION AND RETURN IMMEDIATELY.

Jenez sent back, RECEIVED. WILL PASS ON RECOMMENDATION.

Then he hastily shut the external hatch again and stowed the lamp away. He was prone to letting his youthful imagination run away with him, and the last hour alone had been ample time for his mind to populate the ship around him with all manner of beings, mostly malevolent. But at least he felt safe in the shuttle. He was fairly certain a blast of the underjets or manoeuvring thrusters would deter all but the most determined aggressor. But now he would have to make his way far enough into the craft to re-establish a link via the suit radio with the explorers. Why hadn't Rexton detailed somebody to remain with him to act as a messenger for just this eventuality? Probably because he didn't want to be bothered by messages from the Captain, he decided. But he'd have to take notice of this piece of news.

Jenez closed the shuttle's hatch, checked once again that his sidearm was loose in its holster, and stepped up to the airlock through which the others had passed an hour earlier. Automatically the door irised open.

* * *

Rexton led them up the ramps to the higher levels of the tower, talking rapidly.

'I knew what to expect when we boarded this ship because I've seen one almost identical to it. Years ago we found it drifting in towards the edge of Emindar homespace. Except that unlike this ship it was badly damaged – whether by deliberate intent or accident was impossible to determine for certain. Anyway, it was recovered by military tugs and taken to a high-security research station based somewhere in the outer system – you understand I cannot be more specific as to its location. And there it has remained undergoing painstaking examination and reconstruction. Over the years, as I gained seniority, I have been able to oversee the project.'

'To learn how to use it as a weapon against Nimos,' Sam said automatically.

Sam was feeling fully recovered from her disconcerting experience, and was pleased to find her perceptions and responses functioning normally. Rexton glowered at her, but she simply smiled back sweetly. 'Well, do you deny it?'

'I will not confirm or deny anything,' Rexton said stiffly. 'That craft was empty and abandoned and drifting into our space. It was obvious that a study of it might reveal new knowledge, *perhaps* of military value. Assuming it was, is it a crime to wish to see one's homeworld properly defended?'

He glanced round at them, as though demanding their understanding. Suddenly Sam suddenly felt his oration shift gears.

'Emindar has cared well for me in the past,' he continued in smooth but fervent tones, 'and now I am repaying that debt. I was a homeless orphan from backwoods Melconville. The state raised me and gave me an education and opportunity to make something of myself, and I seized it. Now I've risen almost to the highest office the state has to bestow.'

Sam felt she was listening to lines rehearsed in endless political rallies. It almost sounded as though he were proud of his lack of antecedence. Was that the ultimate politician's appeal to the common man? she wondered.

They turned off an upper main gallery and along a radial corridor.

'It is not your past I'm questioning,' the Doctor said simply, 'but your intentions concerning this vessel and the other craft.'

Rexton continued determinedly. 'The alien craft was obviously of a radically different design. Even in its damaged state the theorists could make some reasoned guesses as to its... potentialities.'

'The potentialities being the creation of a hyperspatial transporter carrying a fleet several light years in a few seconds,' the Doctor interpolated helpfully.

Rexton did not reply.

'A weapon. Told you so,' said Sam.

The Doctor continued, 'I suppose that's why you've been getting Ms Wynter to record everything. In case you can't take possession of this craft, you'll send back the information so that your damaged model can be fully repaired.'

Further denial was obviously pointless. Rexton said, 'You're quite correct, Doctor. In the first craft the core of this tower, the control module and most of the secondary chambers were badly damaged. Repairs and partial reconstruction have taken years. But with even the most superficial visual references of an undamaged assembly, that process may at last be completed.'

The corridor opened out into another of the fin-shaped chambers. It was ringed with control panels similar to those in the time laboratory.

But with one startling difference.

White rectangular labels had been neatly taped beside every one of the hundreds of blocks of switches and banks of display screens. Sam could see the nearest of them quite clearly. On it was printed in large clear type not the indecipherable alien script, but a description of the control's purpose in perfectly legible English.

Chapter Twelve
Ghost

Jenez carefully examined the T-junction that opened off the airlock. He saw the arrow sprayed on the side wall of the middle corridor and stepped towards it. Then it struck him that, as the interference had subsided slightly, the explorers might now be in range of his helmet radio. He was about to call them when his attention was diverted. About a hundred metres down the corridor to his right a cluster of three blue ceiling-light discs were beginning to flicker. He looked at them warily, wondering if it was a power fluctuation. If the alien ship was going to commence another of its gravity shifts and energy discharges, he wanted to be ready to grab hold of some solid support. But why were only three lights affected? Even as he watched, the furthest of the three brightened again. The problem seemed to be correcting itself.

Then the next light along dimmed.

And the last one on the far side brightened.

Then another dimmed.

So odd yet outwardly innocent was the phenomenon that he watched it approach at the equivalent of a steady walking pace for several seconds without any sense of alarm. As it got closer he noted that the shadowy patch of corridor directly under the shifting cluster of dimmed lights was curiously indistinct. Almost as though there was something....

The hairs lifted on the back of his neck.

A faint shimmering wisp of grey mist was gliding silently but purposefully along within the zone of shadow.

Heading towards him.

He drew his gun and began to back away, turning into the transverse corridor the others had gone down. He called out anxiously, 'Urgent: Jenez to exploration party. Can you hear me? Reply please!'

* * *

Rexton had stared at the improbably annotated control room for perhaps ten seconds in stupefied amazement. Then he appeared to recover his composure.

'Ms Wynter,' he said, in a tone that demanded instant compliance. 'Photograph these controls. Record every label. Don't miss anything.'

Lyset began clicking away, while the others continued to stare around them in bafflement.

'But this is crazy,' Manders exclaimed. 'Who did this?'

'I don't know,' Rexton said, 'but I'm not going to pass up the opportunity.'

'It's got to be a joke,' Delray suggested.

'It's possible, sir,' Bendix agreed. 'The Nimosians may be trying to mislead us –'

'The Nimosians haven't had the time to create anything so elaborate,' Rexton said. 'And if they had taken possession of this control room, then they'd be here to welcome us. No, somehow this feels right. Whether we capture this ship or not, we will master its secrets.' He graced the Doctor and Sam with a look of triumph. 'I think the Federation will be very ready to admit us when they learn the power we command, eh, Doctor?'

'I'll be sure to mention it to them,' the Doctor said absently, his own eyes flickering intently round the room. Then, suddenly, he said, 'Keep away from the far wall!'

Lyset, who had been working her way methodically around the control panels, flinched backward. The Doctor stepped quickly up to her side.

'You were about to touch that,' he told her.

Sam looked past Lyset at the half of the control room furthest from the entranceway. Now she looked closely she realised it was slightly blurred, as though seen through a distorting lens. The labels on the panels, which had been clearly legible on this side, suddenly became *il*legible only a couple of metres within the boundary.

Dessel cautiously reached out a gloved hand. Sam saw his fingertips blur as though they had passed into water. He pulled his hand back quickly.

'It went right into me,' he exclaimed in mild surprise. 'A sort of cold tingle. Nasty.'

'What is it?' Delray exclaimed breathlessly. Sam thought she heard a slight and unexpected catch in his voice.

'This room extends along the axis of the ship towards the end that appears indistinct and translucent from outside,' the Doctor said, as he ran his hands along the line of the boundary. 'It must be out of phase with the rest of the structure. Until we understand its exact nature I would strongly advise keeping well clear of it.'

'But we must get through to the other side,' Rexton said. 'Half the controls are in there.' He glared at the immaterial barrier for a moment, then tried bodily to step through it, as though he would defy it by sheer force of will. But after a few seconds he staggered backward, trembling, his face contorted by pain and anger.

'There's a distinction between courage and foolhardiness, Councillor,' the Doctor said sharply. 'You must have patience. We will determine its limits by subtler methods than brute force.'

As Rexton glared back at him with barely contained rage, Jenez's voice sounded over the subdued crackling of their headphones. The pilot was speaking very quickly and urgently.

'... hear me? Come in, please!'

Bendix answered, 'We can hear you, Jenez.'

'I'm in the cross corridor opposite the airlocks. There was a message from the *Cirrandaria*. The Nimosian party has been attacked... and there's something coming towards me right now!'

The Doctor cut in. 'Jenez, keep well clear of it but try to give us a description.'

Rexton took one last frustrated look around the control room, then led the way back into the corridor. They followed him as fast as the bulk of their restrictive suits would allow.

'Can't see it properly,' Jenez said. 'The lights keep going out around it as it moves. It's like a grey cloud of mist, twisting and writhing.'

'Can you see any details?' the Doctor asked.

They reached the central core and started back down the ramps, Jenez's voice growing stronger as they descended.

'No... but I think it's getting thicker... It was moving slowly at first, but now it's speeding up... Wait a minute. There's a shape inside.... Oh God –'

'Run, man, run!' Bendix shouted.

They heard the searing crack of energy weapon discharges from the corridor on the level below, even as Jenez's scream of terror shrilled in their earphones. They reached the gallery they had first emerged upon with the Doctor in the lead and Rexton, Bendix and Dessel at his heels, weapons drawn.

They rounded the corner into the transverse corridor. A handgun, presumably Jenez's, was lying about ten metres along it. Sam could smell scorching and saw a dark blaze on the ceiling. A cry of pain and fear came faintly to them from somewhere beyond the rise of the corridor. They raced along it.

The junction came into view. Sam saw a flicker of movement as something disappeared down the left-hand corridor – the same impression of something half-seen that she had experienced on the surface. They reached the junction and turned after it. Twenty metres down the corridor the ceiling lights were flickering and going dim in rapid sequence. Within this travelling shadow a grey wraithlike form was speeding away from them. It was bigger than a man, but whether it moved on legs or even touched the ground at all Sam could not tell. For a second they saw a spacesuited arm reach out of the amorphous thing and heard another agonised cry. The thing was carrying Jenez.

Bendix cursed loudly.

'Save your breath,' Rexton commanded.

They pounded after the apparition. However the thing was moving, they began to overhaul it.

Then the corridor opened into a broad chamber from which a dozen more corridors led off in different directions. Across the middle was the blurred haze of the interface that they had seen in the control room several decks above them. It must extend right through the ship, Sam thought. The grey thing was heading directly towards it, haloed by flickering lights in the ceiling above. Now Sam could see the more solid form of Jenez twisting and kicking within, as though held by invisible limbs.

Dessel dropped to one knee, sighted his rifle and fired.

The beam of energy hit the thing low down. It glowed as though lit up from within by lightning, and streamers of sparks flashed about its nebulous form. For a second it seemed to waver and grow more substantial. What might have been a head turned round. Sam had the impression of bared fangs and glowing coal-red eyes. A bestial howl of pain or rage reverberated about the chamber.

Then it plunged through the interface and vanished with its struggling burden through one of the farther doorways. The lights in the chamber returned to their normal intensity.

'I hit it with the strongest blast I dared with it holding Mr Jenez,' Dessel said. 'No good.'

Bendix gritted his teeth and thrust an arm into the interface, but was forced to draw it back, clenching his fist as though trying to restore circulation. Dessel looked at Rexton expectantly, but for the moment it was evident he was at a loss.

'I have some equipment in my luggage that may help us get through this,' the Doctor said. 'We must get back to the *Cirrandaria*. There's nothing else we can do here.'

'That sounds sensible,' Delray said quickly. 'Come on.'

Bendix hesitated, looking at Rexton. The councillor nodded reluctantly. But as they turned to retrace their steps, Lyset Wynter said, 'Wait a moment – listen.'

In the silence Sam heard a low groaning. They looked about, automatically raising their guns.

'Where's it coming from?' Manders hissed.

'There,' said the Doctor, pointing to an open archway.

They advanced cautiously. There came another groan, which dissolved into a choking sob.

'Somebody's hurt,' said the Doctor, and stepped forward briskly.

The corridor beyond made a right-angled turn a few metres in. The Doctor rounded this and quickly bent down. 'Give me a hand, Sam.'

Lying there slumped with his back to the wall was a man in a Nimosian-pattern space suit. On the chest was a name tag with LT. M.

TANE stencilled on it. His visor was open. Sam saw two wild eyes staring up at them. Spittle bubbled from his lips and he made vague scrabbling movements as though he was trying to crawl away from them.

'The rest of you stay back,' the Doctor said. 'Sam, take his hand. Let him know you're real. It's all right,' he continued, addressing the wretched figure in the same calming tones Sam had heard him use on her earlier. 'We aren't here to hurt you...' She took the man's twitching hand and squeezed gently, smiling at him as warmly as she could.

Tane's eyes darted madly from one to another of them. His rapid breathing began to slow and Sam felt the tension flow out of him. His head dropped forward and he began to sob uncontrollably.

'What the hell can do that to a man?' she heard Dessel mutter behind her. Sam thought she could guess.

The Doctor tilted Tane's head back until their eyes met. 'I know you've been through a terrible experience,' he said gently but firmly. 'But you are going to put that aside for now. All you can hear is my voice, and I tell you the fear is going. In a moment you will be able to stand up.' There was a hypnotic rhythm to his words. Tane's face had relaxed, looking almost childlike in repose. 'Give him an arm, Sam.'

They lifted the Nimosian soldier to his feet, the Doctor not taking his eyes from him for a second.

'Now we are going to walk out of here. We'll take you somewhere safe where your friends will come to collect you.'

'Friends?' Tane said dully, his eyes focused on some distant place, speaking half to himself. 'The... the ghosts took my friends. I tried to fight them but it was no use. Pulled us right through the hull. So cold. Then they started fighting each other. Dropped me. I crawled away. Heard my men screaming... had to get away from the screaming...'

'Shh,' the Doctor told him gently. 'That's enough. Don't think of it any more.'

The Nimosian nodded obediently.

Gently they walked Tane back into the large chamber and turned for the corridor that would take them back to the shuttle. Just then came a clatter of boots from a side passage.

Half a dozen men in dark-grey combat suits emerged into the chamber. Dessel, Rexton and Bendix automatically raised their guns.

'Don't be stupid,' the Doctor snapped. 'They aren't your real enemies.' He called out to the Nimosians, 'We have found one of your men. He needs medical attention.'

The marines fanned out around them. Sam saw suspicious faces behind their helmet visors and fingers tight on the triggers of their guns. Just what we need, she thought dismally. One of them, wearing corporal's stripes, stepped forward.

'What happened to him? Where are the others?' he demanded.

'We don't know. We only found him a minute ago,' Sam said.

'I don't think he's suffered much physical harm, but he's in shock,' the Doctor explained. 'He must have medical treatment as soon as possible.'

The corporal looked at Tane's blank face, then waved a couple of his men forward. They took Tane gently by the arms and led him aside.

'Who did this?' the corporal asked.

'*What* did this, you mean. The same thing that's just taken our pilot, probably,' Bendix said bluntly.

The corporal's face darkened. 'Describe it.'

'A misty grey fuzzball – but it had teeth and eyes,' Sam said. 'I know what it sounds like but it was real. It took him through there.'

As she pointed across the chamber at the interface, all the lights on the far side began to flicker and dim.

'They're coming...' she heard Tane say softly.

And then the gates of hell seemed to open upon them.

Chapter Thirteen
Dead Man's Hands

The things poured out of the doorways in a nightmarish tide. For a moment they were mere phantoms lurking in the veil of shadow they wrapped around themselves, their forms torturing the eye and imagination with improbable silhouettes and grotesque half-seen skeletons trapped within them. But as they flowed across the floor towards them they grew and became more tangible. Twists of mist condensed into many-jointed arms, tentacles and claws. Virulent colour suddenly erupted out of shadowy grey obscurity and seared itself into the mind: hot blood red, bile yellow, decay green. And the hues flowed into the things and took on their shapes like water soaking through a sponge, illuminating them in all their terrible magnificence. Sam wanted to turn her eyes away, but she could not because no two were alike in size or shape, or held the form they had for more than a few seconds at a time. And their faces and eyes…

'Run!' she heard the Doctor shout, breaking the spell of disbelieving horror that had held them in its thrall. But before they could react the things burst through the interface and fell upon them.

Only then came the sound: a cacophony of howls, shrieks, roars, rasping hisses and hooting wails that should not have issued from any living creature.

Both parties opened fire. Bolts and beams of fire from Nimosian and Emindian weapons tore into the horde, lighting them up from within as though they were made of melting wax. If the sounds the things had made before were terrible, the chorus of rage and fury that issued forth now was ghastly beyond description.

But not one creature fell.

The edges of a hole blasted through a scaled body flowed together and knitted seamlessly; a limb severed by an incandescent cutting beam re-formed.

A Nimosian marine was snatched up into the air by a huge clawed hand belonging to a hulking thing with a bear's body supported by a cluster of spider's legs. As he struggled another claw slashed across him, tearing his suit to ribbons and ripping open his flesh. Simmons was skewered by a tentacle tipped with a metre-long spike, extending from a pulsating mass of bloated flesh that flopped and wriggled across the floor. A black-winged creature with a slobbering needle-fanged frog mouth dived at Bendix, Dessel and Rexton even though their fire was burning holes through its leathery integument, and knocked them to the ground.

Lieutenant Tane had fallen to his knees as his two attendants joined in the fight. Sam caught him under the arms and hauled him to his feet.

An octopoid arm coiled itself about Lyset Wynter's waist and dragged her into the clutches of a ball of writhing black tendrils. Delray was on the ground, weaponless and clutching his arm, shouting Lyset's name. But the thing carrying her vanished in the dreadful kaleidoscope of slashing limbs and stabbing fire.

Then the shrill of the Doctor's sonic screwdriver rose above the bedlam. Arm outstretched, he swung it back and forth. The image from an old horror film of a priest holding back the devil's creatures with a cross flitted through Sam's mind. The creatures' plastic forms shivered like rippling water and Sam saw waves of light and darkness radiating through them. For the briefest moment the things edged backwards, not harmed but perhaps uncertain what the strange sound was. In that momentary respite she saw Rexton snatch something up from the floor.

'To the shuttle – now!' the Doctor yelled.

They ran for their lives through the mouth of the long straight corridor that led back to the shuttle bay. And at their heels came the gibbering, baying nightmare host.

Tane was rolling his head and shouting wildly. The Doctor grabbed his other arm and helped Sam run him along. She couldn't see any Nimosian soldiers. Were they all dead or had they escaped along another corridor? Dessel took up the rear point behind a limping Delray, firing snatched shots behind him in an attempt to slow their pursuers and buy them precious seconds.

Sam ran as desperately as she ever had in her life. She knew she should look only to the front and that nothing could make her move any faster. Nevertheless she could not resist the compulsion to snatch a glance behind them.

What she saw *did* make her run faster.

Behind them the things actually filled the corridor from floor to ceiling and wall to wall. A boiling mass of translucent putrid flesh, hair and scales, rolling over and squeezing their way between their fellows in a blind frenzy of pursuit. Some were growing extra arms to haul themselves along the ladder-like handrails with hooks and talons, while others ran upside down along the ceiling, clinging on with platelike suckers. Bony many-jointed arms sporting uncannily human hands, spined tentacles and chitinous insectile limbs lashed out from the seething mass – limbs that stretched impossibly like rubber in an attempt to catch them in their embrace.

And then they were at the junction. The inner airlock door, sensing their presence, began to open. Before the aperture was a metre wide they were forcing their way desperately through, driven by fear of what was at their heels.

They only just made it. As Dessel plunged through last he was jerked flat on his face and began to slither backwards, struggling and kicking. A thick glistening tentacle was coiled round his leg. Sam and Manders grabbed his outstretched arms and heaved, while Rexton and Bendix fired point-blank into the wall of mottled, slightly translucent flesh that filled the aperture. A beak set in the underside of the thing snapped back at them. But the beast would not release its grip. Slowly Dessel was being pulled back towards it.

The Doctor had the control panel beside the door open and was working frantically on the circuitry within. Suddenly the door began to close, the irising segments contracting about the thigh-thick tentacle. A motor whined in protest as it met resistance. Then, with a spray of blood and yellow slime, the tentacle fell to the floor as the door closed completely. Dessel fell forward, trembling as though from cold and shock. Sam and Manders tore the limb free from around his leg, the suckers coming loose with loud pops, and kicked it aside in disgust and horror. The cleanly severed end flopped and twitched grotesquely for a moment, then lay still.

Dull thuds reverberated against the other side of the door, and Sam could hear the muffled cries of the things rise in a chorus of frustrated rage. The Doctor adjusted his sonic screwdriver and played it over the control panel, which sparked and puffed smoke.

'They won't get that open in a hurry,' he said.

'Gods!' exclaimed Dessel softly, pointing a trembling finger.

The severed tentacle that had almost dragged him to his death was fading into translucency. Before their eyes it became a coil of mist that vanished as though it had never been.

Even as they looked at each other with numbed amazement, a ghostly grey tendril reached through the tightly closed airlock door. Another followed it and another, as though the material of the door itself had sprouted some weird growth from within. They flinched away from the frightening but hypnotic sight. Tane's incoherent whimpers became manic, fitful laughter.

'They won't let us go. They'll never let us go...'

'We're not dead yet,' Rexton said, panting from his exertions but undaunted. 'Visors down and seal your suits.'

Only as he adjusted his own suit did Sam realise he was carrying Lyset Wynter's camera case slung across his shoulder. Before she could say anything the middle door opened and they stumbled into the next compartment of the airlock. As soon as it shut behind them the Doctor fused the door control once again.

'At least it'll slow them down,' he said simply.

Rexton stepped up to the third door. Sam felt the pressure drop and her suit tighten around her.

She half expected the bay to be full of monsters, but the shuttle stood there just as the unfortunate Jenez must have left it. The Doctor punched the unlocking code into the keypad and Dessel began turning the wheel. Above them the roof hatch began to open.

Sam saw a blurred flicker of motion silhouetted against the stars.

'Look out!'

But it was too late. An indistinct grey form dropped through it on to the roof of the shuttle. And then another...

The first indication Argen had that something was wrong was when the marines standing guard on the hole cut in the hull hatchway started firing rapidly downward. A babble of voices came crackling over the distorted suit channel.

'They're right behind us... Dak, look out! Grenades! Take out the roof!'

What the hell was happening down there? Argen thought, even as he began powering up the *Resolve*'s systems. 'Ready on the ramp hatch,' he told the engineer. 'Turret, make ready to provide covering fire.'

Argen saw a marine's head and shoulders appear over the edge of the hull hatchway only to be jerked backwards into the depths. The two guards redoubled their rate of fire. What were they fighting? Could he move the shuttle closer so they could angle the turret gun to –

Grey forms frothed over the pit's edge. The marines fell back, threw their grenades, then turned and ran for the shuttle. Half-seen things boiled out of the pit after them, growing more substantial as they poured out on to the surface under the glare of the *Indomitable*'s lights.

The turret gun spat fire.

The bolts tore through the ghostly horde and exploded behind them in showers of molten hull metal. The living shadows flickered and swirled where the energy pulses struck them. For a few seconds their advance was checked as they spread out. But then they surged forward once more.

Watching in slack-jawed disbelief Argen saw their bodies grow more solid, resolving into a shapeless nightmare of mismatched forms. He felt sickened. Their grotesqueness defied all logic. This was an appalling, loathsome *danse macabre* that was terribly, terribly wrong.

'Run, run!' he shouted aloud to the marines, though they needed no encouragement from him.

The turret gunner lowered his sights and blasted the ground at the pursuers' feet. Something resembling a huge crab with two sets of pincers was tossed aside by the concussion. A thing like a rolling tumbleweed fringed with lashing tentacles was split in half. But the two segments rolled on and after a few metres merged once more as though nothing had happened.

As the two surviving marines reached the *Resolve* the engineer dropped the access ramp and they tumbled aboard. Argen cut in the underjets and they lifted even as the leaders of the horde washed about them like a grey wave. He saw grotesque forms blasted aside and sent tumbling out across the marbled metal plain.

'Yes!' he exclaimed fiercely.

He was fifty metres up when a long, shapeless, translucent limb slapped across the forward viewport before his eyes. One of them was clinging to the hull. He heard a scream from the compartment behind him, followed instantly by the crack of guns. He saw the HATCH CLOSED light on the display panel flicker and suddenly the pressure dropped. The sound of gunfire ceased abruptly. Over his headphones he heard the gunner in the upper turret give one startled yell that ended in a sudden choking gurgle of pain.

Argen engaged the autopilot and tried to twist about, drawing his sidearm, but his seat harness held him back.

Even as he reached for the buckle a grey ballooning mass swelled and bubbled up through the hatchway behind him, taking on a terrible solidity as it came. An extruded limb lashed out. Argen felt the terrific thud as it struck the back of his chair and something seemed to tug very hard at his chest.

He looked down.

A needle-pointed, curving, glassy spike was protruding thirty centimetres out of his suit just below his sternum. He saw, with a detached and surprising clarity of perception, his own blood laced about its tip begin to steam and boil away into the vacuum.

Then the darkness swallowed him.

They were fighting for their very lives.

Bolts of fire crisscrossed the shuttle bay, exploding in showers of sparks as they struck the walls. A thin haze was billowing rapidly out of the roof hatch, from which more of the creatures were dropping on to them every second.

Sam didn't know if their efforts were doing anything but delaying the inevitable, but it was a simple stark choice: fight or die. Except that as fast as they knocked one of the hellish things down, another took its place. And the ones that had been hit flowed like syrup, re-formed, and came back at them again, like creatures from a nightmare that would not end.

Why couldn't they die decently? Sam thought. Or were they already dead?

Were they really fighting ghosts?

She was frantically cranking the roof hatch open wide enough to let the shuttle pass. Dessel stood by her side, his back to the wall, a rifle in one hand and pistol in the other, blazing methodically away at the nightmare horde that clutched and clawed and snapped at them. The Doctor was hunched over adjusting his sonic screwdriver. Rexton and Manders were standing on the *Doria*'s ramp, fighting to keep it clear. Delray, one arm still held close to his chest, was hauling a feebly struggling Tane towards them. Bendix was visible through the *Doria*'s cockpit viewscreen seated in the pilot's chair and powering up the shuttle for launch.

An intense, rapidly pulsing light filled the bay.

The Doctor was holding his sonic screwdriver aloft once more, this time radiating in the optical wavelengths. Again the things drew back. Sam looked at the steadily opening roof hatch. If only they could hold them for a few seconds more.

'It's wide enough!' the Doctor shouted. 'Come on!'

Dessel started forward with them, only to give a cry of pain and drop his weapons.

Ghostly limbs bristling with dark sea-urchin spines had extended from the wall and coiled tightly about him. He struggled for a second then went limp. Sam saw the spines begin to tear into the fabric of his suit. Instinct overcoming her reluctance to use guns, she snatched up his pistol and fired at the spines at point-blank range. The gun flickered and died, its power cell drained. She threw it aside and tore desperately at the glassy limbs with her gloved hands. She felt a numbing cold bite into her bones and a dreadful weariness seep into her, as though the life force was being drained from her body. But at the same moment the length of limb she touched seemed to become more solid, and some of the spines broke off and melted away in her palm.

Still holding the pulsating sonic screwdriver in one outstretched arm, the Doctor reached out with the other and grasped the thing that held Dessel. The glassy limbs became darker and more solid, as though suddenly infused with reality. She could see the pain on the Doctor's face.

'Now, Sam!' he choked out.

She kicked furiously at the restraining limbs. Spines snapped and fell away while their stems crushed into pulp under her blows. Dessel dropped limply to the ground while the remaining limbs released their hold and, threshing madly, faded and withdrew through the wall. The Doctor thrust the sonic screwdriver into Sam's hand, hauled Dessel upright and threw him over his shoulder. They plunged through a knot of grey things clustered about the shuttle's ramp with Sam holding the pulsating screwdriver before them like a talisman, even nerving herself to kick one of the confused creatures aside, ignoring the stab of pain it caused her.

They tumbled through the hatch and it slammed shut behind them. Even as the Doctor laid Dessel down and they fell into their seats the underjets roared. The rim of the surface hatch flashed past just beyond the ports. Then they were powering their way out into free space and the great bulk of the alien ship was shrinking behind them.

They slumped in their seats, too exhausted to speak. Sam saw the Doctor's head sagging on to his chest, as though even *his* remarkable reserves of vitality were temporarily drained. She herself felt like death.

She was so exhausted that she was only vaguely aware that, despite the automatic heating cutting in, the interior of the shuttle was unnaturally cold. It remained so all the way back to the *Cirrandaria*.

'The *Resolve* is clear of the interference zone, sir, but it is not responding to our signals,' the operator reported to Vega.

'They may have been hurt,' Fayle said.

'Override comm default protocols,' Vega said. 'Patch into cockpit camera.'

A new image appeared on the screens. A collective gasp of dismay whispered round the *Indomitable*'s bridge.

Argen was seated upright in his chair, held in place by his acceleration harness. There was a dark stain around a ragged hole in the centre of his chest. Glittering red jewels tumbled slowly past the camera lens: droplets of frozen blood, Vega realised. Argen's bulging eyes were staring sightlessly through his visor. Blood had bubbled and freeze-dried about his lips.

He was clearly quite dead.

Yet somehow, impossibly, his arms were moving.

It was a jerky motion, as though they belonged to a marionette operated by a clumsy puppeteer. But it could not possibly be mistaken for random movement generated by the motion of the shuttle. Argen's dead hands were operating the shuttle's controls, setting the autopilot to return it to the *Indomitable*.

Vega found his lips were dry. He had to lick them before he could speak. 'Sickbay, recovery team to shuttle port at the double.' He looked back at the screen. Argen's hands were motionless again, but he knew he hadn't imagined it.

Fayle was leaning forward and peering intently at the macabre image, almost blocking Vega's own view. But Vega said nothing. Fayle's suspicious nature might not make him popular, but it had saved them from serious trouble more than once in the past.

Slowly Fayle pointed over the back of Argen's chair. 'What's that?'

It seemed like a patch of mist. More blood droplets? Vega wondered. But surely no vapour could remain suspended in the vacuum the telemetry displays said filled the cabin. Yet the longer Vega stared at it the more it seemed to have distinct edges, and even a sort of fluid structure. Then, just for an instant, he thought he saw a distorted parody of a face within the improbable mist.

'Helm, override the *Resolve*'s autopilot. Steer it clear of the shuttle bay. Take it round to our port side out of the Emindians' line of sight. Keep it a minimum of two hundred metres clear of us as you go.'

The remote operator bent over his duplicate controls and the shuttle began to circle the *Indomitable*. In half a minute it had been manoeuvred into position on the far side of the ship from the *Cirrandaria* and placed in station-keeping mode.

'*Resolve* secure, sir,' he reported.

'Good. Prepare a science team, Mr Fayle,' Vega said. 'They are to take out another shuttle and –'

'*Resolve*'s autopilot has been engaged again, sir,' the remote operator interjected. 'External link has been cut.' On the screen they saw Argen's hands moving relentlessly over the controls. 'We can't override again. Main drive activated... now moving on an approach vector.'

The external viewscreens showed the shuttle once again heading directly for them.

'Shuttle bay!' Vega snapped, 'Close hull doors.'

'It's too close for pressor-beam lock,' Fayle said.

Vega took a deep breath. 'The *Resolve* is under hostile control. Target and destroy immediately.'

A string of plasma bolts flared out into the void and connected with the incoming shuttle. It vanished in a swelling brilliant fireball which slowly thinned into a cloud of luminous vapour and faded into nothing.

'The *Resolve* is totally destroyed, sir,' weapons control reported.

'No external damage to the ship,' the systems monitor added.

Vega nodded absently in response, feeling sick inside. For the first time in his career he had lost a ship to the enemy.

But who, or what, *was* the enemy?

Chapter Fourteen
Lost

Lyset Wynter slowly recovered consciousness.

The last thing she recalled was crawling on her hands and knees into the darkest corner she could find and collapsing in a state of total exhaustion. Now she ached all over, she was shivering, and she felt deathly tired. Tight skin around her eyes suggested she had been crying. That was something she hadn't done for years, but perhaps nobody would blame her in the circumstances.

She was huddled at the end of a blind corridor that served no purpose she could discern. The floor was hard but at least nothing was disputing her right to lie on it. If anything did then she knew she would not have the strength to resist or even to run. It felt as though the life and strength had been drained from her. Her skin still tingled from the shock of the passage through the interface, while deep within her burned a different and deeper cold. That was a legacy of the creature that had taken her. If it had held on to her any longer she was sure she would have died. But it had clashed with some other walking nightmare and she had been cast aside like a rag doll in the ensuing struggle. That was when she had made her unsteady escape.

Now all she wanted to do was go back to sleep again, but she knew she must stir herself. She didn't move. The mind is willing but the flesh is weak, she told herself dully. She licked her dry lips and wished she could have a drink.

Idiot, she thought. You must start thinking straight again.

She reached up with an unsteady hand and pressed a button on the side of her helmet. Feeder tubes extended within it on either side of her mouth. One dispensed water and the other glucose tablets. She chewed and sipped, and slowly began to feel better. With a tremendous effort she levered herself upright so that her back was resting against the wall.

She recalled the posture of the Nimosian they'd found. Well, she could sympathise with him, if he'd been through what she had. It was probably only luck that she hadn't gone the same way. She still might, for that matter.

She realised something was missing. Where was her camera? Damn, she must have dropped it. All those pictures lost.

She suddenly began to laugh out loud at the incongruity of her reaction in the current circumstances and had to cram her knuckles into her mouth to muffle the sound. Careful, or you'll lose it, she told herself.

All right, forget cameras. Think survival. What should she do now? Get back to the others, of course. Wait a moment. How long had she been gone?

She checked her suit watch and found it was past six in the morning, ship time. She'd been unconscious for an hour and a half. Would they still be waiting for her? Were they still alive?

She'd been thinking only about herself! Perhaps they were all dead and she was the only survivor. No, she told herself firmly. You must believe they got away. Either they'll wait in the landing bay or they'll come back with reinforcements.

But where was the bay? How far had she been carried? How long might it take to get back there? She tried to work it out rationally.

Excluding the tower structure, the main body of the ship was a cylinder over four kilometres long and perhaps seven hundred metres wide. As they'd discovered, under the hull was a network of corridors. If they ran the full length and width of the craft that meant an equivalent area, laid flat, of nearly nine square kilometres. Multiply that by however many deck levels there might be and it was the equivalent of a small city. She'd be wandering around in it for hours or even days if she wasn't careful.

Well, at least she knew the long level corridors ran lengthwise. That provided basic orientation. If she could find the interface chamber, she could get back to the landing bay.

Assuming the things didn't find her first.

Also assuming the shuttle would still be waiting for her.

The realisation struck her that the others probably thought she was dead already. Poor Don would take it hard. He was more sensitive than most people realised. As soon as she had gathered her strength she must start back.

Back through the interface?

Would she have the courage to face the pain? Even if she threw herself at it would it be physically possible? Perhaps she could get out on the surface and bypass it. Yes, that was an idea. There was plenty of cover so she'd have a better chance of hiding if need be. Now if only she could find an external hatch –

Lyset froze in horror as a faint scuffing came from around the corner of the corridor. She shrank backwards, but there was absolutely nowhere to hide.

A shape rounded the corner and a bright light shone in her eyes, momentarily dazzling her.

'Identify yourself!' a gruff voice demanded.

Her heart leapt in relief. It was a human voice.

'Lyset Wynter, photographer with the party from the *Cirrandaria*. Who are you?'

The light was extinguished and she saw a man in a combat suit. He was holding a snub-nosed shoulder-slung pulse rifle. And it was pointed at her.

'Squadleader Sho, of the Nimosian Space Marines,' he said crisply. 'And you are my prisoner.'

Chapter Fifteen
Conundrum

'Commander Vega,' the Doctor said, leaning towards the comm-screen image of the Nimosian for emphasis. 'The alien ship is extremely dangerous. You must avoid any further contact with it. Apart from the beings we encountered, the ship's systems are active and unstable. Your own men must have told you what it's like inside.'

The Doctor looked desperately tired, Lanchard thought, as did all the surviving members of the landing party currently seated round the conference table. But he seemed to be able to draw on reserves denied to the rest, and his words poured out across space to Vega with undiminished vigour. Vega, however, appeared unmoved by them.

'Your concern for our safety is appreciated, Moderator,' he replied stiffly, 'but I cannot comment on any intelligence our landing party may have brought back with them. In any case we shall not leave this zone of space until additional forces arrive and we are relieved of our duty.'

Lanchard saw the Doctor shake his head with sad resignation, as though he had been expecting just such response. She suspected both she and Vega would rather be anywhere else in the cosmos right now, but each of them was constrained by that same sense of duty and orders from higher powers.

Vega hesitated slightly before adding, 'I must thank you for taking Lieutenant Tane with you. I shall send a transport over for him shortly.'

'Our ship's surgeon, Dr Gilliam, has treated him for minor injuries,' Lanchard said. 'But she says he mostly needs rest and psychiatric care.'

'He shall receive all necessary attention,' Vega assured her, then he added, 'I trust you did not lose too many of your own crew inside the craft... or as they retreated. Our own shuttle experienced some interference from the alien beings during its departure.'

He's being unusually forthcoming, Lanchard thought. Is he fishing for something?

'We were OK once we got clear of the ship, but it was a bit "skin of your teeth",' Sam admitted with weary frankness. 'It was absolute bloody hell in there. Listen to what the Moderator's telling you.'

'We lost three people and have one seriously injured,' the Doctor told Vega simply. 'I suspect your losses were higher. I urge you not to risk any more lives.'

'We have a number of personnel still unaccounted for,' Vega admitted. 'Nimosians do not abandon their comrades, as you should know.'

'At least wait until we better understand the nature of the beings down there and have developed some defence against them,' the Doctor pleaded. 'Then perhaps we can organise a joint rescue mission.'

Rexton looked as though he wanted to object to the suggestion, but was too exhausted to do more than shake his head.

'We shall see,' Vega said noncommittally. 'My flight controller will send you details of our transport's approach shortly. Vega out.'

The screen went blank.

Lanchard examined the haggard faces around her. If it had been as bad over there as their expressions suggested, then she was grateful she had not gone herself. Even Bendix had lost something of his self-assurance, and she noted he no longer looked at Rexton with quite such uncritical admiration. Maybe there was hope for him yet. Rexton, however, though evidently tired, was still clearly determined. Why don't you give in just for once in your life? she thought. But she had to put her personal opinions aside for the moment. Now it was her task to construct a coherent picture of what had happened on the alien ship for her log and the inevitable board of inquiry. Delray spoke up impatiently, making her jump.

'Now we've done with that, what are we going to do about Lyset?'

He had his arm in an improvised sling and had promised he would see Gilliam about it later. But for now he obviously had only one concern. 'She might still be alive. We've got to get her back.' At his side Evan Arcovian nodded in agreement.

'I sympathise, Mr Delray,' Lanchard said. 'But by your own account you barely escaped with your lives. After what has happened I'm not sure I could authorise another landing. At least, as the Doctor says, until we know what we are dealing with.'

'Wynter was a volunteer and understood the risks,' Rexton said bluntly, making Lanchard wish he had kept quiet.

'You're pretty grateful she came, though,' Sam pointed out scathingly. 'All those pictures she took of your precious control panels. You made sure you didn't lose those.'

Delray evidently didn't understand. 'What do you mean?'

'He picked up her camera and case just before we made a run for it,' Sam explained.

Delray flushed. 'Her camera was more important to you than she was!'

'If you mean that I did not let the vital information she had obtained go to waste, you are correct,' Rexton replied unabashed. 'In any case, I could not have saved Ms Wynter. None of us could. You were there.'

'What are you going do with the pictures?' Arcovian demanded.

'Sorry to sound mercenary, Don,' he said quickly to Delray, 'but we've got to face it, just in case. They may be the last ones she took. They belong to her estate. She wouldn't want them lost.'

Delray nodded heavily.

'They are with the ship's photographer,' Rexton explained. 'Fortunately he understands these old chemical imaging systems. I believe he is "developing" the exposed film. I will be having the final images transmitted back to Emindar. The equipment, and those pictures not classified, will be returned to you in due course.'

Arcovian still looked puzzled. 'But why keep Lyset's camera?'

'Because he wants to go down there again and finish the job she started, and that camera is the only one he knows will operate despite the interference field,' the Doctor said.

Lanchard saw that the life and animation had returned to his handsome enigmatic face, as if in a few minutes he had thrown off his fatigue. She felt an unexpected wave of relief at the sight. Nothing was quite as bad as it seemed if he was on your side, she realised.

'I think it's time you explained exactly what we're dealing with here, Doctor,' she said.

Before he could reply, Rexton, who had been eyeing Arcovian doubtfully, said, 'I would rather we didn't go into details at this moment. We must be circumspect about what we tell the passengers. There are certain security implications to be considered first.'

'What are you implying – that I can't keep my mouth shut?' Arcovian said indignantly. 'I'm as patriotic as the next man.'

'We don't care about security,' Delray said. 'We only want to find Lyset.'

'You cannot expect any more volunteers from the crew, for whatever purpose, unless they know exactly what they're letting themselves in for,' Lanchard warned Rexton.

Rexton conceded with dismissive shrug.

'Please continue, Doctor,' Lanchard said.

'As I explained to Councillor Rexton earlier, the alien ship is an experimental hyperspace bridge,' he began. 'Theoretically, if the continuum is simultaneously stressed by high-intensity energy and gravitic waves, then it will warp, forming a tunnel through hyperspace.'

'But how do you play with real gravity?' Manders asked. 'Not the simulated fields we use to keep our feet on the decks, I mean.'

'By using mass, of course,' said the Doctor. 'It's a crude solution but it works. The network of pipes enclosing the main body of the craft not only provides conduits for the transference of energy, but also for degenerate matter. Perhaps even stabilised neutronium.'

'You mean they pump neutronium around the ship?'

'I did say it was a crude process. The actual bores of the tubes would be quite small, perhaps only a few millimetres across. The rest, a metre or more, would be solid, high-tensile synthetic, strengthened by intra-molecular force fields to enable it to withstand the operating pressure. The ship's cylindrical central core would act rather like a dimensional lens system, distorting space to varying degrees depending on the distribution and intensity of electromagnogravitic fields along its length.'

'Doctor, you said those streaks of light we saw at the bottom of the tower well were stars,' Sam said, moving the conversation on to something she could grasp.

'Yes. Distorted images of the stars lying between the two ends of the ship.'

'What do you mean, between them?' Lanchard said, totally bemused.

'The two ends of that ship are really separated by a gap of several light years, forming a stable tunnel through hyperspace between here and somewhere else. That's why one end appears blurred and translucent to us. At the far end of the tunnel that section would appear solid and our end would appear intangible.'

'Is that where those... creatures that attacked us come from?' Delray asked.

The Doctor's face darkened. 'Possibly. They may be beings whose natures are radically different from our own. Or they may be the crew of the ship itself who have been so affected by the ship's function that they are almost totally out of phase with this reality. That's why they appear immaterial to us and can pass through solid matter, though it's clearly easier for them to follow the path of least resistance along conventional corridors.'

'But they kept changing shape,' Manders said.

'It may be their natural state, or it might be the result of dephasing. Their forms may no longer be stable. The experience would probably affect their mental state as well.'

'You mean they're mad,' Delray said bluntly.

'It's possible,' the Doctor said gravely. He glanced at Rexton. 'I told you that technology was unsafe.'

Manders asked, 'Why did some of those creatures look more solid than others?'

'There may be individual variations between them due to other factors we know nothing about. Some may have been so faint we didn't see them at all. But generally they altered in apparent solidity according to their proximity to us. Remember the ceiling lights.'

'The way they blinked out as they passed?'

'Yes. I think they were unconsciously drawing energy from them.'

'They were feeding off energy?' queried Sam.

'Not just any energy. Did you notice those lights were self-contained bioluminescents?'

Manders nodded. 'So?'

'For want of a better description, those beings were feeding off any organic life force. Drawing power from the biomatter in the lights, or us, to increase the level of their own existence. That's why we feel physically drained by our encounter with them.'

'But could prolonged exposure kill somebody?' Bendix wondered. 'Would they suck all the life out of them?'

'Quite possibly,' the Doctor admitted.

There was an uncomfortable silence, then Rexton said, 'How can we fight them, Doctor? Our weapons were virtually useless over there. Even that device of yours only held them back for a few seconds.'

Lanchard realised he was openly asking the Doctor for advice. It was obviously not something he liked doing, but she began to suspect it was a habit people slipped into in the Doctor's company.

'I'm not sure we even should be fighting them,' the Doctor sighed. 'Still, I have some equipment in my luggage that might be useful.'

'But what about Lyset!' Delray begged. 'We can't leave her down there.'

Lanchard said, gently but firmly, 'Until we can find some means of protection from these… these *ghosts*, nobody will land on that ship again. I'm sorry, Mr Delray, but I can't afford to lose any more passengers or crew. At least not until they have a reasonable chance of coming back safely.'

She turned back to the Doctor again. 'Anything else, Doctor?'

'If it weren't for those lost on the alien ship I would advise you as I have the Nimosians: leave this area immediately. But I know there's no chance of either of you doing that.'

'Not until reinforcements arrive,' Rexton confirmed bluntly.

'Would it help if I told you I can arrange for the alien ship to be investigated by a properly qualified research team?' the Doctor said. He looked at Delray and Arcovian. 'I assure you they would do whatever they could for those still on board.'

'So that the Federation would benefit from the alien technology,' Rexton suggested.

'I promise you the Federation would do no such thing,' the Doctor said. 'Their only objective would be to determine the ship's origins and prevent any more such dangerous meddling by whatever race built her.'

'But you're a Federation employee,' Bendix said. 'Are you asking us to believe you'd turn down the chance to learn all you could from that ship?'

'I consider myself primarily a citizen of the galaxy,' the Doctor replied without any trace of pomposity. 'A Moderator must act without fear or favour, not simply for the short-term good of the Federation. I know that ship is dangerous, both in itself and as a potential prize that is further dividing you and the Nimosians. It's as I told you – rather than let any one side have it, I would destroy it utterly.'

He really means it, Lanchard thought. If only Rexton would believe him.

'But what about its crew? What about Lyset and the others?' Arcovian asked.

The Doctor shook his head mournfully, but said nothing. Manders broke the uncomfortable silence that followed. 'This business of the external hatch keyboard locks we found down there still bothers me, Doctor.'

'Yes, you haven't explained how you managed to crack that, Doctor,' Bendix said with more than a trace of suspicion.

The Doctor sighed, drew across a notepad and stylus and began to sketch rapidly, drawing uncannily precise angles and straight lines. In half a minute he had produced a neat replica of the keyboard in question, which he then placed in the centre of the table.

'Sometimes the truth is hidden by the observer's own insistence on seeing complexity where there is none,' he said. 'Look at the squares running down the rows three, four, two, five, three and six in from the left, and then think of the word "unlock"…'

There was a moment's silence and then a rising chorus of exclamations. The Doctor nodded.

'Exactly. The pad simply displays six stylised letters of the alphabet, with a few minor embellishments, rotated through ninety-degree increments. Here the C resembles a V somewhat to distinguish it from a U, and square dots have been added to fill in the Os and Ls, but apart from that it's quite clear.'

'And reading down four, five, four and one in spells "lock",' Sam Jones said. 'It's as easy as that.'

'But it's absurd!' Rexton exploded. 'The ship is unmistakably a product of alien technology. And even if somebody were to have concocted some incredible hoax, they wouldn't have left such a blatant clue behind.'

'Perhaps not, but the fact remains,' the Doctor said. 'I take it you never noticed this anomaly on the ship you found?'

'Its hatches were all unlocked,' Rexton admitted. 'The door pads were hardly a priority –'

'I can imagine,' interjected Sam dourly.

Rexton scowled at her and continued. 'There was no need for the linguists to examine them closely. But they did examine all the inscriptions inside the ship,' he pointed out. 'Except they couldn't translate them.'

'Naturally,' the Doctor said. 'Unlike the hatch keys, those were simply collections of random symbols.'

'But somebody's translated them now all right,' Manders said. 'We saw that in the main control room. But if they're nonsense as you say... that's impossible!'

'Doctor, what does it all mean?' Lanchard demanded.

The Doctor's face became very solemn, and he leaned slightly forward as though about to impart a great confidence. The rest bent forward in turn, gazing at him in expectant silence.

'I only wish I knew,' he admitted softly.

A little later Sam and the Doctor were in the lift descending to the cargo hold. Sam yawned prodigiously.

'I prescribe an hour in the TARDIS's sleep room for you,' the Doctor said. 'Set the neural dampener on eight. Then you won't have any bad dreams.'

'I wish you'd told me about the lock business first,' Sam said, stifling another yawn. 'How am I meant to assist you if I don't know what's going on?'

'The truth is, I'm not entirely certain myself,' said the Doctor with an apologetic smile.

Sam looked at him. Her natural reaction was to believe him, of course, but there was something in his eyes that seemed... distant. Sam took a deep breath.

'Are you telling me the truth now?'

If she was expecting a reaction from him, she was disappointed. 'Absolutely,' he remarked, eyes half open as he scrutinised the bland decor of the lift.

They reached the hold level, exited, and made their way along the passage to where the TARDIS rested. The Doctor glanced at Sam's despondent features and continued, 'If you must gather confidences, there was one other curious detail you may have observed on the alien ship that nobody else, as far as I know, has so far commented upon.'

'What?' Sam asked, feigning disinterest now.

'It concerns the weaponry.'

'The guns didn't work very well against those ghosts, did they?'

'My dear Sam, they shouldn't have worked *at all*! All other devices of any complexity were affected by the alien craft's energy field. Even within the ship our radios were operating very poorly, remember. Why then should contemporary energy weapons, outside the shuttle's counter-interference field, function normally?'

'Oh.' Sam looked at him. 'I didn't even think about it.'

'Neither did anyone else, apparently – not even the Nimosians, I suspect. But we'll have to find an answer before this is over.'

Chapter Sixteen
Soldier

Squadleader Harren Sho's life centred about a small number of jealously guarded certainties. They were not particularly subtle beliefs, but they had served him well thus far. For example, he believed that the space marine corps were the finest fighting force in the galaxy, that Nimos was the most perfect planet created by God – and that you could never trust an Emindian.

His current prisoner gave him no reason to change his mind on any of these points.

She simply looked scared, though she was trying to hide it. Her naked fear made him feel pity and some contempt for her, coupled with a warm glow of satisfaction in his own professional composure. She claimed she was the photographer of the Emindian exploratory party, yet she had no camera with her. When challenged on this point she claimed to have lost it when the ghost creatures attacked them. Sho smiled. He'd been attacked by the same creatures but he hadn't lost any item of his kit in the process. Exactly how he had escaped from them he could not for the moment recall precisely. All he remembered was a confusion of shapes and gunfire and a feeling of cold as a pack of the things had descended on his squad and... No, it was gone again. He must have received some minor injury during the mêlée. No doubt his memory would return in due course. Meanwhile it certainly did not affect his fighting efficiency in any way...

He blinked and realised the Emindian woman was speaking again. Careful, Sho. You're in enemy territory. Concentrate.

'Look,' she was saying anxiously, 'you don't need to take me prisoner. We're both in the same boat. We both want to get out of here and back to our own ships, don't we?'

'So that you can get back to report how well your deception is going?' he hissed back at her.

'What do you mean?' She was not a bad actress. She looked genuinely surprised.

'The voices! You can just hear them over the suit bands if you listen very carefully, but not on our frequencies. Do you suppose it's those creatures? Would they use helmet radios? No, it's your people.'

'It must be the party I'm with, that's all.'

'No, these sound different. You can never quite hear the words. Some special force with new model equipment, eh?'

'I don't know anything about any special forces and I've no idea what's going on here. Why can't you believe me?'

'You can tell that to Commander Vega. I'm taking you back to our ship and we'll find out everything you know.' He paused for effect. 'Easily.'

'This is ridiculous. If we really are responsible for all this, why did those creatures attack us?'

'You *claim* they attacked you.'

'It was in some big chamber. The interface ran right through the middle of it. There were some of your people there as well. More marines. And we found a Lieutenant Tane...'

The relief squad, it had to be, Sho thought. And the lieutenant was still alive. If only he could link up with them. He realised she was still talking.

'Can you hear me? Those ghost things attacked all of us. Your own people will confirm it once you find them.'

'Then it was an act to put us off our guard,' he said, suddenly seeing how it all made sense. 'This must be an experimental weapons-testing base. Those things are some new form of camouflaged combat suit. You're trying to trick us into staying here so you can test them properly.'

'You're paranoid!'

He took her by the arm and pushed her ahead of him.

'I don't care a *jek* what you think of me. Now move! And you keep your mouth shut, unless you want to attract any more of our friends.' He drew his field knife from its belt sheath and showed her the long, dark, reinforced-carbon blade with its razorlike crystal tip and edge.

'This won't make a sound. Give me away to anybody and you're dead, understand?'

She nodded dumbly.

Together they moved off down the long corridor.

Chapter Seventeen
Guilt

The next morning, ship time, the *Cirrandaria*'s crew spared no efforts to distract the passengers' attention from the alien craft and whatever it might contain. Tired holidaymakers, waking from the excitement of the previous night's departure of the expedition to board the derelict, found that the public-address speakers and info screens were alive with announcements of special prizes for the coming fancy-dress night, the attractions of the gymnasia, solarium, deck sports, tri-dee shows and a live theatre matinée. Only a brief mention was made about the results of the expedition itself.

It was implied that the exploration party had encountered something strange on board, but the details were carefully vague. It mentioned, without undue emphasis, that Lyset Wynter and a couple of other crew members were unaccounted for, but there seemed no great urgency about their situation, and in any case it seemed natural to associate Lyset with exotic and dangerous situations. She had always returned safely in the past. And in the strange way that fact and fancy sometimes blurred, the reassuring thought lingered in the back of most people's minds that Don Delray would be there to rescue her if the situation got serious.

The passengers were also gently but repeatedly reminded that the whole business would be over very shortly, when a squadron of navy ships would arrive to relieve them. The Captain had also gently eased the *Cirrandaria* a few kilometres further away from the derelict during the night, reducing its apparent size and prominence. After a day of excitement and speculation the novelty of the situation was beginning to wane. It had been an interesting if slightly inconvenient diversion, but now separation from the focus of interest made it easier to dismiss from the mind. It was evident that the Nimosians were not going to profit from their attempts at salvaging the craft, and so the status quo had been maintained.

Besides, the *Cirrandaria*'s passengers had paid for a luxury cruise and they were determined not to let anything stop them getting their money's worth.

'Why don't you go to the library?' Rhonda Plecht suggested to Lester as she gathered up her wrap.

She was going for a sauna and massage with a couple of new-found cronies (as Lester privately thought of them) who seemed to share Rhonda's view of life. They were steadily working their way through all the diversions the ship had to offer, apparently for the sole purpose of highlighting the minutest deficiencies of the staff, the facilities and their fellow passengers. Still, it seemed to keep her happy, and it allowed Lester a few hours to himself each day.

'Or the lounge on C Deck,' she continued. 'That man is going to give another of his talks on the ancient Pharosens. You'll like that.'

'Yes, dear,' he replied dutifully. 'Or perhaps I might have a go on the topological putting green. I used to like golf.'

'You were dreadful at golf. It was an embarrassment. Such a relief when you gave it up. Well, as long as you keep to putting. Don't try any of those freefall games. You know you get nauseous so easily. You don't want to make a spectacle of yourself.'

Rhonda always had a horror of his committing some social disaster, though that eventuality, as Lester would be the first to admit, had long since passed into the realm of the highly improbable since she had taken over the running of his life. This surrender of responsibility, he acknowledged, had not been without its mutual benefits. She had a better social sense than he did and far more ambition. It was her guidance and encouragement that had enabled him to climb the rungs of the corporate ladder until he had reached the boardroom itself. This cruise had been one of the rewards. And yet, once in a while, Lester longed to do something just for himself – without worrying about the social consequences, or what Rhonda would think.

Rhonda departed and he made his way towards the putting green and its Escher-inspired contours. He could not afterwards explain what impulse led him to visit the Underpool Grille Room first.

The Grille was built around the lower section of the *Cirrandaria*'s main swimming pool, and was largely illuminated by the bluish light that filtered through the large viewports set in the pool sides. One could watch as the swimmers played in the superoxygenated water, which allowed even air-breathers to stay under virtually for as long as they wished.

Lester sat beside one of the ports nursing an orange juice and watched the plunging, twisting forms on the other side of the glass enviously. The water lent even bulky figures a curious grace. Humans were not the only occupants of the pool, and he saw the pseudo-crocodilian form of an amphibian Tritonite glide past with a flick of its tail. Even out here between the stars, it seemed, people were still drawn back to the environment in which they had first evolved.

Might he join them? He wasn't sure he had the nerve to experiment with actual water breathing. Some people's reflexes never allowed them to take in that first lungful. But it looked fun, and he certainly wouldn't get nauseous as he did when he tried freefall games, despite the drugs. He used to be a good swimmer when he was a boy…

He was recalled from his reverie by a tapping on the glass.

Floating just a metre away from him was the young woman he had met at the rail the previous night.

The momentary illusion that he had been accosted by a mermaid was reinforced by her costume of slender strips of iridescent scales clinging tightly to her skin, and which was clearly intended for decoration rather than concealment. He swallowed, trying hard not to stare, and smiled back at her nervously.

She smiled and waved in turn, then pointed upward. With a kick of her long legs she rose to the surface of the pool.

And Lester found himself rising from his table to follow her.

The Poolside Bar was disguised as a section of tropical beach, complete with sand and palm trees, but without mosquitoes. Thatched awnings shaded tables from a convincingly hot artificial sun, which shone out of a blue sky projected on to the inside of one of the *Cirrandaria*'s larger hull domes. At night, by ship's time, the projectors were turned off and the real stars shone down on the pool.

By the time Lester reached the poolside the woman was towelling herself down beside a shaded beach chair. He realised he still didn't know her name and faltered as he approached her. She seemed to read the cause of his hesitation and held out her hand.

'Ingrid Schollander.'

'Lester Plecht.'

Her grip was firm, her hand still cool from the water.

'Did you need to go off so quickly like that last night?' she asked with unexpected directness. 'You missed them leave.'

'My wife. She wanted to get back to sleep.'

'Couldn't you have told her you'd be with her in five minutes? She doesn't run your life, does she?'

Before he had time to think he replied, 'She does, actually.'

He almost bit his lip in embarrassment. He'd said it out loud to a perfect stranger. Just the sort of thoughtless remark Rhonda had warned him about not twenty minutes earlier.

But to his amazement Ingrid laughed. It wasn't unkind laughter or in any way mocking. It invited him to join in, to see the humour of his unguarded response. He managed a wry grin of his own, then found himself saying, 'Can I get you a drink?'

As though in a dream he waved the autowaiter over and ordered a refill for Ingrid's glass and, almost absently, added a stronger drink for himself than any Rhonda had allowed him for five years. Then he found a spare beach chair and drew it up beside Ingrid's.

And they talked.

He found out she was twenty-eight, a partner in a small astromining business and unattached. He in turn spoke about his own work. He found he kept mentioning Rhonda, realising as he did so how much she had shaped his life. It felt incongruous in the circumstances, but Ingrid didn't seem to mind, and listened attentively and sympathetically.

And then they moved easily on to tastes in vids, politics, sport and fashion. It was trivia of no significance whatsoever and an unalloyed delight. She actually laughed at some of the things he said. Deep down he had no illusions that this was the start of some wild affair.

He was twenty years older than she and had nothing she could possibly want. Perhaps it was just her nature to spare him a little time because she felt sorry for him. Well if that was so then he wasn't too proud to refuse. For a little while he could enjoy the pleasure of her company, aware of the envious looks he was drawing from several tanned and muscular young men around the pool.

The difference between Ingrid and Rhonda, Lester realised, was that everything Rhonda did was so calculated, while Ingrid just responded naturally, openly, without any ulterior motive. Ingrid gave while Rhonda took. Ingrid offered her attention freely, and seemed to find pleasure in the all those trivial curiosities and inconsistencies of life that so annoyed Rhonda. When the autowaiter delivered a vile mixed drink to her by mistake, she simply pulled a wry face, laughed, tipped it back into its hopper and told it to try again. Rhonda would have complained to the purser at the very least.

Suddenly Lester saw his watch. How could so much time have passed so quickly? 'I'm sorry. I must go. Rhonda will be back soon to get ready for lunch.'

Ingrid frowned gently. 'Why are you looking so guilty? Have we done anything wrong?'

'No. Of course not. It's been… wonderful. But she wouldn't understand… I mean about us just talking…' He realised he was sounding pathetic.

'You can always say you were cultivating a potential client. Your company deals in management systems. Perhaps we might be interested in them. Or say nothing at all. You don't have to account for every second you're away from her, do you? Doesn't Rhonda trust you at all?'

'She's… overprotective.'

Ingrid looked at him thoughtfully for a long moment, and he found himself melting into the deep blue of her eyes. 'Do you love her?' she asked.

'I did. Once,' he admitted.

'Then stand up for yourself and find out if you still do. Or else why stay together?'

'Habit, I suppose. We've got no children to think of. That might have made a difference, but it never seemed to be the right time to have them.'

'Maybe you should make the time now, before it's too late. Or if your wife doesn't want to, at least find some happiness for yourself.'

Lester wondered if he had the nerve after so long relying on Rhonda to make all the important decisions. The thought was enticing and frightening at the same time.

Ingrid got up, gathered her things and smiled at him. 'I hope I'll see you again. Good luck.'

Lester watched her walk around the side of the pool. She was so beautiful, he thought. Rhonda still had a well-proportioned body and could appear very attractive when they had to attend some business reception. But she never made herself attractive for *him* any more. Perhaps Ingrid was right. He should do something before it was too late.

Then he saw Ingrid's left leg twist under her. Her foot skidded sideways over the lip of the pool and she fell heavily.

Lester was at her side in a moment, catching her just before she slithered into the water. As concerned fellow bathers and staff gathered around them he helped her sit up. Her face was pale and creased with pain.

'Are you hurt?' he asked anxiously.

'Gave my knee quite a crack,' she admitted, wincing as she tried to straighten it.

'It's bleeding… and your other leg's grazed.'

'Don't know how I did it. Almost felt like somebody in the pool tugged my ankle.'

'There wasn't anybody in the water near you,' Lester said. 'I would have seen.'

She frowned for a moment, then shrugged and managed a smile. 'Just clumsy, I suppose.'

'We'll get you along to sickbay to have the doc check your knee,' one of the attendants said. 'Just stay there while I fetch a wheelchair.'

'I can walk there myself, thanks,' she said, politely brushing aside their attentions and looking expectantly at Lester. 'As long as somebody will give me an arm.'

And so, acutely conscious of her warm body resting against his, Lester helped Ingrid to her feet and supported her as she limped away from the pool. He realised that the eyes of the young men who had surveyed him earlier were even more envious now. The sensation, far from adding to his embarrassment, made him feel happier than he had done in years.

Don Delray sat in his darkened room.

It had taken him a while to convince Evan that he was safe to be left alone, and in the end he had to speak sharply to him. He saw the pain in Arcovian's face at his rebuff, which only added to his own misery. He didn't want to hurt the little man's feelings but he had to have some time to himself. He couldn't continue the act any longer.

Slowly he withdrew his arm from the improvised sling, pulled the loop of cloth over his head and tossed it on to the bed. He flexed his fingers. They felt fine. His leg, which had displayed that convincing limp for the past few hours, moved easily as well. He was a better actor than people gave him credit for – perhaps because he was a craven coward.

He thought Lyset sensed the truth, though she never said anything. Arcovian was the only other person he allowed close enough to find out, but his nature tended to blind him to people's failings.

Delray went through to the bathroom, rolled up his sleeve and examined his arm. There was a slight bruise on the elbow. For want of anything better to do he sponged a little cold water on to it. There, he had treated his own injuries. No need to see the ship's doctor after all. Better to keep the sling on for a few days though… He sank his head over the basin in disgust, not wanting to look at his face in the mirror. The bruise was nothing, but then neither was he any more. It had saved his reputation at the cost of his self-respect. And perhaps Lyset's life.

He slunk out of the bathroom and threw himself on the bed.

He'd had no choice but to accompany Lyset when she made it clear she was going to the derelict, despite having a bad feeling about the whole business. Of course he could make patriotic little speeches about standing firm against the Nimosians, but then that was not so hard to say in company, especially when he didn't seriously believe the Nimosians would attack a civilian liner.

Still, he thought he could get away with it. He'd managed in the past when performing those modest stunts himself – getting the best people to set them up, joking on the set about the danger and his concerns, secretly taking a stiff drink just before it was time and then letting it happen. So far it had worked, but it never got any easier. In the fantasy world of the vids he could pretend to do anything. It was real life that scared him, waiting with its unscripted surprises and the big scene that he would foul up by freezing at the crucial moment.

Inevitably, that was what had happened over there on the alien ship.

He didn't think anybody had noticed, during that fusillade of gunfire as those things had attacked them, that he'd been too frightened to pull the trigger of his own gun. He might still have got away with it by grabbing Lyset, who had been coolly taking pictures even as the things bore down on them, if that spawn of a nightmare hadn't snatched her. And there was a moment when he could have fired at it, or thrown himself forward and attacked it with his bare hands. Never mind that it would probably have been a futile gesture, he had been too frightened to move a muscle.

Then he had been knocked over himself by some flailing half-real tentacle. The cold shock had galvanised his thoughts and from then on he had faked it.

He'd rolled about in believable agony so that everybody could see he hadn't just been tapped, he'd been *smashed* to the ground! Nobody could blame him for having lost his gun when he probably had a broken arm. The limp had followed naturally as he'd struggled bravely to his feet. He hadn't lost it even as they'd run for their lives down the tunnel with the ghost things at their heels, because by then he was into the part, and he'd rather really die than let them see he'd just been covering up his cowardice. In the landing bay, that Nimosian lieutenant had been staggering about, so he'd simply grabbed hold of him and dragged him towards the shuttle. That was OK. He'd played that part before: wounded soldier helping comrade to safety. That was heroic enough and nobody expected him to fire a gun while he was doing it.

And then they were clear of the ship and he was alive and Lyset was probably dead. For the rest of his life he would have to live with knowing he could have tried to save her but didn't have the courage.

Then a curious sound penetrated the veil of his self-revulsion. It was a faint whine and rapid snuffling, followed by the whisper of steps on carpet, as though there was an animal in the next room. Numbly he got to his feet and walked heavily through.

But there was no sign of any animal. He looked behind the chairs and sofa but found nothing. The snuffling sound came again, but now it seemed to issue from the bedroom he had just left. How could it have got past him? He returned to the bedroom. It was empty. The space under the bed was hardly deep enough for an animal of any size to crawl under, but he looked anyway. Then, feeling faintly ridiculous, he checked the cupboards. He even looked in the bathroom. No animal of any description. Then he heard the sound right behind him and for a moment felt something soft brush against his leg.

He started violently and kicked out by reflex. His foot passed through empty air. Was he starting to go mad?

Then came a light hesitant tap at the main door. For a moment he wondered if he was imagining that too, but it was repeated again. It didn't sound like Arcovian and it hadn't the briskness of one of the staff. Looking about him nervously, he went to answer it, automatically picking up the sling from the bed and putting his arm back through it on the way. He was committed to the pretence now, unless he found the courage to admit the truth.

Dan Engers Junior was standing outside looking very nervous and glancing up and down the corridor as though he didn't want to be seen. Delray managed to control his voice enough to say heartily, 'Hallo, Dan. What can I do for you?'

'I just wanted to see if you were all right, Mr Delray. My mother said I shouldn't bother you, but I had to know.' His wide eyes were locked on to the sling in horrified fascination.

'That's very kind of you, Dan. I'm fine.' He tapped the sling with his 'good' hand. 'Don't worry, this is just a scratch.'

The boy nodded and smiled in relief, then added, 'I heard them say Ms Wynter was still on the alien ship. Is she all right? When are you going back for her?'

Delray very nearly lost his composure in the face of that innocent question, but somehow he managed to shape a confident reply. 'I'm sure she's all right. We had to leave suddenly and couldn't bring her along, but we'll be going back as soon as we get some technical problems sorted out. Got to have the right tools for the job, you know that.'

'Were there monsters over there?'

'Yes, Dan,' he said simply. 'There were monsters.'

'Wow! Are you going back to fight them?'

'That's right. I'm just getting tooled up ready for them.'

With an expression of great self-sacrifice the boy said, 'You can borrow my electro-gun if you want. And the holster.'

Putting all the sincerity he could into his reply he said, 'Thank you very much, Dan. But I think I can manage with what I've got. Now, I've got to get some rest so I'm really sharp for taking on those old monsters. Bye now.'

The boy smiled and ran off up the corridor. Delray closed the door and staggered back through to the bathroom, tearing off the hated sling, fearing he would be sick at any moment. But on the threshold he stopped dead.

Written on the bathroom mirror in spidery streaks of soap and water was one word:

Coward

Chapter Eighteen
Suspicion

Fayle turned away from the bed where Tane rested and followed Vega out of the *Indomitable*'s sickbay. Behind him Tane continued to stare sightlessly up at the ceiling. Feeding tubes and lines connected him to a medical support monitor. In the corridor outside Fayle spoke to his superior in low angry tones.

'Commander, we must take action against the Emindians.'

Vega looked at him through tired eyes. For the first time since he had taken up service under Vega, Fayle began to wonder if the man had the right character for command.

'To what purpose, Mr Fayle?' Vega said.

'Do you not find it the least suspicious that a party of Emindian civilians escaped from the alien ship with minor losses, while we have lost all but one of our own professional, well-armed crew? And that one *they* return to us so severely traumatised, that he may never recover sufficiently to give us a coherent report of what went on down there?'

'I consider that they were simply luckier than we were, Mr Fayle. For all we know more of our men are still alive and well inside that ship, but without detailed knowledge of the conditions down there we can only speculate. When the second modified shuttle is ready we will learn more. Until then we can only wait.'

'But what about that thing we saw on the *Resolve*? It was using Argen's body to steer it towards us.'

'Possibly an alien life form, maybe an inhabitant of the ship. We shall assess the threat they pose and take whatever action is necessary against them in due course. What has that to do with the Emindians?'

'Their shuttle seemed to suffer no such misfortune. Why did they escape so easily?'

'You suggest they are somehow in league with these aliens?' He shook his head. 'I think it's still better to put it down to chance. After all, we were lucky to intercept their original signal reporting the discovery of the alien vessel. Though perhaps that does not seem so fortunate now,' he added darkly.

'What if we were meant to hear that message?' Fayle said. 'Perhaps this is all part of some plot to lure us here. Is it coincidence that Kale Rexton himself, the most outspoken militarist on the Emindian High Council, was on the *Cirrandaria*?'

'Yes, because if this was all planned as you say, why hasn't Rexton come at the head of a battle squadron?'

'Perhaps there is one, Commander, waiting somewhere just out of detector range.'

'What would be the purpose of such a deception?'

'I don't know, but it does all focus on the alien ship – and as you already admitted, Commander, we do not know enough about conditions on board it.'

'That at least we can agree on. Have you any other suspicions you wish to inform me of, Mr Fayle?'

Fayle replied stiffly, 'I am just performing my duty, sir: informing my commanding officer of possible scenarios relevant to the current situation.'

'Consider me duly informed. Is there anything else?'

'The… fortuitous presence of the Federation Moderator on the *Cirrandaria*. It limits the scope of our actions.'

'As it does those of the Emindians. I think his intentions are quite sincere if misguided… but I suppose you think he is also part of this plot?'

'Possibly. We are in no position to confirm his credentials, sir.'

'You see conspiracies everywhere, Fayle.'

'Only where the Emindians are concerned. I lost my parents on Garroth Five.'

Vega sighed again. 'I'm familiar with your file. I know what part Emindian deceit played in that tragedy. But it was almost thirty years ago and perpetrated by their Covert Operations Agency. Even their own government disowned their actions eventually.'

'Publicly, officially. They had no choice.'

'I have no love for Emindians, but remember we are dealing with a civilian liner here, not a warship.'

'There were families on Garroth. That did not stop the COA.'

'So now you think they are using their own people as cat's-paws? For what possible reason?'

'I don't know, Commander. Yet.'

'Well I can't stop you exercising your imagination, Mr Fayle. But until you have something more substantial than mere supposition to offer me –'

They were interrupted by Second Lieutenant Chen, who came hurriedly round the corner, looking back over his shoulder as he did so, and almost collided with Vega.

'Watch where you're going, Lieutenant,' Fayle barked at him as the younger man started violently.

'Sorry, sir.'

Vega looked at him closely. Chen seemed unusually pale, his brow glistened with sweat and he had an air of nervous unease about him.

'Are you unwell, Lieutenant?' Vega asked. 'Were you going to sickbay?'

'Uh, it's nothing sir. Just a persistent headache. I shouldn't have come really.'

'Get yourself checked out anyway,' Vega told him. 'This crew will have to be on maximum alert for the next two days at least. I can't have anybody at their station who isn't one hundred per cent fit.'

'Yes, sir.'

With another quick backward glance, Rask Chen walked reluctantly into the sickbay.

Chapter Nineteen
Sabotage

Refreshed after her artificially induced rest, Sam found the Doctor in the TARDIS's laboratory.

Despite the complex microelectronic equipment that littered the heavy oak workbenches, the atmosphere was still Gothic. It was the sort of place, Sam thought, that you might expect to find a badly stitched together body lurking under white sheets. Come to think of it, his appearance and period costume...

'Feel better now, Sam?' he asked as she entered.

'Yes, thanks. What are you doing, Dr Frankenstein?'

He had what appeared to be a heavy cylindrical hand torch before him, except that where the bulb and reflector would have been was an array of metallic discs forming a projecting cone. Mounted parallel with the shaft was a standard laser-pencil pointer. A card containing circuitry never seen in any conventional torch was ready to be slid into the hollow shaft.

'A device that may be of use against those dimensionally displaced beings on the alien ship.'

'Call them ghosts. They look like ghosts. They *feel* like ghosts.'

The Doctor smiled gently. 'I don't believe in ghosts. Only mysteries. There's a rational explanation for what they are.'

'I know that, but I don't feel all that rational when I think of them. All right, what does your gizmo do?'

'You might call it a normaliser. It combines some of the frequencies my sonic screwdriver emits, bioelectric wavelengths and a narrow spatial-distortion field. The effect should, temporarily, either make those creatures almost completely insubstantial, so that they can't interact with us, or else substantial and stable enough so that we might attempt to communicate with them.'

'Or at least let us fight them on even terms.'

He frowned. 'That's not like you, Sam.'

151

'I'm sorry, but they really got to me,' she protested. 'Being near them was like… like having all your worst fears made real. I think I know why that Nimosian soldier flipped. He was alone down there too long. At least we had company when we fought them.'

The Doctor looked at her intently. 'If you want to stay in here, you'll be safe.'

'No, I'm going to see this through,' Sam said forthrightly. 'Only…' She smiled at him. 'It's not very cool of me to ask, but stick close, will you?'

He smiled. 'I'll do my best.'

There was a beeping and a light flashed over a mobile intercom resting beside the bench.

'I linked our room phones through to here,' the Doctor explained, punching a button. 'Doctor here,' he said.

Lanchard's voice came on. 'Doctor, could you come up to the bridge, please. We're detecting another energy build-up around the alien ship and I thought you might be interested.'

'We'll be right there,' he promised. Sliding the circuit board into the normaliser, he screwed the end cover into place and dropped it into his pocket. 'Coming, Sam?'

'Right behind you.'

Rhonda Plecht caught up with Lester before he reached their compartment. He would have preferred to have been waiting for her, but nevertheless he managed to face her with a bright and hopefully innocent smile.

'Hallo, dear. Did you have a nice sauna?'

'Never mind about that. Who was that woman I saw you with?'

It was the question he was dreading. He struggled to reply mildly, 'What woman, dear?'

'That half-dressed girl on the promenade last night. I saw you talking to her outside the ship's clinic. I was in the elevator on the other side of the atrium. By the time I reached the floor you were gone. Why was she wearing a dressing gown?'

'A beach wrap, dear. That was Ms Schollander. She'd just come from the upper pool. She'd had a slight accident there and I helped her down to see the doctor.'

'And what were you doing at the pool? You said you were going to play golf.'

'I was, dear, but we met on the way and she invited me for a drink. You're always saying I should take advantage of social meetings. Well, I told her about my work and it turns out she has a share in a mining company and they may be able to offer us some business.' He added desperately, 'Perhaps quite a lot of business.'

'I see,' Rhonda said with a sniff. 'And the other woman?'

Lester blinked in genuine surprise. 'Sorry, dear. Do you mean Dr Gilliam?'

'Of course not. The other one with you in front of the clinic. She was wearing a blue smock dress and had some sort of peculiar headpiece on. I couldn't see her face. She accompanied you when you left.' Rhonda looked suspiciously up and down the corridor. 'I thought you turned down here together. Who was she?'

Lester looked at her in total bewilderment. He was absolutely certain he had walked back from the sickbay quite alone.

The Doctor examined the bridge displays, their coloured lights tinting his pale features. Captain Lanchard and the rest of the bridge crew looked on expectantly. Sam recognised their attitudes. Everybody turned to the Doctor eventually.

'Yes, there is a distinct build-up in the energy field around the alien ship,' the Doctor agreed.

'But it's not quite the same pattern as before,' Lanchard said. 'I must know if we're safe here or whether we should pull back further.'

The Doctor shrugged. 'Who can say? If it's no greater intensity than before then we should be safe. If it's something else…' he shrugged again. 'Perhaps you'd better have the engine room ready to cut in the main engines just in case.'

Lanchard nodded and opened an intercom line. 'Nel? Can you have the main drive ready on immediate standby, please?'

'Captain,' Nel Manders's voice came back rapidly. 'I was just about to call you. There's something... odd happening down here. I don't know if we're seeing things... Perhaps somebody had better –'

Sam leaned over the microphone. 'This is Ms Jones. The Moderator and I will be right down,' she said.

The *Cirrandaria*'s engine compartment contained a linked series of huge machines that comprised the power core, secondary generators and main drive. A workshop housed in a side bay gave access to the shuttle berths. Sam instinctively felt there should be more noise, but the immaculately clean solid-state devices containing almost no moving parts generated only the slightest of low hums, giving little clue as to the tremendous energy contained within them. As they left the lift and passed along the catwalks and stairways that webbed the walls, small sections of the compartments teased her memory with their resemblance to the interiors of fictional starships that had sailed only in the minds of stage designers and all the anorak sci-fi fans back in her own century.

Manders was waiting for them in the engineering control room set between the power core and the main drive assembly. Her face bore an angry scowl, while behind her were several anxious-looking coveralled technicians. She took a few steps away from them before conversing in low tones.

'I don't want to say what I think it is in front of them, in case I start a panic. They're already feeling bad enough about losing Simmons. I had to tell them how it happened. But this is not imagination. There's something down here, all right. It's keeping to the shadows and we've only caught glimpses. We've just found that some of the secondary monitor panels have been tampered with, so it's real enough.'

'Are you suggesting it's a ghost?' Sam asked bluntly.

'I'd rather it was a Nimosian saboteur,' Manders admitted. 'But I don't think an ordinary person could move about the way this thing's been doing. We've made one sweep of the whole compartment but somehow it got behind us.'

Sam looked around anxiously at the looming mass of machinery that surrounded them. Suddenly there seemed too many shadows for

154

her liking. 'But how could a ghost have got in here?'

'It may have come back with us on the shuttle,' the Doctor suggested.

'But we'd have seen it,' Sam said. 'Those things weren't exactly subtle. I mean you'd notice if one was sitting next to you...' She hesitated. 'Though now I think of it, it did seem pretty cold on the way back.'

'We may have only encountered the less controlled creatures so far,' the Doctor pointed out. 'They may be able to remain inconspicuous if they don't attempt to interact with anybody.'

'But what could one of them want down here?' Manders asked.

'That's what we have to find out,' the Doctor said. 'If there's just one, I think we can deal with it.'

'Don't we need weapons?' Manders asked.

'They haven't done us much good so far, so let's see if we can manage without,' the Doctor suggested.

They arranged all the available engineering crew in a line and began a second sweep of the compartment. They moved along every catwalk and aisle between the blocks of machinery, probing the shadows with torches. The Doctor and Sam followed on a little way behind them, Sam armed with the Doctor's normaliser – the operation of which he had rapidly briefed her on – while he carried his sonic screwdriver. Sam found her eyes darting about as they passed between the towering machines. There were so many places for a *real* person to hide, let alone a wraith.

They'd completed two-thirds of their sweep when there was a call from the catwalk almost above her head: 'It's up here!'

Sam saw a grey form woven of mist and shadows flying at the technician, who leapt aside in horror and almost fell over the guard rail, dropping his own torch, which fell with a clatter. Sam stepped back rapidly to get a clear line of sight, pointed the normaliser at the ghostly thing and pressed the button. The device buzzed in her hands as the sighting beam stabbed out and touched the creature.

The thing faltered, writhing as she held the beam on it. The Doctor was at her side adding the shrill of his sonic screwdriver. The creature seemed to be shrinking as the fuzz of half-seen limbs around it contracted. A darker, more substantial shadow was forming inside the haze, resolving into a man-sized creature hunched over on all fours. It uttered something between a moan and a snarl, then it collapsed to the floor of the catwalk.

'We've got it!' Sam shouted.

But even as she spoke, the creature rolled underneath the catwalk guard rail and fell out of their line of sight behind a secondary generator. There was only the slightest of thuds as it struck the floor.

It took them only a couple of seconds to round the generator, but in that time the creature was moving again and as immaterial as before. One of the technicians swung a length of I-beam at it but he was brushed aside. It turned the next corner before they could fire at it again.

'It's heading for the control room!' Manders shouted.

They pounded back along the aisles after it, rebounding off the sides of machinery as they turned right-angled corners. But they were too late.

The heavy blast doors of the engineering control room were closed in their faces. A technician lay slumped beside them. Through a mesh-reinforced transparent port they saw the ghostly form brush across the panels.

'What are those controls for?' the Doctor asked Manders.

'They're the bridge repeater controls. You can steer the ship from there in an emergency. Was that what it was after all along?'

'Possibly. Contact the bridge and tell them to override its commands if they can.' Manders spoke rapidly into her wristcom. The Doctor turned to Sam. 'The shielding will attenuate the beam a little, but try the normaliser on reverse effect. The creature won't be able to operate the controls so easily.'

Sam sighted on the creature through the clear panel and fired. The thing grew paler, but it continued to work the controls. She felt the ship tremble as power was fed into its thrusters. The Doctor knelt beside the frame of the blast door, adjusted his sonic screwdriver, and activated it. There was a shrill whine and a hole began to appear in the toughened metal and ceramic composite.

'They've lost control of manoeuvring and main drive,' Manders said, dropping her wristcom from her ear. She grabbed a toolbox from a locker, pulled a power tool from it and began attacking the recessed bolts securing a floor plate beside the wall of the control room. 'I'm going to cut the circuit directly,' she shouted over her shoulder.

Sam staggered as the ship yawed suddenly, but tried to keep the normaliser focused on the ghost. She realised her fear of it had muted, and not simply because she had something with which she could fight back. This particular creature had acted with purpose, not like some mindless beast from a nightmare. Where there was purpose there was also reason and hope – at least so the Doctor often said.

An engineer who'd been standing clear of the noise of the Doctor's screwdriver to listen to his wristcom shouted, 'Captain says we're heading for the alien ship!'

'Naturally,' the Doctor replied grimly. The hole he was cutting was half completed.

Manders tore off the floor panel, revealing thick bundles of cabling running beneath it. She selected a pair of insulated cutters, reached down and snipped. The drone of the thruster units faded away one by one. The ship steadied. The thick wedge of blast-door material the Doctor had cut away around the lock fell to the floor. He hauled the sliding door open and they confronted the ghost.

'Now keep it solid, Sam, so that it can't slip away through the wall.'

The creature tried to pass them but the Doctor drove it back with a burst of sonic power, penning it in the room. Sam heard its guttural snarls and hisses, even though she could see no mouth that could have issued them. The flickering sequence of shapes and colours the thing ran through made her eyes water. She could not focus on one before it was gone. But she steeled herself not to look away. It was not a supernatural entity but a real creature, she kept telling herself. It must have its limits. The thing was bobbing and weaving from side to side. Mismatched limbs kept reaching out towards them, then shrinking back.

'We've got it frightened!' she exclaimed.

'We want it co-operative, not frightened,' the Doctor said. 'If there's a chance to make contact we must take it. Reduce the power slightly.'

As she did so, he made a deliberate show of putting his sonic screwdriver in his pocket. Then he began to make careful exaggerated gestures with his hands, inviting the thing to calm down, pointing at himself and then it. Then he touched his mouth.

'If you communicate with sound-based language, please do so,' he said. 'I will understand you.'

Whether his words or gestures registered Sam was not sure. But the flickering of body shapes became less frenzied. She had the impression the thing was descending from some violent peak of agitation into relative calm.

Then came a distant clatter of boots on the stairs. Bendix was pounding down them followed by two crewmen carrying rifles.

'Stay back!' the Doctor shouted. But it was too late.

The thing flared into its former rage. Knobbly limbs lashed out, knocking them back from the doorway. The normaliser was dashed from Sam's hands as she hit the deck. There was a shock of cold as it surged past them.

Bolts of gunfire struck the creature. It reared up, swelling with flickering inner fire until its head brushed the ceiling. A terrible bellow rent the air. For a moment Sam saw blazing red eyes and a reptilian jaw full of dagger-like teeth. Then it fell forward on to its attackers. One crewman was dashed aside against a stanchion, the second snapped up into those terrible jaws, even as Bendix kept up his fusillade of futile gunfire.

The Doctor had drawn his sonic screwdriver once more and its shrill note cut through the creature's howls. Sam scrabbled over to the normaliser, swung it round and pressed the trigger. The creature reared back from Bendix, the energy bolts burning its flesh for the first time.

'Manders – where's the nearest external bulkhead?' the Doctor shouted.

'Behind you and left!'

'Sam, we've got to drive it that way. Get around it! Bendix, you can't kill it. We must force it out into space.'

Manders picked up one of the fallen crewmen's guns and added its fire to that of Bendix. Slowly they drove the monstrous being towards the bulkhead that separated the compartment from open space until it had its back to the curving metal wall, snapping at them like a cornered dog.

'Change normaliser polarity when I say so, Sam,' the Doctor said. 'Ready the rest of you… heavy fire, knock it over… now!'

A blaze of gunfire toppled it backwards. Sam switched the normaliser over. The thing became a pale phantom. The Doctor adjusted his sonic screwdriver to emit one last pulse of brilliant light. The ghost fell through the solid hull and was gone.

The echoes died away. Sam found the sudden silence almost deafening. The Doctor turned an angry face to Bendix.

'That was an ill-timed and quite unnecessary intervention. I believe I was about to make some kind of contact with it!'

'With that thing!' Bendix shot back at him.

'At least it's dead now,' Manders said.

'Oh, I doubt that,' the Doctor said. 'It's not alive enough in this universe for simple exposure to vacuum to kill it.'

'All right, Doctor,' Bendix conceded. 'But at least it's gone.' He tapped his wristcom: 'Captain. The intruder has been… dealt with.'

They all heard Lanchard's brittle reply. 'It may be too late. We're on a collision course with the alien ship. If you can't restore control we shall hit it in six minutes!'

Chapter Twenty
Exit

The realisation that Squadleader Sho had been seriously unhinged by his encounter with the ghosts grew within Lyset Wynter as they made their way along the alien ship's seemingly endless corridors. But rather than fear, she found the knowledge kindled a small spark of sympathy within her, and she wondered if he had taken her prisoner more for company than military necessity. She took no satisfaction in having come though her recent experience relatively unscathed, while he had clearly suffered mental damage. He may have had it worse than she had. On the other hand it may have been the fault of his own nature. His type would resist until the last. Maybe it would have been better if he had simply passed out as she had done. She had bent, he had broken.

Twice they hid down side corridors from ghosts, warned by the flickering lights ahead. Only when they were sure the way was clear did they scuttle for the next intersection. Sho was very stealthy in his actions, scouting ahead and waving her on with curt gestures. She did not attempt to escape. She had no doubt he would kill her as he had threatened. Besides she had no better idea of which way to go, and he did provide a certain measure of security. She couldn't face the thought of wandering alone down here either.

But after a while she began to worry. If they had been headed back towards the interface they should have reached it by now, even allowing for the possibility that the ghosts had taken her further away from it while she'd been unconscious than she had estimated. And she was using the corridor handrails more often to steady herself as she leaned forward. The corridor seemed to be steepening under them, though it remained perfectly level to the eye. Suddenly she understood what was happening.

'We're going the wrong way.'

'Shut up,' Sho hissed.

'I thought you knew which way to go. You're as turned around as I am.'

'I told you –'

'Look, why can't you admit making a simple mistake? You can feel where the centre of gravity is. We must be getting near the far end now, not the middle. All we've got to do is turn round.'

Sho was breathing heavily, his eyes constantly darting from side to side. Perhaps she should simply let him work it out for himself in his own time, she thought.

Then the lights along the corridor began to flicker.

Sho bundled her down a side turning and into a wall niche. He crouched down with his rifle held at the ready. The reflected flickering of lights got closer and she held her breath. She heard a faint whisper of marching feet. The lights opposite their turning dimmed.

She caught a glimpse of the group as it went by. But they were not like the other ghosts they had seen.

Their forms were grey and translucent, but they were smaller and roughly humanoid. Moreover, they seemed to be dressed in bulky padding or armour. She had an impression of heavy gauntlets and oversized helmets. They were also carrying long sticks or poles, together with some other unidentifiable bundles of twisted ropes slung across their shoulders. Unlike the other creatures, these beings moved with deliberation. One helmeted head turned to look down their side tunnel as though searching for something, making her jerk back into the shadows.

Then the lights brightened again and they were gone.

Sho rose from his crouch and turned an accusing face to hers. 'What were they, then? They weren't like the others. Some of your own guards looking for you?'

'I keep telling you I don't know. I don't care! I just want to get out of here. Listen. Before you found me I was thinking of finding an external hatch and getting out on to the outer hull. We can get back to our shuttles from there, or maybe signal our ships, and we shouldn't have to keep dodging these creatures along the way.'

Sho considered, clearly viewing any suggestion Lyset made with automatic suspicion. But eventually he had to acknowledge the logic of the idea. 'We'll try it. But if it's a trap –'

'Oh, please, shut up about traps. Give your paranoia a rest. Let's start looking for ramps or ladders. There must be some service hatches or something around here.'

They found what they were looking for down another cross corridor. One of the alcoves in its walls was deeper and higher than the others. There was a small irised hatch built into the ceiling and recessed horizontal slots set into its back wall leading up to it, which were obviously intended to serve as the steps of a ladder. Sho climbed them cautiously. The hatch had a simple wheel set beside it, which Sho turned. The hatch opened. Beyond was a small bare chamber.

As he examined it Lyset felt a sudden tremor run through the ship's structure and a distinct rising throb of power. She swarmed up the ladder after Sho. 'I think we should get out of here before something else happens,' she said urgently.

Sho closed the hatch. Another ladder led to a second hatch above their heads. It looked like a similar sequence to the airlock system leading off the landing bay. Lyset closed the faceplate of her suit and felt it pressurise. Sho opened the upper hatch leading to the second chamber. She expected another keypad lock, but there was none. The third hatch opened on to the hull.

They emerged in the narrow channel between two massive pipes. Towering over the end of the channel was a rising series of curving walls, encrusted with pipes and conduits and crowned by a great spire. It was one of the ring structures that surrounded the ends of the ship's main hull. They'd travelled as far as they could go.

Then Lyset frowned.

'Wait a moment. If we've gone the wrong way, this should be the fuzzy translucent end of the ship.' There was only static on her radio. She touched her helmet to Sho's and repeated the question.

'What of it?' he growled back.

'Well, why does it look perfectly solid?'

The puzzling irregularity must have penetrated even Sho's narrow mind. A few metres away was a support bracket for the pipes. He climbed it and stood on the upper curve of the pipe. Lyset followed and looked about them.

'Oh, Gods!' she exclaimed softly.

Chapter Twenty-One
From a Well of Stars

'This is the Captain speaking. Prepare to abandon ship. This is not a drill, I repeat, this is not a drill. Make your way quickly but calmly to the nearest lifeboat stations. Members of the crew will be there to guide you. Do not stop to collect any personal belongings...'

The *Cirrandaria*'s Young Adventurers room was a confused mass of screaming children, costumed entertainers trying to usher them through the exits and parents, frantic to find their offspring, fighting their way in against the flow. With a gasp of relief Jeni Engers pushed forward and clasped Dan junior's hand so hard that he protested. 'Mummy – you're hurting me!'

He was not afraid, she realised. It was all part of the entertainment to him. She fought to keep her own voice steady. 'Now we must go to the lifeboats,' she told him.

'Will Daddy be there like the Captain said?'

'Yes, he'll be there.'

Despite the injunction, Rhonda had insisted they stop to collect her handbag. With an uncomfortable insight Lester realised she was so used to controlling and arranging life to suit herself that she acted as though no disaster could possibly overtake the ship until she was safe. Now she was chiding others to move more quickly and berating those who were carrying any extraneous personal items.

As they moved with the flowing tide of confused and frightened fellow passengers, Lester scanned their faces in the hope of seeing Ingrid. He had discovered that her cabin was only two corridors away on the same deck as theirs, and thought she might be making for the same lifeboat station. He couldn't see her, but comforted himself with the thought that somebody as practical and level-headed as she was would not let herself get left behind.

* * *

Ingrid Schollander pulled and twisted the handle of her cabin door, but it refused to open. It was jammed or locked – but who would want to lock her in at a time like this? She pounded on the door but if anybody heard her over the general commotion they did not respond, and the door was much too strong for her to break down.

For a moment she leaned against it, sobbing with fear and anger. Then she remembered the cabin phone. She scrambled across the bed and punched the emergency call button on the unit built into the headboard. Nothing happened. The operating light remained dark. She pressed the button frantically and slapped her palm against the speaker. Something rattled ominously inside it, but the unit remained quite dead.

Delray heard Evan Arcovian banging on his door over the sound of running feet and raised voices.

'All right, I'm just coming, Evan,' he called out automatically. 'You go on. Take care of yourself.'

But he didn't make any effort to leave his compartment. If the ship was lost then so was any hope of rescuing Lyset. In which case there was no point in his living. Why not just sit here and let it happen?

The unseen shuffling continued moving about the room and again something soft brushed his ankles, but he ignored it.

Then a faint voice seemed to whisper in his ear, 'Taking the coward's way out again?'

Rexton arrived, panting, on the bridge. His clothes looked crumpled, as though he had slept in them. Even he had needed rest to recover from his encounter on the alien ship, Lanchard noted absently. He should have been making his way to a lifeboat like the rest but clearly he didn't classify himself as an ordinary passenger. He took in the readings on the displays and the swelling image of the alien ship with professional composure.

'How long until we hit, if we can't get the engines on line?'

'Less than five minutes now,' Lanchard said crisply.

'You can't evacuate the entire ship in that time.'

'I know – but there's no other choice. With the gravity field that thing generates accelerating us we'll be smashed to pieces for certain.'

Which meant she would die. He knew as well as she did that, by ancient and well-founded tradition, until everybody had been safely evacuated a captain could not leave her ship.

'There's one other thing I can do,' she said, opening the general distress channel. 'This is the SC *Cirrandaria*. Our main drive has been sabotaged and we are out of control and on a collision course with another vessel. We are preparing to evacuate the ship. Any craft receiving this message please give immediate assistance.'

Of course they both knew the only ship that could possibly respond in time was the *Indomitable*.

Out of the corner of her eye she saw Rexton open his mouth as though to protest, but he said nothing. Either his instinct for self-preservation overruled his pride and hatred of the Nimosians, or else he realised there were times when the needs of common humanity came first. She wondered which.

Vega strode through on to the bridge from his ready room, where he had been snatching half an hour's sleep.

'Report,' he snapped.

'The *Cirrandaria* is now on an unpowered trajectory that will cause her to impact the alien vessel in four minutes,' Fayle said. 'Her lifeboat ports are opening.'

'Put us on to an interception course,' Vega commanded. 'Ready the tow beam. Communications, inform them that we will attempt to bring them about on to a safe course. They must not try to eject their lifeboats while we are making the beam lock.'

In the engine room the Doctor and Manders were working frantically over the cable conduit to restore engine control. Sam could only look on anxiously, holding torches and passing over tools on demand. It was evident that it was far quicker and easier to sever connections than it was to repair them correctly. Still, the task would normally take only ten minutes. Unfortunately, they didn't have ten minutes to spare.

Manders, her arms thrust deep into the void under the floor plate as she microwelded and reinsulated the wiring, said, 'With the gravity field that ship generates we'll need all the manoeuvring thrusters working to alter course in time. And I don't think we're going to make it.'

'Are the inertial gyro rings still functioning?' the Doctor asked.

'Yes.'

'Then forget the thrusters and concentrate on getting the main reaction drive operational. Bendix,' he called out to the first officer. 'Tell the Captain to use the gyros to turn the ship ninety degrees to our present course, then cut in the main drive as soon as it's functioning. A second or two of that will shift our trajectory enough to miss the alien ship. By the time we fall back towards it again we'll have everything fully operational.'

Bendix transmitted the suggestion up to the bridge. He reported back: 'The Nimosians are going to try to lock on a tow beam and pull us clear.'

'Perhaps they aren't as bad as you've been making out,' Sam said.

'The Captain says she'll implement your suggestion anyway – just in case,' Bendix added.

The *Indomitable* manoeuvred over the falling *Cirrandaria*. The tow-beam controller was aligning the emitters so that the beam would strike the liner over its centre of gravity to prevent it tumbling.

'Still getting the erratic energy readings from the alien ship, Commander,' one of the monitors reported.

'Does it match the patterns recorded during the previous gravity shift?'

'No, Commander.'

'So, they chose this very moment to try something new,' Vega said softly, glancing at Fayle. 'Well, Mr Fayle. Does that strike you as more than a coincidence when the Emindian liner has just reported being sabotaged?'

'Yes, Commander,' Fayle said stiffly.

'I agree. All hands, move to amber alert status. Report any unusual observations directly to the bridge.'

'Beam targeted and locked, Commander.'

'Power up slowly. This is not a military craft we're grappling. Engage main drive to begin deceleration.'

On the bridge of the *Cirrandaria* they felt the gradual force of the tow beam take hold. The *Cirrandaria*'s own artificial-gravity fields shifted to compensate, keeping the floor under everybody's feet.

'We are slowing, Captain,' the helmsman reported.

'Tow beam is holding,' the engineering systems monitor reported. 'Structural stress within tolerances.'

Lanchard ran a finger across her brow and found it damp with sweat. She spoke into her wristcom. 'Captain to all lifeboat stations: continue embarking passengers but do not attempt to launch unless directly ordered. There's a chance we may save the old ship yet.'

'Captain!' the crewman monitoring the external sensor displays called out. 'The energy fluctuations are increasing on the alien ship. The readings are... well, they're going crazy.'

Rexton was staring intently at the magnified image of the ship on the big screen. Lanchard saw that its more substantial end was presented almost full on now, the tunnel mouth looking uncomfortably as though it was gaping wider to meet them. Within was a pit of darkness – no, streaks of light were starting to form.

Even as she watched they resolved into starlike points. It was like looking down into a well on a star-spangled night. They grew brighter and blurred and vanished again, falling into the depths. Then, out of the darkness, she saw a red glow that flickered and shimmered but grew steadily stronger. The glow became diffuse, swelling until it filled the mouth of the huge shaft. It was pulsating more and more rapidly. Then with a surge of power it expanded and filled the screen.

A column of ruddy-tinted sparkling radiance erupted from the shaft and struck *Cirrandaria*.

Chapter Twenty-Two
Cavern

The end of the alien ship rested inside a huge, approximately ovoid, cavern. Their torches could illuminate only the nearest rock face with any clarity. The rest was lost in almost total darkness, broken only here and there by a few faint yellow-white glimmerings which might have been artificial lights several kilometres away. The far end of the ship faded into the uncertain gloom.

Sho turned to Lyset, looking wild-eyed and angry, and touched helmets. 'What is this place?' he demanded.

'Well, it's not Kansas, Toto…' The ancient literary allusion was lost on Sho. She said as evenly as she could manage, 'How should I know? The Doctor – the Moderator – said this whole ship was an experimental hyperspace bridge. Well, it looks like he was right. Crossing that interface must have taken us somewhere else.'

Sho appeared to calm down slightly. 'Then I shall reconnoitre. If this is where the controllers of the alien vessel have their base they may have brought some of my squad here. They may still be alive.'

Lyset wanted to get back to Don and the *Cirrandaria*. But this discovery was so fantastic that, despite her recent ordeal, it piqued her curiosity. If only she had her camera. A trembling underfoot reminded her of one reason why they had left the ship. Maybe it was worth exploring until it settled down again.

'If we're going, let's go.' She looked about her. 'Is that some sort of gantry?'

In the dim light it was just possible to make out a framework tower extending from the rock wall. It connected with the flange structure about three hundred metres from where they stood, holding the great projecting horns clear of the cavern walls.

'Yes,' Sho said. 'Probably to prevent the craft from drifting. We shall climb down it to the cave floor.'

They set off across the pipework field beside the flange wall.

Climbing it would be like mounting a series of small cliffs smothered in tree roots, she thought. But at least there would be plenty of footholds.

As they proceeded the whole cavern seemed to rotate about them. The ship's own local gravity field was stronger than that of whatever place they were in, and so down remained in the general direction of its long axis. Lyset suddenly felt sick and she reminded herself firmly that a spacesuit helmet was no place to throw up.

Her steps were getting lighter and she began to bounce in exaggerated strides across the hull. It was as though she was wearing seven-league boots. The alien ship's centre of gravity was changing again. If it shifted all the way, she thought, they would effectively be at the top of a four-kilometre sheer wall! Sho must have realised the same thing, for he lengthened his own strides.

They didn't need to climb the first flange wall. A single bound carried them to the top. Three long strides took them to the second. Another bound. They soared over the next terrace top. They were definitely getting lighter. As she touched down she felt a vibration through the soles of her boots. Then the gantry was before them. It had seemed spiderlike from the distance and dwarfed by the alien ship's hull. But close to she saw it was formed of a latticework of heavy beams. A final leap took them to its base. Running up inside the framework was a ladder with rungs a metre apart, ideal for a low-gravity environment. They began to climb hand over hand.

After they'd ascended only a hundred metres her legs were gently pulled away from the ladder in the direction of the invisible far end of the alien ship. The centre of gravity had shifted, but distance was moderating the effect. Lyset was breathing heavily by now and her arms were beginning to ache. She wondered if she could attract Sho's attention long enough to suggest they take a rest now they were out of danger. Then she blinked. Why was it getting brighter?

A dull red glow was emanating from the huge tunnel mouth below her, illuminating the depths of the cavern. She climbed faster.

Two-thirds the way up the ladder all relative gravity faded away as the field of the ship and the surrounding cavern equalised. Sho swung about gracefully and she copied him. She needed to push to get herself started down again, but then she could glide, letting the side rail of the ladder slip through her fingers. The radiance was extending into a misty sparkling haze about the mouth of the shaft. By its light she saw balconies studding the walls about her, and the dark mouths of smaller cave openings, planed shelves of rock and strips of window reflecting the light in the distance. The ship was a massive dark cylinder hanging above them, apparently supported by several slender pylons similar to the one they were climbing.

Sho's hand slapped her leg. She looked down and saw rock floor just below them. She slowed her rate of descent and hit ground, staggering slightly even though the gravity was less than that on the alien ship. A path, looking as though it had been cut by a laser, led away from the base of the pylon and twisted between the rugged upthrusts of rock.

Should we follow it? she wondered. Then she saw Sho staring upward, rifle unslung and cradled ready in his arms. She followed his gaze. Smoke seemed to be pouring from several of the dark cave openings opposite the glowing hull mouth. What was happening now?

Then a sense of scale asserted itself. It was not smoke.

Fire blazed from Sho's gun even as his mouth opened in a soundless scream.

Chapter Twenty-Three
The Shadow Host

The impact as the red glow enveloped the *Cirrandaria* was transmitted through the tow beam to the *Indomitable*, making the ship shudder.

'An energy beam of unknown composition has surrounded the Emindian ship,' a monitor reported. 'It's acting like an attractor field, pulling the ship towards the shaft mouth.'

'Increase power to main drive by one half,' Vega said. 'We're going to rescue the Emindians even if somebody else thinks otherwise.'

In the engine room they felt the *Cirrandaria*'s hull groan under the increased strain as Bendix relayed the news from the bridge. Lights began to flash urgently on monitor panels.

Manders lifted her head out of the floor hatch to call out, 'Everybody suit up. Repair teams to emergency stations. Close all airtight doors. Activate reserve pressure curtains.'

'Bendix,' the Doctor called out. 'We'll be finished in another minute. Have the Captain turn the ship all the way round. Then we'll use the main drive to pull free.'

The main bridge monitor screen was filled with the image of the glowing tunnel mouth, slowly growing larger despite the counterthrust of the *Indomitable*. As she stared more intently Lanchard noted that the beam had a subtle structure. The sparkling points within it, like dust motes caught in sunlight, were descending through the centre of the column and rising in a ringlike formation about the outside. It reminded her of a circulation pattern in a column of liquid. And they were caught in its apex, unable to break free, slowly being sucked down into the centre.

She frowned. There was something else rising up the outside of the beam. Darker fuzzy patches she could not resolve. She magnified one quadrant of the image to the maximum. It was a hazy grey cloud with irregular edges. Beside her Rexton drew in his breath sharply and gave vent to a curse which was suddenly cut short as he regained his composure.

'Ghosts,' he said tonelessly. 'Hundreds of them. They're going to attack us.'

They had just scrambled into emergency pressure suits when the ship's speakers came to life: 'All hands to armament lockers. Unidentified beings are riding the beam up to the ship. They may attempt to board us.'

Bendix started to move, his face very pale.

'Your weapons are useless,' the Doctor called after him.

'So? You expect us to give up without a fight?' Bendix snapped. He was already halfway to the lift.

'No. That wouldn't be the human thing to do,' the Doctor acknowledged gently.

'This might help them,' Sam said, holding up the normaliser. 'We've got to try. Maybe we can hold them off until you can get the main drive fixed.'

'All right, Sam. Be careful.'

She saw the concern in his face and felt the familiar frisson it sparked within her. One of the things she was most proud of in her life was that this man truly cared about her.

She ran after Bendix.

'Have the Nimosians cut their beam for a few seconds so we can eject those lifeboats that are full!' Rexton said. 'At least some of them will get away.'

Despite the full thrust of the *Indomitable*'s engines they were still slowly descending tail first. There was nothing more they could do.

'They may not have the power to pull free of the beam from the derelict,' Lanchard snapped, fighting back a sense of sick despair. 'Even if they did, what if those things attack them in open space?'

'It's an acceptable risk.'

'I will not gamble with the lives of my passengers! Acceptable risks are for soldiers. Gods damnit! We shouldn't be here playing your games. I should have told the board what they could do with their directives. People are going to die because I wasn't brave enough to stand up to you!'

The main screen was filled by fleeting images of shadows without bodies. In the last moments before they struck, Lanchard saw, against all reason in the vacuum of space, that they had wings.

Such was the confusion on the upper port lifeboat deck that the ghosts' arrival went almost unnoticed at first. People were still pressing forward while others were being turned aside from boats that were full. Children were crying, adults were shouting and families were desperately trying to stay together – all tinted by the red light streaming in through the viewports. The cries of those who saw the first shadows melting through the hull wall on to the deck were drowned in the greater uproar.

They were almost invisible at first – feeble flickering things whose batwings shrivelled away as soon as they touched solid matter, as though the effort of maintaining them had drained their strength. They became no more than cold wisps of grey mist blowing through the throng. Then one of them wrapped itself around a man.

As he screamed in pain and fear the ghost grew, as though feeding on his very life force. It swelled into a translucent thing of teeth and claws and boneless clinging arms, and the people scattered from it in terror. As it became more real the man's struggles weakened, and he faded into grey translucence. Clutching its prize, the ghost ran at the hull and leapt, sliding through the solid metal and glass and pulling the man with it.

The shadows began to pluck people from the panic-stricken crowd. Each victim melted into insubstantiality and was carried back through the hull into the red haze. Anybody who tried to bar a ghost's passage was knocked aside by a fleetingly solid limb, or slashed by claws and talons.

Into this nightmare came Bendix and a handful of armed crewmen, with Sam at their heels.

A shadowy form lunged at them. Sam caught it in the beam of the normaliser and it materialised into a thing with a crocodilian head set on a lion's body, carrying one extra pair of legs. The crewmen fired, knocking the creature out of the air and sending it tumbling backwards. It writhed and twisted under the gunfire, metamorphosing into new forms that swallowed the blast holes in its body even as they were formed.

'Do it like we did in the engine room!' Sam shouted.

They forced the creature back to the hull. At the last moment Sam reversed the normaliser's polarity and it fell backwards and was gone.

Down in the hold Manders withdrew her arms from the cable conduit and said into her wristcom, 'Captain, main engines back on line!'

The engine room trembled as the power flowed into the impeller banks while the ship's frame groaned again under the new load.

The Doctor sprang to his feet. 'Which is the quickest way to the hold from here?' he demanded.

Delray heard the distant sounds of battle but made no move to leave his cabin. Once a shadowy form slid through the wall. There was a fierce snarling and snapping of unseen teeth. With an unearthly scream of pain and rage the ghost retreated. The growls subsided again to a low whine. Delray hardly noticed.

The voice was deep within him now. There was nowhere to run or hide. It was confirming what he most feared about himself.

'The *Cirrandaria*'s main engines have cut in,' the monitor reported to Vega. 'Motion towards the alien ship is decreasing again.'

'Maintain thrust at this level,' he confirmed. 'Any sign of system failure due to proximity to the alien ship?'

'None yet, sir. We are twenty-nine hundred metres from the craft. Estimate descent will cease at twenty-six hundred.'

We'll just make it, Vega thought. On the screen was a view along the tow beam. Tiny grey forms could be seen circling the *Cirrandaria* like wasps around a hive. Every few seconds one would emerge from the ship, actually through its hull, and tumble freely down the core of the beam and into the central shaft of the alien vessel. It looked as though each of them was carrying something.

'Sir, something else is coming up the beam. It's larger than the other creatures…'

A vehicle glided through the hull of the *Cirrandaria* as though it was no more substantial than air and dropped into the mêlée on the lifeboat deck. It was a glittering craft the size of a small shuttle but apparently made of mist and soap bubbles: a vehicle less substantial than its crew, whom Sam could see riding inside it even as it set down on the deck. They were manlike figures in bulky armour, who piled rapidly out through the vehicle's hatchways. They carried tridents and nets in the manner of ancient Roman gladiators.

And they started attacking the ghosts.

Where energy bolts had passed through them with little effect, the primitive and apparently insubstantial weapons of the newcomers trapped and stabbed and drew blood and ichor from the ghostly veins. The ghosts turned upon the warriors, but their blows and slashes glanced off their plated armour.

It was as she was trying to make sense of this unexpected turn of events that Sam saw Jeni Engers.

She recognised her face clearly through the simple globe of her emergency pressure suit. She was holding on to the arms of a small figure in another suit who could only be Dan Junior. A ghost had the boy by the legs. Sam lunged forward through the throng, raising the normaliser and shouting for Bendix, even as Dan Engers Senior threw himself at the creature that was trying to steal his son. A thick tendril lashed out and smashed him aside. A second blow knocked Jeni over backwards. Before Sam could line up a clear shot, the ghost, with Dan wrapped in its cold embrace, ran at a viewport, dived through it and flew out into space.

Just then one of the armoured warriors threw a net over Sam and pulled her off her feet.

* * *

A ghost, drifting through the cargo stacks of the hold, had almost prevented the Doctor from reaching the TARDIS. But he had driven it away with his sonic screwdriver and managed to get within the TARDIS's own shielded walls. Now he was working frantically over the control console.

His first priority had been to prevent the ship crashing. Now, perhaps, he could do something about the intruders.

'The normaliser functions as intended,' he muttered to himself as his hands flew across the controls, 'confirming that the ghosts are susceptible to frequencies nineteen to thirty-seven... combine the characteristics and channel output through the ship's power distribution grid... allow for containment and amplification within the hull... cross fingers and –'

He threw a final switch.

The lights throughout the *Cirrandaria* began to pulse rapidly. Pieces of electrical equipment started up of their own accord and several immediately fused. A low drone of power reverberated through the length of the ship, rising rapidly to a shrill whine that drilled into the brain. The humans who heard it winced and covered the earpieces of their suits.

The ghosts fled.

Like fog shredded before the wind, they billowed through compartment walls and out through the hull, there to drop away into the central vortex of the red beam and return to where they had come from. And the armoured warriors also departed in their impalpable craft. And with them went Sam Jones.

Two minutes later, by which time the labouring engines of the *Cirrandaria* and *Indomitable* lifted the two craft five kilometres from the alien ship, the red beam flickered and died away as though it had never been.

Chapter Twenty-Four
Through the Tunnel

The terrible cold numbed Sam's body and mind. She just had sense enough remaining to clasp the normaliser to her chest, though she no longer had the feeling in her hands to operate it. For that matter she could hardly feel *anything* about her properly. The only good thing about the cold was that it had apparently numbed her fear.

She was in a grey twilit world, all fuzzed at the edges and almost bleached of colour. She lay helplessly entangled in the net on the insubstantial deck of the armoured warriors' ghostly craft. Four of its crew of six sat with their feet resting upon her – which she would have resented had she the strength – with their weapons held ready. Outside in the glowing red mist of the beam the ghost creatures spiralled thickly about them on their batlike wings. Sam muzzily realised there were figures struggling feebly in their grasp, and automatically tried to spot Dan Engers. Turning her head to follow them down she found herself looking through the craft's transparent deck.

And through her own outstretched forearm.

She could dimly see the bones and even a suggestion of the muscles around them, wrapped in the transparent layers of her suit. She had become a ghost!

The fear at last penetrated her sluggish brain and she had to fight to stay in control. The Doctor wouldn't panic, she told herself firmly: he would reason.

They knew touching the ghosts made them more solid, but obviously the process worked in the other direction. In their dealings so far they had made only brief contact with them. But evidently if the contact was extensive or prolonged, the living person became equally out of phase with reality. That was why everything appeared so hazy to her. Part of the light normally intercepted by her retina was simply passing through it and the rest of her insubstantial body. And it was in that state that she had been taken through the hull of the *Cirrandaria*. But was the change permanent? No! That was why they were resting their feet on her. It was only their continuing contact that stopped her regaining normality and falling through the hull of their almost nonexistent craft.

It meant her condition was reversible. She would not remain a ghost for ever!

She clung to this rationalisation even as the craft dived into the gaping tunnel mouth of the alien ship.

Around her were stars, smeared and distorted as though by a funhouse mirror. Then she felt space pressing in about her. The craft, the warriors and her own body were being sickeningly twisted and stretched. The stars contracted to pinpoints once more, blazing brilliantly as they flew past. The cold deepened. She wanted to cry out but she couldn't move. It was the interface effect, spread out along the entire length of the shaft. Time slowed to an eternal moment. A few trillion kilometres and several aeons crawled by.

Her stomach knotted again and she writhed in pain as the process slowly reversed. The far end of the tunnel opened around them and they were clear.

She heard sounds that might have been muffled words.

Craning her neck, she saw that one of the two warriors seated before the craft's glassy control console was swaying from side to side and flailing about with his arms. His comrade seemed to be trying to restrain him. The warriors seated about her started forward as though to help, but it was too late.

The disturbed one rose from his seat, tearing at his armour, which was splitting and falling away from his body.

Then a rock wall came out of the darkness straight at them.

If they had been in a normal state of being they would have been smashed to pieces. As it was, the crash resembled hitting foam rubber. But evidently they were still travelling too fast to pass cleanly through as they had the hull of the *Cirrandaria*.

The craft sank a few metres in, buckled and disintegrated.

Sam, still bundled in the net, was thrown through its fragmenting hull and hit the rock wall. She felt its substance soak into her flesh before peeling away again and letting her go. Then she was falling slowly into darkness, the life coming back to her as she receded from the ghosts and their craft, sharing her store of reality only with their net, which remained tangled about her.

By the time she hit ground the rock felt as hard as it should have – and the impact knocked the senses from her.

Chapter Twenty-Five
Aftermath

Bendix spoke regretfully to the Doctor.

'Your assistant was heading for the woman and child. We were right behind her when we were hit by a ghost. It took one of my men and knocked me over.' He touched the fresh bandage on his forehead. 'By the time I'd got back on my feet, the warriors had already bundled her into that craft of theirs. Then your alarm, or whatever it was, started up and they all simply poured out of the ship back through the hull. There was nothing I could do. I'm sorry.'

The Doctor's face was a pale, set mask. The others round the table looked on sympathetically.

'I wish we'd left when you suggested,' Lanchard said to him. She thought of Dan and Jeni Engers, whom she had visited in the sickbay while Dan was having his injuries treated. The look on their faces would stay with her for a long time. 'Now we can't leave. Not with all those people missing. Unless you think there's no hope…'

'There's always hope,' the Doctor said firmly. A little animation seemed to flow back into him. 'We'll have to go after Sam and the others who were kidnapped, that's all.'

'Into the ship?'

'Not quite. Into the interdimensional tunnel that runs through the middle of the ship. The hull already formed the initial hyperspatial bridge, and now they've used it to open the main corridor. But I can't determine where the other end lies, so there's no other way but to travel along it. My instruments show it's passable for the moment, but it will inevitably collapse in a few hours.'

'What if that red beam appears again?' Lanchard asked.

'The vortex field? I doubt it. It's a secondary hyperspatial effect. The creatures needed it to launch their attack. Vacuum may not harm them, but they can't move themselves through it. I suspect their wings were to work against the resistance of the beam. If you keep clear you won't be troubled by it again.'

'What about those humanoid warriors?' Bendix asked. 'They seemed to be fighting the ghosts – at least at first.'

'I have no idea what their motives are – yet. But if they still have Sam then we will certainly be making contact with them,' the Doctor assured him. 'But now we must get ready.' He fished a piece of paper out of his pocket and handed it to Manders. 'How soon can you produce, say, four of these?' She unfolded the sheet to reveal a hand-drawn circuit diagram and a set of specifications. 'It's a normaliser, like the one Sam had. They seem to be our best defence against the ghosts.'

'Yes, we'll certainly need all the protection we can lay our hands on,' Rexton agreed. 'We underestimated those creatures. On the ship they seemed to be no more than wild animals acting purely by instinct. But this attack was very deliberate. The one that got aboard examined the engine room systems, then set the ship on a very precise course to take it within range of that beam.'

'I take it you are prepared to accompany another party to the alien ship, Councillor?' the Doctor asked.

'I am,' Rexton said.

'But our objective is not the ship itself but whatever lies on the far side of it,' the Doctor pointed out. 'That is most likely where the passengers have been taken. Unless, of course, you're still thinking of trying to recover the data from the other half of the control room beyond the interface. Logically that should be accessible from the other side. But be careful, you may find it quite literally a ghost ship now.'

Before Rexton could reply Lanchard said sharply, 'May I remind you my ship and its complement *have* been put at risk, Councillor, so I am at liberty to leave this zone of space as soon as I am able. Remember also that you will get a volunteer crew to accompany you on a *rescue* mission, but *not* for more intelligence gathering.'

Rexton had the sense not to protest. 'Suppose I get a chance to obtain the data myself?'

'At your own risk,' Lanchard conceded. 'It must not jeopardise the safety of the others.'

'Agreed,' Rexton said.

He doesn't lack courage, Lanchard thought. Aloud she said, 'Nel, how quickly can you make more of these devices of the Doctor's?'

Manders had been scanning the diagram. 'Most of this looks pretty standard. I think I can use some regular items. Say a couple of hours. That is if it has priority over repairing the main drive, Captain. It's pretty well burnt out.'

'How long to fix that?'

'A ship's day, maybe thirty-six hours.'

Lanchard pinched the bridge of her nose, realising how tired she felt. 'If there's the slightest hope, we must try to recover passengers. We can hold our position with thrusters until then.'

'Good,' said the Doctor. 'Now I'd better have a word with Commander Vega. I think he'll want to be involved in this.'

'You don't mean to ask the Nimosians along?' Rexton said incredulously. 'They cannot be allowed to see –'

'It's too late, Councillor,' the Doctor interjected sharply. 'After what's happened it won't take them long to deduce the alien ship's purpose. Your secret's out. Start thinking of some compromise, because this is one trophy you won't be taking home.'

Rexton glared back at him but said nothing.

'And I'd also like an item of my luggage moved from the hold into the *Doria*,' the Doctor added. 'I've a feeling we may need it.'

'I shall complain to the shipping line,' Rhonda Plecht said angrily. 'It's quite intolerable. We were crushed into that tiny lifeboat for no reason at all.'

They had returned to their cabin once the all clear had been given. Rhonda had apparently taken in the damage done to the ship and the sight of the injured being tended with the same critical eye she turned on an unmade bed. The general atmosphere of fear and uncertainty touched her not at all.

'It was an emergency, dear,' Lester pointed out. 'And we were lucky enough to avoid being attacked by those ghost creatures.'

The argument did not seem to count with Rhonda. That sort of thing happened to other people and certainly shouldn't be allowed on a well-run cruise. Lester knew she wasn't very good at empathising with the suffering of others. It was not callousness exactly, more an inability to accept simple misfortune. She believed life was what you made it and if it went wrong it was somebody's fault – probably your own. Except in her own case, of course, when somebody else was to blame.

'Do you think it might be good business to check on Ms Schollander?' he said casually. 'As a prospective client, I mean. See that she's come to no harm.'

'Yes, that might be a good idea. But don't be too long, Lester,' she said absently, looking at a message flashing on the room's infopad. 'Well really, they've put back the restaurant openings by two hours…'

Lester slipped out and made his way quickly to Ingrid's cabin. He found an apologetic steward just leaving and Ingrid looking pale and drawn.

'Are you all right?' he asked anxiously.

She forced a weak smile. 'It's nothing. I was just locked in my room when the call came through to abandon ship.'

'What?'

'Somebody seems to have played a badly timed practical joke on me. They also sabotaged my phone so I couldn't call for help. I suppose I'm lucky one of those creatures didn't find me. They said they were terrifying. The steward only heard me banging on the door after it was all over.'

'But who'd want to do such a thing?' Lester said. 'How could anyone want to hurt anybody as nice as… I mean, it could have been dangerous.'

She smiled at him. 'You are kind,' she said. And she kissed him on the cheek.

'Where were you, Don? You had me thinking they'd taken you with them.'

Arcovian's face was a picture of concern as he confronted Delray in the door of his cabin. Delray said simply, 'I had some thinking to do, Evan. I was all right.'

'Thinking! While those ghouls were tearing the ship apart! Don, you don't look right. It's worry about Lyset, I know. You gotta see the doctor.'

'No. It's something I must sort out for myself. Just leave me alone. Please.'

'You won't do anything… foolish, Don?'

'I've been doing foolish things all my life. But I'm not feeling suicidal, if that's what you mean. That would be the coward's way out… and I think I've got past that stage.'

And he closed the door firmly.

Of course he was not really alone. Now he could just make out a grey fuzzy shape on the floor, but he no longer feared it. He now knew what it was and, though the knowledge sickened him, he was beyond fear.

The burst of sound and light that had driven the other ghosts away had not removed them. The voice had cried in pain while the thing on the floor had howled. But they had not left him. Perhaps they had courage. It was more than he had.

'Fine words,' said the voice inside his head. 'Think you can live up to them?'

'I don't know,' Delray said huskily.

'You took Evan for granted, but he was better than you deserved. But you'll never be able to make up for that.'

'I know.'

'Do you know the ghosts took young Dan Engers?'

Delray sank his head into his hands. 'No… not the boy.'

'That's right. The one who thinks you're a real hero –'

'Shut up!'

'You can't shut me up. You're stuck with me for ever.' There was a suspicion of a bitter chuckle. 'Maybe longer.'

'What about Lyset?' he asked desperately.

'Maybe it's too late for her as well. That depends on you.'

'What do you mean?'

'Look on the bed.' The voice was suddenly leaden.

'What?'

'Just do it.'

He walked stiffly through to the bedroom. He knew there was something terrible there, but he also knew he had no choice. When he saw what it was, all the guilt and anguish within him was released in a cry of utter despair.

Chapter Twenty-Six
Command Decision

'Commander Vega,' the Moderator they called the Doctor said, his earnest face filling the screen, 'you have demonstrated your common humanity by coming to the aid of the *Cirrandaria*. Now follow that impulse through to its logical conclusion. Very soon we shall be taking a shuttle into the hyperspatial corridor that has been opened through the centre of the alien vessel. If you have managed to modify a shuttle of your own, will you come with us? If we can pass through successfully it should allow access to the far side of the interface where your lost men may very well have been taken. If any have survived you may be able to rescue them.

'We shall transmit a schematic diagram of a relatively simple device called a normaliser, which can be used to alter the phase state of the creatures we have called "ghosts". It does them no permanent harm but it does make them more vulnerable to conventional weapons and even physical attack. If you can replicate these devices you will be as well protected as we ourselves.'

Fayle said, 'You simply want the protection of our superior fire power to help you recover your own people.'

'Your superior fire power is useless without the device I have mentioned,' the Doctor pointed out. 'The logic of organising a joint mission is inescapable.'

'When our fleet arrives –' Fayle retorted.

'You will lose even more brave lives in a futile effort to fight something you do not understand,' the Doctor interrupted. 'Please believe what I am telling you. Try to think beyond the prejudices which have shaped your lives for so long. This is not a prize for either you or the Emindians.'

Vega had to admit there was something compelling in his words. But the thought of a joint venture with the Emindians was disturbing to say the least. 'I will consider your proposal, Doctor. You shall have my answer in one hour.'

The Doctor smiled warmly. 'Thank you, Commander.'

His image was replaced by the circuit diagram of the normaliser, which Vega had relayed to the engineering department. Then he turned to Fayle.

'Well, do we join with the Emindians on this? We haven't much time to decide. Our own instruments show that the discontinuity within the alien ship is slowly decaying.'

'The Moderator is very persuasive and silver-tongued, Commander,' Fayle said. 'He may even be sincere. But I cannot trust any arrangement in which Rexton is concerned. Has the Moderator succeeded in purging him of his "prejudices"? I think not.'

'No. But will we let our pride prevent us from recovering our lost men?'

'As soon as the second shuttle is ready we can go ourselves.'

'But that would mean going without the Doctor's support. I feel he is a man with uses. Perhaps I should have been more open with him earlier.'

'If you mean about the attempted alien infiltration we suffered, it would have been a sign of weakness to have admitted it, Commander.'

'So, unwarned, they were infiltrated in turn and we had to put our ship at some small risk to rescue them. Innocent lives were lost unnecessarily. Is it surprising that I feel a certain responsibility?'

'You have shown the Emindians every leniency in the circumstances.'

'Do you think I have been too accommodating, Mr Fayle?'

Fayle's face set. 'It would not be my place to say, Commander, unless I believed your actions directly endangered the success of the mission or the safety of the ship.'

'Do you doubt my competence... or loyalty?'

'No, Commander. I only say that, if the choice had been mine, I would have pursued a different course of action. I know where my duty lies.'

'Yes, we both want what is best for Nimos. In the end it comes down to making the right choice.' He looked at a monitor which showed the live image of the alien ship. 'But what is the right choice where that thing is concerned? I have a bad feeling about it. If we win it for Nimos, will history praise or curse us?'

There was a diffident knock on the cabin door.

'Enter,' said Vega.

Rask Chen came in. He looked acutely embarrassed but determined. He stood before them stiffly 'I request special permission to send a hyperwave message to my brother, sir,' he said.

'Your brother,' said Vega. 'He's on the *Starfire*, isn't he?'

'Yes, sir.'

'The ship is on active duty in a potential danger zone, Lieutenant,' Fayle reminded him. 'Channels are kept clear for official traffic only.'

'I have checked the relevant regulations, sir. Personal correspondence may be sent in cases of special need at the Commander's discretion.'

'Oh,' said Vega. 'And what is your special need, Lieutenant?'

'I am… concerned about my brother's health, sir.'

'Is he ill, then?'

'Not that I know of, sir.'

'Then what are you talking about?'

Chen's expression became more intense. 'I am just… worried about him, sir.'

'Do you mean some sort of intuition?' Fayle asked. 'Have you suddenly developed second sight?'

Fayle glowered at the young officer, his look saying more eloquently than words what he thought about his troubling them with such nonsense at a time like this. But Chen stood firm.

'I don't believe so, sir. I just have a strong feeling he may have suffered some sort of injury.'

Vega considered the young man for a long moment.

'Is your concern interfering with your work, Lieutenant?'

Chen hesitated. 'It is a distraction at times, sir,' he admitted.

'Then in the interests of crew efficiency I will permit the call. Just keep your message short, understand?'

'Yes, sir. Thank you, sir.'

Vega passed on the authorisation to the communications room and watched Chen depart with a smile. Fayle however was frowning.

'You think I'm being overindulgent again?' Vega asked.

'I think the crew are letting their imaginations get the better of them. This uncertainty is not good for morale. We need to take the initiative.'

'I intend to do just that, Mr Fayle. I think I will take up the Doctor's offer. You will have command of the ship while I'm gone.'

'You mean to lead the mission personally, Commander?'

'Does that trouble you, Mr Fayle? Do you feel unequal to your part?'

The question caught Fayle by surprise. 'No, Commander, of course not,' he said quickly. 'But –'

'No buts. I am accompanying the expedition. I want to learn the truth. According to the Doctor that vessel creates a tunnel through hyperspace. That would make it a very valuable device, but is it the miracle it sounds? Is that what Rexton is after, or is there something else? Whatever the thing is that has cost so many good lives, I want to be sure it has been worth the sacrifice.'

Before the hour was up two hyperspace messages were received by the *Indomitable*. One was a personal response to Rask Chen, simply assuring him that his brother was perfectly well. The second, in code to Vega, gave details of the ships that were on their way to support his position. Due to refitting delays on the *Starburst* it had been replaced at the last minute by its sister vessel, *Starfire*.

Chapter Twenty-Seven
Garden of the Lost

Lyset could have simply walked away from Sho after the army of winged ghosts had passed into the tunnel. But pity for the wretched man held her back.

After firing up at the grey horde until the power pack of his gun was exhausted, Sho had scrabbled his way into a fold in the rocks and curled up in a ball like a frightened child. If the ghosts noticed his volley of wild shots they did not respond to them. Presumably they had more important business elsewhere. In a minute the last of them vanished and it seemed that they were alone in the vast cavern once again.

Lyset cautiously edged over to Sho and tried to rouse him but he simply curled up tighter. He was obviously in shock, perhaps unable to face his own fear. It was painful to see even a Nimosian soldier reduced to such a state.

She sat beside him, keeping watch for any new danger while trying to work out what to do next. In the light gravity she could possibly have carried him some distance, but which way? Their suit oxygen wouldn't last for ever. They would have to return to the alien ship if they couldn't find a breathable atmosphere elsewhere on this lump of rock. Unless there was an artificial supply somewhere she was doubtful of their chances. From its gravity she suspected the place was a minor asteroid, so there was no possibility of its having a natural biosphere. Did any of those tunnels dotting the cliffs about her lead to pressurised chambers? If they did, was the air breathable? And who controlled this place anyway – the ghosts or some other force?

She was not sure how long she sat there, but she was suddenly roused from her deliberations by Sho. He got to his feet, pulling her up beside him, and touched helmets.

'Now we shall reconnoitre the enemy base,' he told her.

She gaped at him in amazement. Not a word about his collapse. No questions or excuses. She saw him look at the power warning light blinking on his gun with evident surprise, and mechanically replace the battery with a fresh one from his backpack. He doesn't know it happened, she thought. He's denying it even to himself.

They set off along the levelled track that ran across the cavern floor to the nearest of the dark openings, a slight flick of the toes being enough to carry them forward in the fractional gravity. The mouth of the tunnel was four metres across, its rough edges trimmed smoothly back in places. Perhaps it had originally been a natural volcanic vent modified to suit other needs. The rim and mounting of a heavy circular blast door had been fitted to it. But the door itself now stood flung wide, twisted and ripped almost in half as though by an explosion. The tunnel beyond was dimly illuminated by widely spaced red emergency bulbs set in its ceiling, but otherwise it was totally bare.

As they started down it, Lyset took one last look back at the cavern and the alien ship. What she saw made her grab Sho's arm and shout, 'Run!'

The ghostly horde was pouring back out of the interdimensional corridor. At least Sho did not try any futile heroics this time. He ran with her.

So it was that neither of them saw the craft carrying Sam drop clear of the returning swarm and smash into the cavern wall.

Sam came to feeling desperately sick and dizzy, automatically feeling her suit and helmet for any sign of damage before she was fully awake. But all seemed intact. She was on the Dreamstone Moon. She was –

She blinked and forced her eyes back into focus. Where the hell was this?

She couldn't have been unconscious for more than a few seconds, she realised, because above her the last of the ghosts were disappearing into the cave mouths, caught in the soft red light of the hyperspace tunnel. And one of them, she realised, was carrying a figure much smaller than the others.

Could it be Dan Engers?

The pair vanished into a tunnel only a couple of hundred metres from where she lay even as she wriggled out of the cold windings of the warriors' net. She still had the normaliser in her hand. Pushing herself upright, thankful for the low gravity, she tottered unsteadily after them.

They had run several hundred metres and taken three side turnings before Sho signalled a halt. Lyset looked anxiously back the way they had come, but there was no sign of pursuit.

Cautiously she felt the side of her helmet. She had grazed it against the side of the tunnel when she had bounded too high in the low gravity. As she did so she became aware of a low hissing over her earphones. The impact must have thrown the external switch of her suit radio. But where was the crackle from the alien ship? She tapped the side of her helmet until Sho understood and switched his own set on.

'We must be insulated from the interference effect by separation and the intervening rock,' he said tersely, when they had established communications. 'But you will maintain radio silence. Others may hear us. Reduce your signal strength to minimum.'

They tramped on, Sho scouting each corner and intersection before they turned it. At the fifth of these he stiffened as though in surprise. Lyset peered curiously over his shoulder.

There was a feebly glowing sign mounted over an alcove halfway along the next stretch of tunnel. It was a very familiar symbol to anyone who had worked in spacesuits for any length of time: a yellow cube with a large O2 displayed on each face.

Within the alcove was a rack containing oxygen canisters, suit batteries, water reservoir refills and squeeze-tube helmet rations. There were a few gaps in the racks and a thin film of dust over everything.

'This is one of your bases,' Sho growled, examining the items.

'This is standard over half the sector,' Lyset retorted. 'They'll fit your suit as well as mine.'

'These are not Nimosian brand names,' he said, waving a squeeze-tube in her face.

'So it's an old supply dump. This could have been here for years... look.' She picked up one of the oxygen canisters. 'The seal's intact but the gauge reads three-quarters. The rest must have leaked out... and this one's only two-thirds full...' Frowning, she checked the row of batteries. 'None show full charge. This stuff really *has* been here for years.' She looked about her uncomfortably. 'Nobody would neglect a service point like this, unless... Where are all the people? Are the ghosts the only ones left?'

'All I know is this is not a Nimosian installation,' Sho said. 'I shall attempt to ascertain its location,' he added, as though quoting a phrase from an instruction book. 'The High Command will be interested to learn of –'

'What was that?' Lyset said.

It was a whisper like the wind through the branches of a tree, rising and falling but never quite dying away. Except that here there was no wind, and the only sounds were coming over her helmet radio. It grew stronger and resolved into separate voices that were too indistinct to understand. But the tones were clear enough. There was wild excited jabbering, plaintive wails, a desperate pleading. None of it sounded sane.

'It's the ghosts,' she said.

A sudden itching down her spine made her spin round, even as three nebulous forms appeared round the corner and moved towards them. Lyset turned to run, only to find two more ghosts blocking the tunnel in the other direction. They were trapped.

Sam stumbled desperately on, just keeping the grey wraith and its burden in sight.

A desperate initial dash had brought her within sight of it before it had vanished in the maze of tunnels. Now she wondered whether, if she could get close enough, she should risk a shot with the normaliser. Would the ghost harm Dan in response, or could it be chased away? The trouble was she had no other weapons to take advantage of any weakness the normaliser might induce. Could she use the device on the negative setting and push the ghost so far out of phase that it could no longer physically hold Dan? But it might drain more 'reality' from him as it did so. How much life was there in a small boy?

The tunnels seemed endless and Sam began to worry about finding her way back. The one certainty she clung to was that the Doctor would not abandon her. If he still thought there was a chance that she was alive he would come looking. The question was, could she stay alive until he found her?

A dimly lit cavern, perhaps a hundred metres wide, opened before her. The wraith sped quickly across it while Sam held back for a moment, fearing she might be seen in the open. The floor was dotted with curious plants. They had slender stalks and bulbous heads, like lost funfair balloons trailing the ends of their strings on the ground. They were pinky grey and so pallid that they almost seemed translucent...

She looked again more closely, then recoiled violently with a choking cry of fear and disgust.

They were not plants, but caricatures of child-sized people curled up into balls and enclosed in transparent membranes, eyes tightly shut in perfect, tiny, expressionless faces. They were tethered, or rooted, to the ground by what she now saw were trailing umbilical cords. All were perfectly still and silent; whether dead or merely resting she could not tell.

Sam turned her eyes away from the dreadful things and fought down the reflex to vomit. She had no idea how they got here or what they meant, only that the ghosts seemed suddenly almost wholesome by comparison. Yet she had to pass between them to continue.

Crossing through the terrible forest was a nightmare that would long haunt her. She was terrified that she might touch one of its macabre inhabitants. She felt the despair of living death all around her. All she could do was fix her eyes on the dark opening on the far side through which the ghost had passed, and edge her way forward. If any of the grotesque things around her had stirred as she passed, she knew she would turn and run.

Sick with relief, she reached the far side and sprinted into the next tunnel, hoping the ghost carrying Dan had not got too far ahead.

Around a corner she came upon a translucent, blue, shimmering curtain emanating from a continuous emitter strip cut into the rock and stretching across the width of the corridor. A pressure curtain. Well, at least that was understandable technology. She pushed through it, feeling the resistance of the air on the other side. A few metres on was another curtain and another, each holding back a little more air than the previous one.

When she was through the last one, the sensor on the arm of her suit said the atmosphere was breathable. She opened her visor and sniffed cautiously. The air was musty but tolerable.

Faint sounds came from around a corner ahead, which was glowing with bright artificial light. She held the normaliser ready and crept forward.

It was Dan's voice. He was sobbing and shouting, 'It's not true! Take me back! I want my proper mother!'

Tough kid, Sam thought. He could have been totally traumatised by now. Perhaps he's already seen worse on the vids.

She peered round the corner. The chamber beyond was a dead end. There were crates and boxes scattered about the walls, giving the impression of an abandoned storeroom. Dan was standing in its centre, almost enveloped in the folds of his junior spacesuit, with his helmet open. Two ghosts were also in the room, but neither for the moment was threatening him. One was smaller and almost human in outline, the other larger and flickering unstably, flashing with bursts of angry colour. It was to this one that Dan was speaking.

'You're not real, you're not real!' he screamed.

Hold that thought, Dan, Sam said under her breath. Just give me a second and they'll be as unreal as I can make them.

But even as she raised the normaliser, the smaller ghost moved forward and touched the larger. It began to shrink. The flickering ceased, and gradually it seemed to solidify into a new form.

Sam gaped in utter astonishment at what it was.

Chapter Twenty-Eight
In the Ruins

Lanchard stared at the strange container that was being loaded into the belly hatch of the *Doria*, then at the Doctor.

'The probe Vega destroyed was also a blue rectangular box,' she said. 'We never saw it clearly, but it must have been about this size.'

'Really?' said the Doctor innocently.

'Yes. What did you say it was again?'

'A sort of mobile laboratory and holdall. Full of useful odds and ends. More distinctive than the usual set of matching plaid cases, don't you think?'

How can he joke at a time like this? she wondered, grateful nevertheless.

Rexton appeared carrying an extra pack in addition to his life-support unit and Wynter's camera. Lanchard wondered just how far he would go to get his precious information. He'd been in private communication with Emindar for much of the last hour. He gave the Doctor's box a curious glance, then appeared to dismiss it from his attention.

The team comprised the minimum complement necessary to allow as much room for the return of survivors, assuming there were any. Apart from Rexton and the Doctor there were just Bendix as pilot and a couple of Dessel's security staff. All were armed and each had one of the Doctor's normalisers. Nel Manders's technicians had managed to produce six of the devices within the deadline.

They were just about to board when a voice said, 'I'm coming, too.'

It was Don Delray, already suited up. His face was impassive, his voice level, his manner determined but also curiously detached.

'I thought you were injured, Mr Delray,' Lanchard said.

'There's nothing wrong with me,' Delray assured her.

'This will be more dangerous than last time,' Lanchard pointed out.

'I know,' Delray said. 'I've had first-hand experience of what we're

201

facing, remember. Let's say I've learnt from it.'

The Doctor was looking at him very closely. 'I think if Mr Delray wants to come he should be allowed to, Captain. We need people we can trust to keep their heads. You won't let us down, will you, Mr Delray?'

'No, Doctor,' Delray replied. 'Not this time.' There was something compelling about the man's eyes, Lanchard realised.

'Draw arms from the locker, Mr Delray,' she said. 'You leave in two minutes.'

There was only a small crowd on the promenade deck, as most passengers were still keeping to their cabins or the inner public compartments. Lester Plecht, however, was among those at the rails. It was only correct and only proper to show moral support, he had told Rhonda with uncharacteristic assurance.

He was looking hopefully about for Ingrid Schollander. Instead he found himself standing next to Evan Arcovian. The other man was looking devastated and dabbing his eyes unashamedly. He had the manner of one who has to confide in somebody, even a total stranger.

'Don's going after her,' he said. 'I tried to talk him out of it but he was determined. Never seen him like this before.' He faltered. 'Trouble is, I have this feeling in my gut that I'll never see him again.'

Lester was not really paying attention. Ingrid wasn't here and he was getting a headache. There was a persistent buzzing in his ear he could not seem to get rid of. Maybe the stress of the last few days had been too much for him. Perhaps he should see the ship's doctor as soon as the shuttle had departed.

'There they go,' said Arcovian, his voice breaking as he pointed. 'Take care, Don.'

Bendix kept glancing at Rexton out of the corner of his eye as he steered the *Doria* to their agreed rendezvous with the Nimosians. The councillor sat beside him in the co-pilot's seat, staring ahead with intense concentration. The last time they had taken this journey, Bendix had unquestioningly considered Rexton to be the most important man on the mission. But now he found his attention divided between him and the Doctor. In many ways they could not be more unlike, yet both possessed the same intriguing aura of power that was hard not to admire.

There was also something different about Delray this time, but he was not sure what it was. The last few hours seemed to have changed the man. There was a chill about him, and a couple of times Bendix had seen him absently reach down by his feet and run his hand over empty air.

There was a blip on the forward scanner display. It rapidly resolved into the image of a slightly larger craft than their own.

'It's the Nimosian shuttle,' Bendix said, opening a channel. To his surprise Commander Vega's face appeared on the screen.

'This is the shuttle *Dauntless*,' Vega said briskly. 'We are ready to make entry. I suggest maintaining a minimum separation of one hundred metres during the passage through the hyperspatial corridor.'

'Agreed,' said Bendix.

'I see you have decided to take personal charge of the mission, Commander,' Rexton said.

'I never ask my men to do anything I will not do myself,' Vega replied. 'Besides, I wanted the opportunity of meeting you face to face, General.'

'I hope you won't be disappointed, Commander.'

'I'm sure I won't be.'

The Doctor leaned forward into view of the comms-link camera. 'Commander, the passage through the tunnel may be rough, both physically and mentally. I suggest you set your autopilot so that your ship will slave on to ours if you lose manual control.'

'And what makes you think your craft will maintain independent control any better than ours?' Vega asked.

'Because, if Councillor Rexton will oblige by changing seats with me, I'll be ready to take over if Mr Bendix is incapacitated,' the Doctor responded simply.

Curiously, nobody protested. Rexton vacated his seat without a word.

Bendix turned them on to a direct course for the alien ship. In a minute the interference effect had drowned the link to the *Cirrandaria*. The dark mouth of the tunnel swelled, seeming to gape wider as they neared it, obscuring the rest of the ship as it grew. He could see a faint red glow in its depths at the centre of a halo of twinkling darts of light.

They passed within the great arcing rim of the shaft, the familiar stars of normal space becoming a shrinking circle behind them. But there was no corresponding circle ahead where the other end of the shaft should have been. It seemed to stretch away to infinity. Bendix felt his heart skip a beat. The void within the shaft suddenly contorted. A sudden sickening wave of nausea overtook him as some invisible force reached into his body and twisted. His vision blurred and his thoughts fragmented. Dimly, he realised that the shuttle was tumbling and he knew they were at the mercy of powers far beyond those of its feeble engines to oppose. All he could do was keep them steady. But his hands had become useless things lost somewhere light years away from him. He could not operate the controls. They were going to smash into the side of the tunnel.

Then the *Doria* steadied.

The Doctor was bent over the controls, holding them on course. Bendix had an impression of clenched teeth, pale skin beaded with sweat and blue eyes colder than any glaciers and sparkling with more determination than he had ever seen before.

Somehow he held them steady through the endless agony of dislocation.

Then a dark circle was rushing towards them and they were clear of the tunnel. Rock walls glittering in the ship's lights. Off to one side was the Nimosian shuttle, its motion mirroring theirs. A broad planed ledge of rock appeared out of the darkness and the Doctor set them down upon it as gently as a thistledown.

For a long moment there was only silence as they collected their wits. Then Rexton said gruffly, 'Thank you, Doctor.'

Vega's pale image spoke over the comm screen. 'I also thank you, Doctor. But where are we?'

They peered out into the huge cavern illuminated by the darting circles of their spotlights. Bendix saw the Doctor straining his eyes, hoping to see some sign of those they had lost. But there was nothing. Rexton had eyes only for the bulk of the alien ship, hanging like some huge grub in its rocky cocoon.

'I don't know,' the Doctor admitted, after a minute's intense study of their surroundings, in answer to Vega's question. 'I have some equipment on board which might tell us, but it will only function properly outside the interference field of the alien ship. I can't see any signs of survivors from the raid in here.'

He adjusted one of the spotlights to play over the wall opposite the mouth of the ship. It picked out the dark circles of several cave mouths. 'But there are plenty of places they could have been taken,' he said. 'If there is any chance of finding them, and your missing crew, then it will be down there. They look wide enough to take both shuttles through in this low gravity.'

'Agreed, Doctor,' Vega said.

Rexton took one last look at the alien ship, then returned to his seat. His face was creased in thought.

Bendix lifted them on low-power underjets and minimal thrusters and steered them towards the nearest of the caves, feeling the *Doria* pitch gently as it moved away from the sharp gravity gradient surrounding the hulk behind them. The *Dauntless* followed and they passed into a long smooth-sided tunnel some fifteen metres across.

'Looks like an excavated asteroid,' Bendix commented. 'It might be honeycombed with tunnels. How do we know they took our people down this one?'

'We don't,' said the Doctor. 'But we must begin somewhere. When we're clear of the interference we may know more.'

'Something up ahead,' Rexton said.

The shuttles slowed, gliding up to a blackened metal ring that encircled the tunnel. The huge plate of an armoured door lay beside it, blown completely clear of its mountings. Close by it, partly buried in the thin scree of dust and rock fragments, were half a dozen twisted shapes. They were bodies. Skulls grinned up through shattered helmets. Blackened skeletal hands seemed to be reaching out in supplication through torn and melted fabric. Beside them were the remains of machinery. One larger item might once have been a self-propelled energy cannon, though it was now reduced to a twisted pile of wreckage. It was impossible to tell who had been attacking or defending the asteroid base.

'This did not happen recently,' Vega said. 'But many years ago there was certainly a battle here. Our instruments are picking up radiation traces. Possibly weapon residue.'

'We can't afford the time to examine them properly,' the Doctor said. 'Let's keep going.'

The tunnel ran on before them as they glided cautiously forward. Side passages opened off it but all seemed quite empty. Occasional blast marks scarred the walls, but there were no signs of ghosts or their captives.

Bendix calculated they had travelled about four kilometres when they came to a pair of doors. The outer had been twisted and buckled while the inner was intact but standing open. Bendix took them carefully through. A rock ledge under them faded away into the darkness on either side. The Doctor stared through the forward port intently.

'There's something here,' he said. 'Turn off the external lights and let your eyes adjust.'

They did so. Slowly, like a moonlit landscape growing into being, their surroundings became visible. It was another cavern slightly smaller than the one that housed the alien ship. But unlike the rough walls of the former, these were sculpted into sweeping glassed terraces, picked out here and there by the feeble glimmer of emergency lights. Between them were projecting docking booms and transfer tubes and the dark mouths of hangars and launchways. It was unmistakably a commercial starport.

Or what had once been a starport.

The glass on the terraces was shattered, docking booms were bent and twisted, wreckage littered the lowest levels. It had not been spared by the conflict that had apparently swept through the rest of the base. But what filled Bendix's mind, as he took in details of the ruins, was a growing sense of shocking familiarity.

'We're home,' he choked out.

'What are you talking about?' Rexton snapped.

'Don't you see? The derelict must be in the navy base. We've passed through to the commercial section. This is Starport on Em Minor. *Cirrandaria*'s home port!'

'He's quite correct,' Delray said simply with infinite sadness, causing the Doctor to look at him curiously.

But Bendix hardly heard him. 'What's gone wrong... What's happened...?'

He took the controls and sent the *Doria* skimming across the port to where a pale disc of light appeared to hang in the roof. The *Dauntless* followed in their wake.

'That's the main access shaft,' Bendix said breathlessly. 'There's only one like it...'

The *Doria* soared up the shaft that cut through half a kilometre of rock and burst into open space. The crater-pocked surface of a small asteroid moon shrank beneath them. Overhead hung Emindar in gibbous phase, filling half the sky, the outlines of its continents unmistakable.

But it was no longer the blue and white globe he had left twenty days before. The oceans were grey; where green forests had been there were only brown stains. Ugly phosphorescent glows played about the horizon of its nightside hemisphere. They were the scars of total planetary war. Emindar was a dead world.

Rexton gaped openly in disbelief, his iron control broken by the image of the one thing he held dear above all others in ruins. Even from the *Dauntless* came gasps of dismay.

'A corridor through space... and time,' said the Doctor, filling the awful silence. 'I said you couldn't manipulate one without affecting the other. I think this is your future.'

Chapter Twenty-Nine
Standoff

Lanchard could tell that Captain Sargro of the *Hermes of Cyrene* was not a happy man. But orders were orders. His ship chanced to be the only one in the sector within range, and with the necessary capacity to evacuate their two hundred or so Federation passengers.

Now the *Hermes* was docked with the *Cirrandaria* and Sargro was contemplating his new charges gloomily. He was more used to cargo that didn't expect four-star accommodation and cuisine. The *Hermes* was a freighter with limited passenger space and personal facilities. It would be a long trip to the nearest Federation port for both evacuees and crew.

Evan Arcovian had also returned to his vigil on the bridge, looking more distraught than ever. However, at least he was keeping his opinions to himself. Lanchard would have liked to spare him a little time for consolation, but she had other worries of her own.

Several Emindian citizens wanted to join those leaving on the *Hermes* and had to be told bluntly that there simply wasn't room for non-Federation passengers. To complicate matters further a few Federation passengers, who had lost friends or relatives in the ghost attack, wanted to stay behind in the hope that the rescue party might yet bring them back. The Engerses were of course among them. Eventually, on advice from head office, Lanchard had them all sign waivers confirming they were staying of their own free will and absolving the company of any subsequent liability.

In the circumstances the abilities of the *Cirrandaria*'s crew were stretched to their limits to calm upset, anxious or plain belligerent passengers. But until the main engines were repaired or their own forces arrived, those who were left would simply have to be patient. How the company was handling the matter of those Federation citizens killed or taken by the ghosts was a job for lawyers and politicians. Lanchard could only put a copy of her orders in the safe ready for the inevitable board of inquiry. For the moment she was concerned only with ensuring there were no further losses.

That depended on maintaining a very fragile status quo.

She assumed the *Indomitable* would not instigate any overt action against them after having gone to the trouble of saving them only hours before – even though she felt Fayle, Vega's second in command, was a less than sympathetic character. But what if the Nimosian reinforcements arrived before their own?

An hour after the *Hermes* docked with them, that was just what happened.

The detectors gave little warning before dark-grey predatory forms slid out of the darkness like sharks. They could identify the bristling bulk of a carrier, accompanied by two heavy cruisers and two destroyers: an entire battle group.

The carrier took up station beside the *Indomitable*, disgorging fighter wings which began circling like bees round a hive. The other craft took up sentry stations where they could watch space for the inevitable arrival of the Emindian forces. It was not long before a priority call came through for Lanchard.

'This is Admiral Mokai, commanding the carrier *Starfire*,' said the severe, beribboned figure on the screen. 'You are in Nimosian-controlled space. You will relinquish any claim on the alien vessel and leave this sector immediately.'

Lanchard had been expecting something like this and was ready with a suitable reply.

'Our government disputes your right to any claim on this sector of space, but, in addition to that, be informed that we cannot leave. First, our main drive is under repair and won't be fixed for another day at least. Second, we have a shuttle down inside the alien vessel on a humanitarian mission. They are looking for some of our passengers and crew who have been abducted by hostile forces. You can check with the *Indomitable*. They saw what happened and have a shuttle down there as well. Now if you will excuse me I have a ship to run.'

She cut the connection, wondering whether Mokai was merely being perverse or hadn't been fully briefed on the latest situation. A sudden thought struck her and she called up the purser's office.

'Have the last of the Federation passengers transferred to the *Hermes* yet, Oscar? No? Good. Lose their baggage. That's right. And don't find it again until I tell you.'

She switched to engineering. 'Nel, send a tech to the docking port. Make sure there's a problem with the tubes to the *Hermes*. Yes, you heard: find a problem. Anything, just keep that ship next to us until further notice.'

Suddenly Captain Sargro and his ship had become their best insurance against the Nimosians. They wouldn't dare try anything while a neutral Federation vessel was present. Now it was simply a question of waiting for their own forces to arrive. For some reason that prospect did not reassure her.

Lester took his headache along to the clinic. He felt slightly guilty because he knew they were still treating far more serious cases in there. But the pain was getting quite intense and the annoying buzzing, whispering sound was still with him. And there, quite unexpectedly, was Ingrid, wearing a white smock over her casual wear, assisting the nurses as they tended the beds of the injured.

She smiled when she saw him. He could manage only a foolish, 'So you're helping out here.'

'Well they're very short-staffed and I did do a basic therapeutic course once. Are you all right? You do look pale.'

He felt embarrassed explaining his relatively trivial complaint, but Ingrid was very sympathetic. She found him a seat in the extended waiting area and promised she'd find a nurse as soon as one was available.

In due course a nurse came, examined him briefly and said it was probably delayed shock. She put a small cerebral modulator on his forehead and gave him a couple of pills. After a few minutes the headache eased and even the whispering buzz seemed to fade a little, possibly masked by the bustle in the surgery. Lester found himself strangely content to sit quietly in the corner, watching the activity around him and knowing Ingrid was nearby.

'At last, there you are!'

Rhonda's voice jerked him back to reality so forcefully that the modulator fell off. As he scrabbled on the floor to recover it, he became aware that Rhonda was staring across the busy waiting room with a deep frown on her face.

'Why did she leave like that? Who is she, Lester?'

'Who, dear?'

'You know perfectly well, who. The woman I saw you with in the corridor. She was talking to you. But I see now it wasn't a headpiece she was wearing: it was bandages. Quite unsightly. Don't tell me you didn't see her this time.'

'But I didn't,' he protested.

'Nonsense! Why are you lying to me? What is going on between you?'

'Nothing, my dear.'

But he pleaded in vain. For the first time ever he saw serious distrust and suspicion in her eyes. And, which was almost more shocking, a hint of fear.

The unexpected discovery that his brother was now only a few kilometres away from him did not ease Rask Chen's troubled mind. He could still not talk to him directly with the Emindian forces expected at any moment and a general alert in effect. So he sat hunched over his section of the control board with his head bowed, occasionally pinching the bridge of his nose in the hope that it would all go away.

Fayle re-entered the bridge looking sterner than usual. He'd been on the link to the *Starfire*, briefing Admiral Mokai for some time. Vega had left him with a lot of explaining to do and it didn't appear as though his report had been well received. Fayle was clearly looking for somebody or something on which to vent his anger and Chen was the unlucky one who caught his eye.

'Sit straight while you're on my bridge, Mr Chen!' he snapped, as he took his own seat.

'Sir!' said Chen, trying to pull himself together. But Fayle wasn't to be so easily satisfied.

'Are you sick, Mr Chen? Or are you having more of those troublesome "feelings"?' he added with more than a trace of sarcasm.

This drew curious covert glances from the rest of the bridge crew and made Chen feel even worse. 'I would rather not say, sir.'

Fayle's face darkened. 'I asked you a question, Mr Chen. I expect an answer.'

'I... just can't tell you, sir,' Chen grated.

'Then you are relieved of duty, Mr Chen. Report to sickbay. If the surgeon cannot find anything wrong with you, go to your quarters and stay there until you do have a satisfactory explanation!'

Stiffly, aware he was the focus of many pairs of shocked eyes, Chen got up and left the bridge.

'What sort of ship are you running, Captain Lanchard?' Sargro demanded an hour later, his face pushed up close to the camera pick-up so it filled the screen. 'I've never known it take so long to embark twenty people, or fix a pressure coupling.'

Lanchard was listening with only half an ear. Her attention was divided between monitoring the progress of the repair work on the engines and watching the Nimosians on the high-mag monitor. Their destroyers had made several close passes over the alien ship but they had so far not attempted any actual landing. Was their reticence due to caution or technical problems? And when would the rescue party report back? What had they found on the other side of that thing?

'Sorry, Captain,' she said vaguely. 'We've had a difficult time here. Just be grateful you'll be leaving soon.'

'But when will –'

Lanchard saw a new set of blips appear on the master navigation screen and interrupted. 'Very shortly, I should think, Captain. Yes, any minute now, in fact. Goodbye and good luck.'

She switched channels. 'Oscar, find the Fed evacs' luggage and get it aboard top speed. Call off the engineer and be ready to seal off. Let's get the *Hermes* out of here. We don't need it any more.'

Six battlecraft dropped out of hyperspace and spiralled cautiously in towards the alien ship, the Nimosian squadron and the

Cirrandaria. As the *Hermes* finally undocked and sped away they took up their positions in a defensive sphere, spilling fighters and attack craft from their hatches. The screens showed a dreadnought, two assault carriers and three light cruisers. The two sides were very evenly matched, Lanchard thought.

A new face and uniform appeared on the screens.

'This is Commodore Gelbert J. Sternby from the ESS *Korgon*, commanding Task Force Alpha. This is an Emindian protectorate zone. All Nimosian-registered vessels must leave this area at once.'

Mokai came back on the general broadcast channel.

'This sector of space was claimed illegally. We have declared an emergency exclusion zone...'

The battle of words continued. Lanchard wondered if either side really knew what to do next. They couldn't simply snatch the alien ship away with a tow line or beam, and the presence of parties from both sides somewhere in or through it complicated matters even further. Still, while they were arguing at least they weren't fighting. Who had said: 'To jaw-jaw is always better than to war-war'?

She realised just how sick of the sight of the alien hulk she had become. It almost felt as though she would never be free of it. The Doctor had been right: it should be destroyed.

A call from the Emindian fleet came through on another channel. It was a harassed-looking technical officer.

'Lieutenant Prothero,' he announced himself briskly. 'Captain, I need to speak to your engineer urgently. We've duplicated the neutraliser according to her design, but the field collapses when we try to expand it to cover any vessel over thirty metres long.'

'She's too busy trying to repair our engines. Look, can't you tow us clear? We've still got two thousand Emindian civilians on board.'

'We can't spare a ship at the moment, even for civilians. You can see how evenly matched we are with the Nimosians.'

'Well, I can't spare my engineer. Of course, if you could send a team over to lend a hand...'

Understanding dawned on Prothero's face. 'Ah. I'll see what I can do.' And he broke the connection.

Almost immediately a call came through on her wristcom direct from Dr Gilliam. There was a strained edge to her normally controlled voice.

'Captain, will you please come to Stateroom Three C at once.'

'Why? That's Delray's cabin, isn't it?'

'Yes. A servo cleaner found... something in here and alerted a steward. He called me. Please come down now.'

'This is hardly a good time for me to leave the bridge. What is it?'

'Sorry, but I can't explain. You have to see this for yourself.'

There was something disturbing and compelling in her tone. Lanchard handed over the watch to her third officer and made for the lift.

There was a sickly-looking steward standing guard outside the compartment. He ushered her in without a word. Inside Gilliam, also pale-faced, said, 'It's on the bed,' she said simply. 'It's a body... or at least I think it is. Be ready for a shock.'

Lanchard took a deep breath and stepped into the bedroom.

Lying full length on the bed, hands folded peacefully across its chest, was indeed a body. An ethereal body, as translucent as any of the creatures that had attacked the ship. But this was no monster. It was unmistakably human and female in form. She could see the translucent veils of clothing over a haze of musculature enveloping the skeleton within. It was like some trick of medical imagery, except that it was no illusion.

Nerving herself she bent over the face, trying to ignore the angular lines of the perpetually grinning skull beneath the skin, concentrating only on the external contours. Then she caught her breath and started backwards.

'Yes,' said Gilliam. 'I recognised her as well.'

It was Lyset Wynter.

Chapter Thirty
Tears of a Ghost

Lyset waited to die. Sho was swinging his gun round in wilder and wilder arcs, as though he couldn't decide which target to fire at, futile though the action would undoubtedly be. Any second she expected him to roll up in a ball. Any second she expected the wraiths to swarm over them. But for some reason they hesitated.

The voices came again over the radio, and now they were just strong enough to be intelligible.

'Nimosian... High Command... installation... location...'

They were toying with the words Sho had been speaking just before they appeared, as though they'd been listening to him. But how could they hear radio frequencies?

'Mission orders...' the reedy voice continued. 'Secure objective for Nimos...'

Sho was standing stock still. 'Nimos?' he said. 'Who fights for Nimos?'

There was a pause, then, 'We... fight for Nimos.'

She saw Sho's eyes widen and chin lift defiantly. 'I am Squadleader Sho of the Nimosian Marine Corps. Identify yourselves! Name, rank, number!'

The wraiths moved forward and Lyset shrank against the tunnel wall. But they paid her no attention. She saw legs crystallise out of the flicker of half-seen forms, then bodies and heads. They had become humanoid shapes dressed in combat suits. Nimosian combat suits, she realised. And then shades of five soldiers stood before them, wavering and flickering slightly, but bearing no relation to the nightmare creations they had been moments earlier. And the first of them saluted Sho. She saw a pale face, blank and expressionless, in which glassy lips moved, and heard over her radio a faint, 'Robb, G. Private – 738594.'

And the next one.

'Sorven, L.B. Corporal – 960251.'

And the next…

Lyset felt dizzy, her mind trying to cope with the incredible concept. The ghosts were, or at least had been, people. Nimosians! How?

But Sho appeared to harbour no doubts or reservations. He was behaving as though he was inspecting the guard. Had his own madness somehow interacted with theirs? The group finished giving their details, and Sho said, 'Report on your mission.'

This seemed to puzzle them. They shifted their feet and their forms began to flicker more strongly, becoming blurred and defocused.

'Have you located the enemy headquarters?' Sho asked quickly. The simple question steadied them.

'Yes… yes.'

'Are they holding any of our men prisoner there?'

'Yes.'

'Are there others like you still free?'

'Some…'

'Then we shall find them, formulate a plan of attack and free the prisoners. Lead on.'

For the first time the ghosts looked at Lyset. One pointed a spectral hand. 'Is she friend… or enemy?'

'She's my prisoner. Part of the conspiracy. She will be properly interrogated in due course.'

'To touch a solid living thing… makes us stronger.'

'Then use her,' Sho said lightly. 'She's just an Emindian.'

Lyset tried to run, but many cold immaterial hands clutched at her, sinking through the fabric of her suit and into her flesh. The warmth and life flowed out of her. The tunnel turned dim and grey. Even the slight weight of her body seemed to slip away.

'Enough,' she heard Sho say faintly. 'You must ration yourselves. Form up!'

All but two of the soldiers released their hold. They assembled with Sho in the lead and marched off. Lyset was dragged after them, her trailing feet sinking a little into the hard rock floor with only the slightest resistance.

* * *

The two ghosts in the small cave with Dan Engers Junior had become a man and woman dressed in casual clothes.

And she heard Dan junior say, 'Mummy… Dad?'

What? Sam thought, straining her eyes. The figures were misty and translucent, their features almost impossible to make out from any distance. The female was holding out her arms in a gesture of desperate longing to the child, who was backing away fearfully. Sam took a deep breath and stepped into view, holding the normaliser ready.

Dan Junior turned to her and cried out in surprise and relief, 'Ms Jones!'

The female ghost saw her and her human form began to dissolve away as she stretched towards Sam, talons growing on her arms, her jaw distending, eyes blazing. The male tried to hold her back. The two figures rippled and wavered as though they would both break down. She could see that the man was shouting, but his words sounded as though they were distant echoes:

'Jeni – hold on! Hold on!'

Sam hit them both with a blast from the normaliser. They writhed and momentarily seemed to harden. Then they were two ghostly people once more, clinging to each other in pain and grief. The woman was crying while the man was calling out to Sam, his words arriving as whispers: 'It's all right. She won't hurt you. She can't help it.'

Sam held out her hand to Dan Junior and he caught hold of it gratefully. His eyes were red-rimmed and still wide with fear, but otherwise he seemed unharmed. Then she steeled herself to step right up to the ghosts and stare into their faces.

They were the images of Dan Engers's parents.

Stay calm, she told herself, wishing the Doctor were there. He would reel out some wonderful explanation off the top of his head which, even if nobody could understand it, would make them all feel a lot happier. But there was only herself and a frightened child and two… ghosts. She had to say something constructive.

'Do you know who I am?' she asked loudly.

The ghostly version of Dan Engers Senior peered at her, as though she was as indistinct to him as she was to her.

'I think.. I remember you. Back on the ship… before it happened. So hard to think straight… nothing changes. No before or after, just now.'

The absurd but inevitable question got past her lips before she could stop it. 'Are you dead?'

'We… don't know. Perhaps. If not… I wish we were.'

The despair in the feeble words cut her like a knife. The being that looked like Jeni Engers lifted her head. 'I had to see Danny once more,' she said. 'Just for a while…'

'Our Dan is… gone,' her husband explained, his words coming with an effort as though he was forcing them into a coherent form. 'He's back there in the cave with the others who retreated to the womb. Jeni went a little crazy after that and joined the mad ones for a while, but she remembered enough when the chance came. She knew where Dan would be on the other ship. I couldn't stop her, but I knew she'd bring him back here. She just wanted to hold him again. Just once more.'

The woman gently slid out of his arms and crouched down before Dan Junior, reaching out an insubstantial hand to his cheek. But he flinched back.

Sam said, 'Dan, let her. She doesn't want to hurt you.'

'But she's so cold.'

'You can bear it for a few seconds, can't you? Be brave. I think it would be a kind thing to do.'

'But… she can't be my mum. My mum and dad are back on the ship. They're safe, aren't they?'

'They were when I last saw them,' Sam said carefully, realising she had no idea even if the ship was still in one piece. 'Now come on. Let her touch you.'

The boy trembled but held still. The phantom fingers brushed his cheek. Sam saw tiny stars of light form below her eyes. It seemed that ghosts could cry.

No, forget the supernatural, she told herself. There were no such things as actual ghosts. An image of the things in the outer cave returned and her resolution wavered for a moment. How could dimensional phase shifts explain them, or the doubles of the Engerses standing before her? Later, later, she told herself. She had more immediate concerns.

'You know Dan can't stay here,' she said. 'I've got to take him back to the ship. His parents… his other parents will be worried about him. I'll tell the Doctor about you. He'll do all he can to help. Somehow. I promise.'

The ghostly version of Jeni Engers had dropped her hand from Dan's cheek and bowed her head. Her companion put his hand on her shoulder. Dan Junior looked at her with curious eyes, then knelt before her so that he could look up into her face.

'There may be nothing anyone can do,' the man said. 'It may never end… or it might start all over again. You see, we can't remember how it began!'

Sam didn't understand half of what he was saying and now was not the time to waste talking.

'I'm sorry, but we must get back to the alien ship. I know the Doctor will come looking for me and that's where he'll start. If he's there you can tell him all this yourself.'

The man nodded slowly. 'I'll go ahead first to see if it's safe. The mad ones were there the last time.' He looked sorrowfully down at his wife. 'Let her stay with him a little longer. She won't be any trouble.'

He left the cave, moving one leg stiffly. Sam remembered the real Daniel Engers being hit by the ghost – his own wife it now seemed! – when Dan was taken. Hadn't he fallen clutching at his leg? 'Nothing changes,' he had said. How long had they been here?'

Sam suddenly felt very tired and sat down on a packing case. How would she explain this to his real parents? Or *were* these his real parents?

For a while neither the ghost nor Dan Junior moved or spoke. Then Sam saw Dan tentatively reach out and touch her hair, which formed a misty halo round her head. He shivered slightly but did not pull back. His fingers brushed across it, momentarily adding substance until it caught and reflected the light like dewdrops in the sun.

'Is it really you, Mum?' he said.

Sam must have dozed, for suddenly Engers was standing before her. Dan Junior and the ethereal image of his mother were sitting close together amid the loose packing cases on the other side of the cave. There was no fear between them now, only sadness.

Sam blinked. 'What is it?'

'Shuttles came through the central core of the alien ship. One was Emindian, the other Nimosian, I think. They are headed for the port.'

'The port?' Sam realised there was so much she didn't know. 'Never mind. Can you take us there?'

The two shuttles rested side by side on a twilit terrace of the dead starport. Vega had ordered his marines into a defensive circle about the craft. They were all armed with copies of the Doctor's normaliser. He wondered how soon they would have to use them.

A large blue box, apparently belonging to the Doctor, had been lowered from the Emindian shuttle's belly hatch and easily set right side up in the low gravity. The Doctor had then disappeared inside it, promising answers to impossible questions. Curiously, Vega realised the box resembled the probe he'd ordered destroyed during the initial confrontation with Lanchard over the alien ship. (Had that been only two days ago?) They never had discovered where it had come from – too much else had been happening to allow time for such speculation. Anyway, it must just be a chance resemblance since the probe had been destroyed and could hardly now be a piece of the Doctor's luggage. Yet, there had been something odd about the light that had poured out of its doorway, and for a moment Vega had thought he had seen…

No, he must have been mistaken.

The other members of the Emindian party stood about looking numbly at the desolation of their home port. Even Rexton seemed overawed and lost for words. Vega almost felt sorry for him. The image of dead Emindar would haunt his own dreams long enough as it was.

The Doctor emerged from his box. Behind the faceplate of his helmet he looked grave as he turned to the Emindians.

'I'm sorry, but I had to confirm certain facts. There's no doubt about it. We are a little over twenty years in the future, relative to the time you think of as the present. Emindar is dead and abandoned – destroyed by pollution from radioactive, chemical and biological weapons that were used in the war with Nimos. From the decay readings, this war ended a year after we crossed the hyperspatial bridge that brought us here.'

'But that's ridiculous, impossible!' Rexton exclaimed, coming out of his torpor.

'It's true,' said Delray in an earnest but curiously flat voice. 'You know where we are as well as the rest of us. You saw what's left of Emindar. Do you think all this could have happened since we left and nobody back home told us? Believe him.'

Rexton could only shake his head, as though determined to deny the truth to the bitter end.

Bendix asked the Doctor, 'But how can you know these things?'

'I'll explain shortly,' the Doctor assured him. 'But I'm afraid there's more. I take it this base has a hyperwave communicator. Where is it?'

'The communication centre's over there.' Bendix pointed to a building on the next terrace up. 'Why?'

'Because if it's still functioning, it will be the quickest way to prove the rest of what I have to tell you.' He looked at Vega. 'You must come as well.'

Vega felt a sudden coldness touch his heart.

With a small escort of guards they tramped across the terrace and up a broad flight of steps. The nearest of the building's external airlocks was still intact, a long-life emergency bulb still burning forlornly above it. The marines entered first, then waved them inside. There was minimal pressure within and they kept their suits sealed. The interior appeared undamaged, but when Bendix led them through to the main operations room, they found a few desiccated corpses and some blackened scars on the walls. The equipment, however, seemed largely undamaged. Bendix examined the active displays. Solid-state switches still functioned and brought more screens into life.

'The reserve batteries have fifty-six per cent power. Enough to activate the relay. Backups are on line. The system checks functional.' He suddenly looked lost. 'But who are we calling?'

'That's up to Commander Vega,' the Doctor said, 'but I suggest he should attempt to contact his High Command on Nimos. If he can.'

'What are you saying, Doctor?' Vega demanded, knowing already.

'That Nimos is also dead, destroyed in the same war as Emindar. I'm not being cruel, but you must convince yourself that I am speaking the truth.'

Vega turned to the console, adjusted the settings and called the High Command. Its channel was never left unmanned. But there was no reply. He tried Government Central, Spatial Dispatch, the Commercial Shipping Co-ordinator's Office, the emergency channel...

They were all dead, filled only by static.

'If there was a war they may have changed frequencies...' he said desperately. But he knew he was clutching at straws. There was nobody there to respond to his signals. They were gone.

'Nimos suffered even more than Emindar,' the Doctor said sadly. 'It will never be habitable again. All that remains of your two peoples are handfuls of scattered survivors who will settle on far distant worlds and try to forget their past. This sector of space has been so badly traumatised by the war that it will remain a shunned backwater for millennia –'

'How do you know this!' Vega demanded, his composure strained almost to its limits. 'You can't be a Moderator. What are you?'

'I'm a time traveller,' the Doctor said with simple dignity. 'A Time Lord. And I would like to help you if I can.'

'Help us!' Bendix almost shouted, breaking into a sudden outburst of despair. 'We've lost our families, our homes... How can you help us?'

The Doctor took him by the shoulders and stared straight into his eyes. 'You and your companions still live,' he said with passionate unwavering conviction. 'You're virtually your worlds' sole legacy. That must not be lost to the universe. Who knows? You may yet have a part to play in the greater whole. Don't give up.'

'I'll never give up,' Rexton said, his voice brittle. 'My duty is to my planet. I will not let it become what we have seen out there. We will go back and stop it.'

'Unfortunately,' said the Doctor, 'that may not be possible.'

They stared at him in horror.

'What do you mean?' said Vega. 'You just said we shouldn't give up.'

'I mean this is how it has been and will always be and you have become inextricably linked with it. Your past and future are feeding off each other. What we've experienced on the other side of the hyperspatial tunnel and now what we've seen here suggests this is all part of a self-perpetuating loop in time, centred around a single alien ship.'

'But there are two ships –' Bendix began.

'Quiet!' Rexton barked, glaring defiantly at the suddenly suspicious eyes of the Nimosians.

'No,' said the Doctor almost wearily, 'there is only one ship. There has always only ever been one. Haven't you realised that yet? It's part of the loop and we've all been drawn into it. And there may not be a way out.'

Chapter Thirty-One
The Warning

The long silence following the Doctor's words was broken by one of the marines calling urgently over the helmet circuit:

'Movement outside! Two figures approaching... I can see right through them!'

'Wait!' the Doctor said. 'Do they look human?'

'Uh... yes.'

'Are they armed?' Vega asked.

'Not that can see, sir.'

There was a strange expression on the Doctor's face. 'Let them pass. I think we've been expected.'

The two figures entered the communications room a moment later, with marines edging backwards about them, keeping them under their guns. A man and a woman in uniform, as pale as wraiths but moving like humans and without any outward menace. There was something very familiar about their uniforms...

'Captain!' Bendix choked out.

The woman was the image of Captain Lanchard.

And the man, Vega realised, was the image of himself.

The others saw it too, glancing incredulously back and forth between them. Vega felt himself come as close as he ever would to blacking out, but with a supreme effort regained control. He would not show such weakness in front of foreigners.

The two figures halted in the centre of the group. They held up their wristcoms with very deliberate gestures before beginning to speak into them.

'Search for their channel,' the Doctor said, adjusting his suit frequency receptor.

On maximum amplification, their words came through faint but clear: '... can you hear us now?'

'Yes,' said the Doctor loudly. 'We can hear you.'

'I thought I remembered coming here,' said the thing that looked like Vega, 'but I could not be sure. It was so long ago…'

'We thought it best to allow you time to discover some of the truth for yourselves,' said the ghost of Lanchard. 'Now there is no need for concealment. *Cirrandaria*, power up.'

Out across the dark hollow of the port the graceful form of the starliner appeared hovering by a docking boom. It was glowing softly from within, lit by a thousand faint lights. At its heart pulsed the unearthly radiance of its power core, all encompassed by a structure seemingly as insubstantial as spun glass. It was startlingly beautiful yet so forlorn amid the ruins.

'I think I'm beginning to understand what's happened,' said the Doctor, 'but please explain anyway.'

'We shall,' Vega heard his doppelgänger say. It looked into his eyes. 'You will believe me, if nobody else. There is little time left, but you must learn the truth so you won't make the same mistakes. I think something will happen soon…'

'Don't you know?' he asked.

His image touched its head as though trying to concentrate. 'Nothing changes for us. We do not age. All memories are now and the past at the same moment. We think twenty years have passed. Is that correct?'

'That's right,' the Doctor confirmed. 'Go on.'

'Something will happen back there, on the other side of the space-time corridor, that will make us like this. But none of us can remember what. I and many other Nimosians found ourselves on the *Cirrandaria*. There was no sign of the *Indomitable*. The ship was drifting in space as you see it now. There was no response on the hyperwave. Only the radio functioned, and that barely at all. So we came here. I think the trip took a long time. Hard to tell when you don't feel hunger… you don't sleep. And the engines don't interact with the continuum as they should…' He trailed off vaguely. Vega felt sickened to see himself so incapable.

'And when you got here?' the Doctor prompted.

'It was like this,' the Lanchard image continued. 'We found the alien ship in the navy port. We remembered it from before. They must have brought it here as the war was coming to an end, but we think they were overrun before they could use it.'

'How did the war start?' Rexton asked intently.

'We don't know. There are records here saying the loss of the *Cirrandaria* helped start it, but the details are confused. Not that it mattered. That was the end for many of us. They went mad. We had to confine them below decks. When you are like this and forget who you are, when you stop concentrating... your mind shapes your body. You change. Sometimes you become something out of your nightmares.'

'But not all of you,' Bendix said.

'No,' the Lanchard ghost admitted. 'Those who can best keep control guard them. It's dangerous; their madness is infective. Guns don't work well against them so we made armoured suits, and use nets and tridents made out of materials from the *Cirrandaria*. Those are the only things that still feel solid to us – apart from the alien ship. It seems to exist in many different states of being. We can just manage to work with its systems. We found that the controls on its bridge were labelled. They showed it was meant to work through time and space. So we tried to learn how to use it. We had nothing better to do...' She laughed bitterly. 'And time was not a problem. We had to stop it happening again.'

'But even if you could change the past, you might simply cease to exist,' the Doctor said.

'That would be a release,' Vega's ghost said. 'Don't you see? We can't die!'

Bendix's expression was tortured. In the silence that followed he said, 'Captain, I have to know: am I here?'

The shade of Lanchard looked at him curiously for a moment, then said, 'I remember... it's Bendix, isn't it? No, you're not here.' She glanced at Rexton. 'Nor are you. Perhaps that means you survive.'

Rexton's lips tightened, but he said nothing.

The Doctor, his face very grave, said, 'I will do all I can to help you. But by using the alien ship, you may have made things worse for yourself.'

'It wasn't how we planned,' Lanchard's ghost explained wretchedly. 'Just after we activated it some of the insane broke free and scattered all over the base. We had to recall the crew from the alien ship to help recapture them. We tried to keep them away from you, but some got past us. Otherwise we would have been there to meet you when you boarded the first time, to explain and to warn you. But instead some of the more controlled ones must have got on to your shuttles when you first arrived. Others hid, waiting to try to cross over if you came close enough. It's contact with living things, you see. It's the only time you can feel properly, to remember what it was like...'

She trailed off, as though exhausted by the effort of speaking, or by the memory of what she had lost. Her image seemed to grow paler and shivered slightly.

Vega's ghost continued, 'We finally recaptured most of the remaining insane ones when they returned from their raid on you. We took advantage of their trap to send a shuttle to bring one of you back here, so we could show you the future. It would have returned the person safely later, but it crashed.'

'It was Sam Jones, my assistant,' the Doctor said quickly. 'Is she all right?'

'We don't know. I am sorry.'

'Where are the other people they took?' Vega asked.

'The survivors are being kept safe a little way from here. Most are badly shocked and do not understand what has happened to them. You must take them away. They are a... temptation while they remain here. I think there are ships back there preparing to fight. You must stop them. Tell them what you have seen. Both for Nimos and Emindar.'

Vega nodded. 'I'll tell them. If they will believe me.' He looked at Rexton. 'Will you help prevent this tragedy, Councillor?'

'I won't let this happen to Emindar,' Rexton stated bluntly. He glanced at the Doctor. 'Even if he says there's no chance of changing anything.'

'I didn't say there was no chance,' the Doctor corrected him. 'There may be a slim possibility of making some slight modification to the timeline, and you wouldn't be human if you didn't try to take it. But if there is to be a change, it must be made at a crucial junction in the course of events. The place where a single word or action has the greatest effect.'

'Well, I don't believe the future is immutable,' Rexton said defiantly. 'Whatever you say, while there is free will, there are always alternatives!'

'Free will may be where it all began in the first place,' the Doctor replied heavily. He turned to the ghosts. 'Please take us to the survivors. Let's do what we can for them.'

The survivors had been housed in one of the port lounges that still held its pressure. They huddled together in a state of utter bewilderment, shrinking back from the heavily armoured ghost people who stood guard over them. There were a handful of Nimosian marines, a few crew from the *Cirrandaria* and thirty or so civilian passengers. There was a rising murmur of surprise and hope when the rescue party appeared.

Vega looked for Lio Reng amid the haggard faces. Some were curled up on makeshift pallets made from chair seats. He examined them all, but Lio was not among them. He turned despondently to see the same expression of dashed hope on the Doctor's face.

'My assistant is still missing,' he said. 'And a couple of others I was specially hoping to find. One was a small boy.'

Vega was moved to say, 'They may still be alive. I am also missing some men. We shall not give up.'

The Doctor smiled faintly. 'No, we won't. But we must get these people out of here first. Can we fit them all into the shuttles?'

'Just about. If we can get back through without crashing.'

'Now we've been through once the autopilots can be set to fly a reverse course.'

'And if the hyperspatial tunnel has closed?'

'There is another way back. You might say I brought along some insurance just in case. But I'd rather not strain this part of the continuum any more unless I must –'

A voice came over the helmet radios. 'Doctor, where are you?'

The Doctor's face lit up with joy. 'Sam? Sam, are you all right? Where are you?'

'Very close, I think… yes, I can see you now. Just a minute…'

And very shortly a young woman had entered the room, trailing a small boy and two more ghosts in her wake, and was hugging the Doctor as well as pressure suits would allow. Their pleasure at being reunited was palpable and even Vega had to smile.

'Didn't I tell you to take care of yourself?' the Doctor chided her gently.

'Sorry,' she said. 'But it got a bit complicated. I did find Dan Junior…' She lowered her voice and spoke urgently. 'The ones with him are the ghosts of his parents, I think. Do you know what's going on here?'

'More or less.'

'Can we do anything to help?'

'I'm not sure.'

'Have you seen anything of Lyset?' Delray asked Sam.

'No. I'm sorry. But we did see some ghosts gathering as we came here. The Engerses think they're Nimosian soldiers that have never got on with the rest of them here. They seem to be up to something. They may be headed this way. I heard someone speaking to them over the radio: a Squadleader Sho? From the way he was talking he sounded a bit loopy.'

'Sho!' Vega exclaimed. He switched to the military band. 'Sho, this is Commander Vega. Do you hear me? Sho, respond. This is an order.'

'This is Sho,' came the cool response. 'I have located the enemy base where they are holding our men, Commander. I have assembled a force to effect entry and release them. We are attacking in one minute.'

Vega realised his double was by his side. He could just hear him say, 'He must mean the ship. There are over five hundred insane on board. If too many get out at one time we shall never control them.'

'Listen, Sho,' said Vega. 'Recall your men and await further orders. Do not attack the ship.'

There was a puzzled silence, then, 'We don't leave marines in enemy hands. We take care of our own. Every loyal Nimosian knows that!

You're not Commander Vega!'

And the circuit went dead.

'If there's going to be trouble we must start getting these people to the shuttles,' the Doctor said. 'Come along all of you...' He frowned and scanned the room. 'Where's Rexton... and Bendix?'

Sealing their suits, they piled out through the airlock. Down on the lower terrace the *Doria* was taking off, scattering the ring of guards.

'Rexton!' the Doctor shouted into his microphone. 'We need the shuttle to take people back to the ship.'

Rexton's voice came through clearly.

'They won't need taking back when I've finished. If this is the future then I'm going to change it. Nimos may die, but Emindar is going to live!'

Chapter Thirty-Two
Breaking Point

Lanchard agreed with Gilliam that Wynter's 'corpse' should be taken back to the sickbay, though there was nothing Gilliam could do except put it in storage. On closer examination there was a deep wound in her chest, perhaps from an energy weapon, that must have proved almost instantly fatal. But the body showed no signs of decay. However, Gilliam admitted she wasn't even sure how to obtain an accurate temperature reading. It looked as though it had been preserved in some way shortly after death, but just how she could not begin to speculate.

'This is beyond me, Captain. What do you do with a dead ghost?'

The 'body' weighed almost nothing. Gilliam and an orderly with a strong stomach lifted it on to a powered stretcher. Their hands sank with unnatural intimacy into the flesh, which was resilient but drained the heat from them. When the covers were folded over it they seemed hardly distorted by the form underneath, almost as though there was nothing there.

But there was something, Lanchard thought. It could not be ignored even though she wasn't sure what it implied. For the moment she would follow the book, which required that a formal identification be made. With Delray absent that meant asking Evan Arcovian. The prospect of subjecting that poor little man to more grief was not a pleasant one, but it had to be done.

Rhonda Plecht did not notice Arcovian coming out of Dr Gilliam's office a short while later, as she entered the extended medical centre. The look of utter despair on his face did not register with her at all. She had more important things on her mind.

Rhonda had come directly from her cabin, where she had been arguing with Lester. Arguing! Lester never argued. But there he was actually defying her, and looking as though he was enjoying it.

She stopped one of the regular nurses impatiently as she hurried by.

'You had a passenger helping out in here a little while ago. Young blonde woman, Scholl… something. Is she still here?'

'Ms Schollander? She's down the end there, I think…'

But Rhonda was already on her way.

The Schollander woman was tidying an empty treatment cubicle. Rhonda stepped inside, pulled shut the temporary curtains behind her and said without preamble, 'My husband Lester Plecht was in here earlier. I saw you with him. But who was the other woman?'

Ingrid Schollander wearily brushed back a lock of hair that had escaped her cap. 'I beg your pardon?'

'She was wearing a blue smock dress…' Rhonda realised it resembled the garb bedpatients wore, and added, 'She must have been having treatment here. She had bandages on her face. Who was she?'

'I don't remember anybody else apart from the nurse.'

'I saw you both with him the other day. You must know her.'

'Yes, I was with your husband the other day, but there was no other woman.'

'Don't lie to me, you stupid girl! What are you trying to hide? Is there some sort of conspiracy between the three of you?'

The younger woman's mouth set in a firm line. 'Look, I'm very busy. In case you hadn't noticed there are a lot of people here who need help. Why don't you stop browbeating that poor husband of yours and lend a hand? You might learn a bit of humility along the way. And don't call me a stupid girl!'

'How dare you speak to me like that!'

But Ingrid Schollander did not shrink or turn away. Instead she stepped closer and said, 'I can speak to you however I like. I think you are a very selfish woman, and I don't know why Lester has put up with you for so long.'

Rhonda was not used to being defied. Suddenly she felt terribly afraid that this juvenile, so full of the warmth Rhonda knew she lacked, and her unknown co-conspirator would somehow steal Lester from her. In a sudden panic she thrust out a hand to push her away.

She honestly had not realised she'd picked up an instrument from the tray beside the bed. It was as though her hand did not belong to her. The thing fitted neatly into her palm and hummed slightly as she clenched it tight. It slid so easily into the middle of Ingrid Schollander's chest.

For a moment the young woman looked at her with wide surprised eyes, reaching up as though in disbelief to the handle of the instrument protruding from her chest. Then with a single and oddly slight gasp of pain she fell backwards on to the bed.

Rhonda stared down at her for perhaps ten seconds, seeing the dark stain spreading across the front of Ingrid's overall. Then she edged out of the cubicle through the curtains. A few people glanced at her curiously. They must have heard something of their argument but had been too busy with their own duties to investigate. They didn't know what had happened. They wouldn't know until somebody opened the curtains again. In the general state of things that could be several minutes.

Numb with shock, face expressionless, Rhonda walked briskly past them and out into the corridor.

She had to think. This was not something she had planned. How would it affect them socially? Lester's career would be damaged. Did they know somebody who could help them, to explain that it had all been an accident?

There was something sticky on her hand. She held it up and saw it was blood. There was a smear on the side of her dress as well. The realisation helped decide her priorities.

First she must wash and change.

Fayle entered Chen's cabin with the most peremptory of knocks. Borix, who'd been sympathising with Chen, excused himself and made a discreet exit, leaving Chen standing uneasily before the *Indomitable*'s second in command. Fayle came straight to the point.

'In a few hours we shall have enough shuttles protected from the interference effect to make a mass landing on the alien ship. The Emindians will probably try to stop us. One way or the other I need every single member of the crew to be at full strength. Your record has been excellent up to now, Chen, so I'm giving you one last chance to explain the problem and pull yourself together. Otherwise I'll have you declared unfit for duty and sent home for reassessment. Do you understand?'

'Yes, sir.'

'Can you guarantee to give one hundred per cent to this ship?'

Chen looked wretched. 'I want to, sir... but he won't let me.'

'What?'

Chen's eyes seemed to be focused at some point over Fayle's shoulder. 'He keeps telling me to get out of here or else we're all going to die. I know it can't be who it seems, but I can't make him go away. I only heard him at first, but now I'm beginning to see him, too.'

'What are you babbling about, man?'

'My brother!' Chen shouted back. 'I know he's on the *Starfire*, but he's also here right now. I swear it! And he's only got one arm!'

Fayle gaped at him in disbelief, then growing anger. 'You're finished, Chen. You've let that ship get to you. Can't you manage without imagining your brother's here to hold your hand? There's no place in the service for weaklings...'

And to emphasise his last point he stabbed a scornful finger into Chen's chest.

A cold hand grasped his wrist, twisted his arm behind him and slammed him against the wall. Fayle spun about in a blazing rage to face his unseen assailant, only to have the furious words boiling up inside him die in his throat.

A man-shaped shadow seemed to stand in the cabin between him and Chen. Fayle couldn't help but notice that the shadow's left arm was missing.

Lanchard was in the shuttle bay to welcome the craft that had just arrived from the *Korgon*. The party included not only the engineers that Prothero had promised, but relief medical staff, too. At last the military were showing they were good for something besides posturing, she thought. Then a call came through from Gilliam.

'Captain, one of our civilian helpers has been murdered. We think we know who did it…'

Lester Plecht hardly had time to register his wife's return to their compartment before she had swept through to the bathroom. He followed diffidently after her, determined to make up for the earlier row. If only she would listen to him for once.

To his surprise he found she had torn off her dress and had flung it on the floor. It had a dark stain on its side. Rhonda was bent over the sink scrubbing furiously at her hands. The water was running pink.

'Rhonda… what's the matter? Have you hurt yourself?'

She turned a ghastly drawn face to him, even as she continued washing. Flat words tumbled out. 'It was an accident… I didn't mean it. She shouldn't have spoken back to me like that. It was very impolite.'

'Who, dear? What accident?'

'But she probably had it coming; scheming to take you away like that. Must find that other woman. She'll confirm it.'

'Rhonda… have you hurt somebody? Who? Tell me!'

Her eyes suddenly wouldn't meet his. 'That… Ingrid person you were so friendly with. It was an accident. I didn't know what I was doing…'

Lester felt the life drain out of him. 'Is it bad?' he asked faintly.

'I don't know… I think she may be dead.'

'"May be"…? "Don't know"? You mean you left her? You didn't get help!'

'It was too late!'

'You mean…'

'Yes, all right, she was dead! So you see I couldn't get involved. Think what people would say –'

Lester hit her with the force of all the little resentments that had grown within him through the years.

Rhonda fell to the floor, her hand going to her bleeding lip, too amazed by his action to make a sound. He looked at her, then at his fist. For the first time ever he'd shut her up. For the first time he had her complete attention. For the first time he mattered.

As though in a dream he stepped forward and grasped her by the hair.

When Castillo and a couple of security men arrived two minutes later, Rhonda Plecht was lying unconscious in the bathroom, her face in a growing pool of blood. Her nose, several teeth and her jaw had been broken as though by a frenzied assault. There was no sign of her husband.

Lester Plecht ran desperately through the *Cirrandaria*'s maze of passenger-deck corridors. The ship's routine had been so disrupted they were not that busy. Those few people he passed only stared at him curiously.

He was appalled at what he had done. If only it had been simply revenge for Ingrid it might have been crudely justified. But that had been only the spark. It had really been his own revenge. Now he had made himself as bad as Rhonda and destroyed the memory of Ingrid's brief, uncomplicated friendship. He had to get away. But how could he? Where could he go?

As he stumbled on it seemed that harsh throaty laughter followed him.

Admiral Mokai studied the tactical display on the screen in the *Starfire*'s battle room impatiently. They dared not get too close to the alien ship, the focus of all their attention, until they had negated its interference field. Therefore neither side could form a proper close protective globe around it because it limited their room for manoeuvre. So both capital ships were holding station more or less on opposite sides of it, shielded by a constantly shifting screen of supporting craft. Each watching the other in case they left some sort of tactical opening.

How could the Commander of the *Indomitable* have undertaken a joint mission to the alien ship with the Emindians? Mokai wondered. Unless he had some idea of gaining an advantage by it. His second, Fayle, had not been very helpful, and had hinted that his commander was going soft. But Fayle sounded bitter and resentful, so how reliable was his opinion? Mokai cursed softly under his breath. How was he supposed to fight if he couldn't rely on the quality of the men under him?

The civilian liner also posed a problem. A shuttle had been sent across to it from the *Korgon*. Who or what had been in it? If hostilities broke out the *Cirrandaria* would have to be taken care of as cleanly as possible…

His thoughts were interrupted by a message.

'Urgent call from the *Indomitable*, sir. Officer commanding says he has received some sort of warning. He says there's going to be a disaster.'

'What? Where's this supposed to come from?'

'A source on our ship, apparently.'

'On our ship? The man must be mad.'

'He did sound, er… a little excited, sir,' the operator admitted.

Lester found himself on the deserted lifeboat deck. There was still debris from the attack in corners. A few small, lost, personal scraps, dark stains that the robot cleaners had not yet been able to lift from the expensive wooden deck boards. Opposite him was the row of lifeboat hatches.

He rushed to the nearest and hauled on the hatch handle. It opened easily and he scrambled inside, slamming it shut behind him. He did not know there were safety locks to prevent what he was attempting unless the abandon ship alarm had been sounded. But these had not reset after their previous activation.

He'd seen enough of the internal layout earlier to know where the controls were, and strapped himself in before them. Normally every lifeboat should have been manned by at least one qualified crewman. But they had been constructed with emergencies in mind and the possibility that, in extreme circumstances, they might be operated by untrained personnel. The essential controls were large, easy to operate and very clearly marked.

He released a protective cover, threw a switch, twisted a large red handle and punched a green button.

'Launching sequence activated,' came an impersonal synthesised voice. 'Brace for ejection. Five, four, three…'

The alert sounded on the bridge, but by then it was too late. The lifeboat erupted into space in a cloud of gas and fragments of sealing strip. Immediately it turned by itself and headed for the nearest Emindian ship.

Inside the lifeboat the computer voice said, 'Autohoming activated.'

Lester stared at it aghast. He didn't want it to take him to an Emindian ship. He would just be brought back to the *Cirrandaria* again, to face reality. His eyes fell upon a button marked OVERRIDE. He pressed it.

'Target overridden. Selecting new objective.'

The lifeboat swung round towards the next Emindian ship.

'No, no! You stupid machine,' Lester shouted, hitting the override again.

Then he thought he heard the same laughter in his ear that had followed him along the corridors. But he could see the whole interior of the compartment from where he sat and it was quite empty.

But it didn't *feel* empty. Instead it began to feel very cold.

The Emindian task force, alerted by the *Cirrandaria*, tried to capture the wayward lifeboat with a tow beam. But the small craft proved an unexpectedly elusive target, almost as though there was something about it that was preventing their beams from making a full lock.

Mokai broke off his somewhat confused conversation with Fayle when the strange antics of the lifeboat were brought to his attention.

'Sound amber alert,' he ordered. 'They may be trying something.'

As all the Emindian ships had been eliminated from the autopilot's options, it dutifully hunted for a new safe haven for its passenger, and promptly turned towards the Nimosian fleet.

Had he been thinking clearly Lester would never have allowed the boat to continue on its new course. But by now he was hardly thinking at all. His mind filled with vague notions about claiming political asylum. All he wanted was to be free of the intolerable burden of what he had done – and what he had lost.

'You can't get away from me that easily,' said a rasping voice in his ear.

'Scanners, what's inside it?' Mokai demanded.

'Can't be certain, Admiral. Looks like a standard Emindian lifeboat, but it reads oddly. Like nothing I've seen before.'

'Put a beam on it and hold it clear of us.'

'Can't get a proper lock, sir!'

'Impact in twenty seconds, sir!'

Mokai scowled. There was only one option left.

Lester was on his knees scrabbling at the main hatch of the lifeboat, not caring that, even if he could have opened it, he would have been blown out into space. He felt a stab of cold in his arm and turned fearful eyes upward. A shadow was forming out of thin air: a shimmering grey image of a woman in a plain smock with a curiously indistinct face.

A translucent hand reached up and peeled off the bandages and he saw the ruin of her face.

Lester had the time for one final scream of terror that mingled with Rhonda Plecht's ghostly, slurred laughter, before the Nimosian fighters blasted the lifeboat into incandescent vapour.

Chapter Thirty-Three
The Circles of Hell

The *Doria* sped back through the long tunnel to the cavern that held the alien ship. Bendix was hunched over the controls, his face creased with anxiety.

'What can we do to change anything if there was only ever one alien ship?' he asked, keeping his eyes fixed straight ahead. 'We've seen what happened to it. You heard the Doctor.'

'The Doctor is a self-confessed liar who masqueraded as a Moderator,' Rexton retorted. 'Would you believe every word he says? Besides, the original ship we salvaged was badly damaged. This one is perfect, without any sign of repair work. They may be linked, somehow, but there are two of them.'

'But he knows about time.'

'Does that mean he invariably tells the truth? And even if he is some sort of time traveller, would you give up without a fight if there was the slightest chance of saving Emindar?'

Bendix wavered visibly. 'No, sir. Not when you put it like that.'

'Good man. Just get me to the ship and I'll do the rest. If they really have cleared it of those monsters we should have no trouble. If there is going to be a war, Emindar is going to have the weapon it needs to win!'

Rexton knew that his time had come. It was as though all his life had just been a prelude to this moment, when his actions might shape the future of entire worlds. He was going to make a difference at last.

Within his narrow world, Sho was as contented as he could ever be.

He was going into battle at the head of a combat team. All they'd needed was a good talking to to get them back into shape and focused on the mission again. They were really responding to his leadership, almost as though they were obeying his thoughts. He didn't care whether they were dead or something else; at heart they were still Nimosian soldiers.

He realised they still had the Emindian woman with them and briefly debated leaving her. But she was no burden in the light gravity and there was still a bit of life left in her. He would need to find a few more like her to keep the men strong. He might even find a use for her himself.

His small force were gathered on the high terrace supporting the docking boom to which the ghostly form of the *Cirrandaria* was moored. One of the hatches it connected to was open, with only a couple of guards standing by it. They were obviously not expecting trouble.

Even now the men he'd detailed were working their way along the underside of the boom out of sight of the guards. Once they had neutralised them the rest could cross by the upper walkway directly into the ship. If they were quick they could release the prisoners before the enemy knew what had hit them. Then he would have an army behind him!

His daydream was shattered by the faint voice on his helmet radio.

'*Cirrandaria*, close all external hatches. A hostile force may be about to attack the ship.'

They had been betrayed! But who by? The false Vega? The girl?

But his men had reached their objective. He saw them vault the rails and fall upon the guards before they could seal the hatch.

'Forward!' he cried, and ran in long bounding strides along the walkway with the rest of his men, dragging Lyset after him like a rag doll. He would deal with her once he had taken the ship.

Inside the hatch ghostly forms were fighting. Nets were being thrown and tridents thrust. But his men were pressing inexorably forward. With a fierce yell he loosed a spray of automatic fire into the mêlée, which passed through friend and foe alike without noticeable effect, and leapt in after them.

He had taken half a dozen steps into the misty insubstantial interior of the ship before he realised his error. The deck gave like a sponge under his boots, separating coldly around them as he sank up to his ankles. He floundered forward another step, plunging down to his knees, looking for something solid to catch hold of but finding nothing. Even in the low gravity the deck was too insubstantial to support him! Lyset Wynter was struggling feebly but sinking as well. Then his legs were kicking in emptiness as the deck slipped up over his chest, imparting the slightest feeling of constriction, then closed over his head.

He dropped slowly into a corridor on the next deck, scattering a crowd of insubstantial figures who had been running in apparent panic along it. He sank up to his waist in the floor and slid from sight in seconds, despite making desperate paddling strokes to try to resist his fall.

They dropped again and again at a leisurely but inexorable rate, leaving the scene of combat far above them. He was being taken from his men when they most needed him! Suddenly they were sliding through the undercurve of the hull and there was nothing below but fifty metres of vacuum before the very real and solid surface of the next terrace. They dropped freely away from the soap-bubble ship, tumbling slowly as they fell, and hit the ground.

In the low gravity it was the equivalent of a fall of a little over two metres on Nimos. Sho hit with his knees together and legs bent to absorb the impact, rolled expertly and came up unharmed. Lyset landed awkwardly, bounced, and dropped back limp and winded.

'Squadleader Sho!'

The voice came over his earphones. It seemed familiar. A small party was heading along the curve of the terrace towards him. Some were ghosts, others solid real people. Some were wearing Nimosian uniforms.

'Sho!' came the voice again. 'Remain where you are. That's an order.'

It was the traitor Vega. He must have warned the liner of the assault. Now he and his fellow turncoats were coming after him. Sho looked desperately up at the glowing intangible liner above him, but there was no way he could return to it. All he could do was buy his loyal men time to release their comrades. He gathered up Lyset's limp form in one arm and held his rifle to the side of her helmet.

'Stay back or she dies!'

They skidded to a halt and he heard a confused babble of voices. He backed away until he had the wall of the next terrace behind him. How far away was the nearest ramp leading up? A hundred metres. He began edging sideways.

A figure detached itself from the group and stepped towards him.

'Stay back!' he warned.

'I can't do that,' the man said flatly, almost without emotion. 'You see, I know you're going to shoot her anyway as soon as you get clear of us. That is what you mean to do, isn't it?'

It was, but how did he know? Sho was certain he hadn't told anybody. He was getting confused. The man continued advancing.

'So there's nothing to lose by trying to save her. I owe it to her. I let her down once before, but I won't do it again. In a moment you'll have to point your gun at me, and then you die. Or you'll kill Lyset and then you'll die anyway. I'll kill you, I promise that. If you drop her and run maybe you'll live. That's the only way out.'

He was less than five metres away now.

Sho jerked his gun away from the woman's helmet and fired at the man, who clutched his side and fell to the ground, even as an indistinct form launched itself from the shadows. Cold fangs buried themselves in Sho's gun arm. He heard a ferocious snarling growl seemingly right inside his suit. He shrieked in pain, dropped the woman and with his free arm clubbed at the thing that was attacking him. But then the man was up again, tackling him low and knocking him to the ground, pinning him by the chest. The unseen thing continued to tear at his arm and he felt the pressure dropping in his suit. But all he could see was a fist holding a pistol filling his field of view, the muzzle rammed against his faceplate.

'I told you,' said the man.

Then the gun slowly sagged, limply, and the weight on his chest vanished as the man toppled sideways. Sho heard shouts of 'Pick him up... I've got her... back to the shuttle... they're coming!'

The teeth released their grip on him. He reached over weakly and tried to close the ragged tears in the arm of his suit, but he hadn't the strength. Above him he saw the *Cirrandaria*. A grey mist seemed to be pouring out of her. It was his men! They had released the prisoners! He had won!

Even now some were dropping down from the upper terrace, falling like thistledown in the gentle gravity. Wait. His eyesight was fading but there was something wrong. They were falling as men, but by the time they touched the ground they had become...

No –

And so the insane host fell upon Harren Sho, and fed until they had drawn the last scrap of heat and life from him.

The *Doria* emerged into the cavern containing the alien vessel and Rexton realised why he had not recognised it earlier. Apart from the gloom, walls had been blasted out to accommodate the huge craft. The war must have forced them to abandon the deep system security research complex and bring it here.

But that would mean this *was* the same ship as before.

He was getting confused. Damn the Doctor's tales! Focus on your objective, he told himself.

They berthed the *Doria* in a twin of the bay they had used on the forward side of the alien ship's central tower. This time they would be on the far side of the interface. Now all they had to do was reach the control room.

Rexton led the way through the triple-doored airlocks with his gun ready, while Bendix held one of the Doctor's normalisers. But the ship was totally still and silent, with no ceiling lights giving their telltale warning flicker. All the ghosts of whatever kind, and the Nimosians, too, must be back in the port with their hands full. Rexton could hardly have arranged it better. By the time they followed him here he would have accomplished his objective.

He led Bendix along a transverse corridor, hoping that what he remembered would be there. It was. A round hatch in the ceiling at the top of a recessed set of rungs. He continued along the corridor, counting hatches until he reached the fourth. Then he started up, through the hatch, and into a long segmented shaft that stretched above him for two hundred clear metres. They were inside one of the vertical rod structures that ran up through the projecting laboratory modules on the outside of the tower. Service access shafts, they had classified them as.

They climbed up and up, past four side hatches leading off the shaft. The fifth Rexton opened and stepped into another small triple-doored airlock, gasketed to allow for movement of the tower module. Beyond it was a large chamber ringed with curving banks of instrument panels. The chamber was divided halfway across the room by a shimmering blurred curtain.

'It's the other side of the control room,' Bendix said, 'beyond the interface.'

Rexton was already unslinging Lyset's camera. 'I never leave a job unfinished,' he said. 'With details of the rest of the main control functions they will be able to complete the repairs on the other ship. Then we shall have a device which will revolutionise the tactics of space warfare! Imagine being able to project a fleet right into the heart of an enemy system, even into orbit round its home planet! Now keep watch.'

He began working his way around the chamber, recording the array of neatly labelled controls. Bendix watched him for a minute in silence, between anxious glances at the interface and the service hatch. Then he said hesitantly, 'Councillor, if this is the original ship you found years ago, and the ghosts found these labels already here, where did they come from?'

'The team working on the ship, of course,' Rexton said.

'But where did they get the information from? You said they hadn't worked out the control functions. I can see there could be millions of possible combinations here. Did they work it all out in that last year of the war – or label them up from the pictures we're just going to send them? Isn't that a paradox, a loop in time?'

Rexton hesitated, then said firmly, 'Paradox is just a word. It's an admission of ignorance. I only care if it works!'

He finished snapping the last of the panels, wound the film on and ejected the cartridge. He held it up before Bendix. 'This is the most valuable item you will ever see. It's more important than your life or mine.' He slipped it into an outer pocket of his suit and closed the seal firmly. 'If anything happens to me, you are to see that it gets back home by any means at whatever cost. Understand?'

Bendix nodded grimly. They started down the service shaft again.

They were almost at the bottom when the ceiling lights began to flicker.

It was a sight Sam would never forget. She had not realised how closely the concentric descending terraces of the port resembled the description of Hell from Dante's *Inferno*. But now they had really become a twilit hell, populated by souls as lost as any the ancient Italian had ever imagined.

The rule of the insane had begun.

They poured in a living stream out of the *Cirrandaria*, metamorphosing and changing even as they went, taking the form of every monstrosity that could be dredged from the darkest depths of the mind. Armoured guards went down before them, losing their own human forms as they fell. Dark and terrible things passed overhead, leaping and springing like monstrous grasshoppers.

They ran before this unstoppable tide towards the remaining shuttle. Sam had Lyset Wynter slung over her shoulder – no burden in this light gravity, her weight even improved the traction underfoot. The Doctor was carrying Delray. Around them Vega's men fired at their pursuers with blasters and their copies of the Doctor's normalisers. Things flickered out of existence or fell to the ground, cut and burned, thrashing about as they regenerated and re-formed. The advance faltered and broke around them, but it did not halt. Sam saw hopping creatures pouring at incredible speed back through the tunnels leading to the other cavern and the alien ship. They want to use it to attack the real *Cirrandaria* again, she thought. And there are ten times as many of them now.

Ahead she saw that the evacuees from the spaceport lounge had been caught in the open ground halfway to the Nimosian shuttle. Flashes of fire from the guards around it told them it was already under assault.

'Even if we have time to get them all on and they let us take off, there isn't going to be enough room!' Vega said.

'Then we'll use the TARDIS,' the Doctor said.

'What?'

'My blue box. Trust me!'

They arrived at the TARDIS, skidding to a halt in sprays of dust. The Doctor opened the door. Vega held back doubtfully. Sam pushed past him with her burden, through the TARDIS's equivalent of a pressure curtain and into the improbable neo-Gothic spaciousness of the interior.

'See – there's room for everybody,' she said.

Vega recovered himself and spoke over his radio: 'Abandon the *Dauntless*. Fall back to the Doctor's machine.'

Sam laid Lyset down in the nearest armchair and unfastened her helmet. She looked exhausted and very pale, but otherwise unharmed. The Doctor came in with Delray. There was a blackened scar on the side of his suit. He wasn't moving.

'Help get the rest inside, Sam,' the Doctor told her.

She ran out of the doors again and started shoving the shambling, confused survivors through them. One of the first was Dan Engers Junior, propelled through by the shades of his parents. But they shrank back from the interior of the TARDIS as though it was painful. Suddenly she knew they would not be coming with them. All Sam could do was mouth through the visor of her helmet, 'He'll be safe – I promise.' Their faces were those of the twice dead as they turned away.

She was practically throwing the survivors though the door. The remaining Nimosian marines formed a tight circle about the TARDIS, guns and normalisers stabbing out into the wall of slavering, clawing, slashing things that bore down upon them. Even as she watched something with folded legs and snapping mandibles dropped out of the darkness and snatched a marine away. A tentacle curled around the side of the TARDIS and she felt its cold caress. She kicked furiously and crushed it against the box's side.

There were only four human ghosts left now: Vega, Lanchard and the Engerses, holding back the insane horde with tridents dropped by the guards. The final few survivors tumbled inside followed by the marines and Vega. Sam saw Jeni Engers's ghostly form melt into a black spidery shape and spring away. Her husband snatched after her and was gone. Lanchard was pulled down by the horde and vanished from sight. The ghost of Vega turned to them, his body flickering and breaking up. His features dissolved until only his mouth and one pleading eye was left. She saw his lips shape the words 'End this!'

Then the TARDIS's door closed with a heavy boom, shutting out the nightmare.

Sam sagged against the wall, fumbled with the catch of her helmet and pulled it off. The air of the TARDIS was warm and candle-scented, and held the friendly mustiness of a library. It smelled wonderful.

Then she turned her head and saw they were not quite done with loss and pain. Lyset Wynter was kneeling by Delray's chair. The Doctor stood over them looking grave.

Sam pushed through the numbed, bewildered crowd of survivors that still huddled close to the doors. Young Dan was standing there, almost unnoticed. God, she thought, he's watching his hero die. She tried to lead him aside but the boy pulled away and the Doctor gave a tiny shake of his head. All she could do was hold him tightly.

The boy said in a tiny voice, 'Was he brave?'

'Yes, he was very brave,' Sam said.

Distantly, inexplicably, she thought she could hear an animal whining.

Then a grey mist lifted from Delray's body, took shape and stepped aside. It was the image of Delray formed in shadows and half-lights. Lyset looked from it to Delray's still form and back again almost without expression, as though her normal responses of fear and shock had been drained dry by what she had so recently endured.

'We had to get it right this time...' the ghost said, his words like the wind whispering across the grass. The Doctor gave the hint of a sad, knowing smile.

The slight movement of Delray's chest ceased.

There was a thin mournful howl from nowhere – a lament for an insuperable loss. They all shivered. Delray's ghost began to fade away. It looked down at itself, then at Lyset. 'Don't be sad…' A low, grey, vaguely doglike form appeared at his heels. 'You'll have to look after Evan… Maybe you can stop this happening to him…'

Then he was gone. The thing at his heels gave a last whine, then it too was no more.

There was a long silence, broken only by the shuffling of feet of the still dazed survivors, and Lyset Wynter's stifled sobbing. The Doctor looked on – sad yet also deeply thoughtful. Of his own volition Dan Junior stepped up to Lyset's side and, in an unexpectedly mature gesture, put a consoling hand on her shoulder.

Sam stood beside the Doctor and asked softly, 'Evan? Did he mean Arcovian? But that thing with him seemed like a… dog.'

The Doctor nodded. 'Madness takes refuge in many forms. The need to escape from reality, balanced by the ties of love and devotion, shaped by the way a person had been treated in life. Think about it…'

Sam felt desperately sick and confused. 'This has got to end,' she said with a shudder. 'If you can't help those poor creatures out there, then put them out of their misery. You must do something!'

'If I can, Sam. Delray has shown there may be a way. But first we must take the survivors back to the *Cirrandaria*. Then we'll need more power.' The Doctor pulled down hard on a lever in its brass housing. 'If we are going to change anything, we'll have only one chance to get it right!'

Chapter Thirty-Four
Convergence

'We're trapped!' Bendix said, his face stark with fear.

Below him at the bottom of the shaft the lights of the corridor were flickering and failing.

'Steady,' Rexton warned him, his own mind racing. 'Back to the control room. Don't make a sound.'

They scrambled back up the ladder and sealed the airlock doors behind them. But the interface still confined them to half the chamber, and it seemed no barrier to the ghosts. Rexton saw Bendix looking at him with desperation in his eyes.

'Patience,' he said confidently. 'The way may be clear in a minute.'

While they waited he prowled the control room, his eyes flicking across the hundreds of neat labels adorning the panels. At last he had the precious information; all he had to do was pass it on.

The sign saying EXTERNAL MONITOR caught his eye. It headed a block of the large multicoloured buttons and a couple of domelike protuberances. Cautiously he touched one of the buttons at random. Nothing happened. Perhaps the system needed to be activated first. There was a black button out of sequence. He pressed it. A clear glass screen rose out of a narrow slot in the panel before him. An image came instantly to life on it showing the view along the great hull of the ship. Bendix joined him excitedly.

'Can you see inside as well?'

'Let's check the external hatchway is clear first. Remember them dropping in on us the last time we left.'

He called up a quick succession of images, discovering that pressure on the domes panned or dipped the cameras. He began to see an order in the layout of the buttons that corresponded to the views he was getting. 'This should be it.'

It did indeed show the external hatch over the bay where they had left the *Doria*. But the hatch was open. And, even as they watched, the

Doria rose out of it, rolling unsteadily from side to side. It cleared the hull, banked suddenly and sped off into the gloom of the huge cavern.

'They've taken it...' Bendix said dully. 'But why –'

'It doesn't matter, it's gone,' Rexton said. He would not be defeated, he would not!

'How do we get back?'

Rexton waved him into silence, looking about him at the serried ranks of buttons and labels. If the Doctor could work it out without any guidance at all...

'We'll just have to take the whole ship with us,' he said.

The TARDIS materialised in its original landing place in the *Cirrandaria*'s hold. The door opened and the Doctor walked briskly out, followed by Vega, Sam, leading young Dan Engers, and the first hesitant rescuees.

'You understand we have arrived here at the same time as if we had travelled back through the hyperspatial tunnel in the shuttle,' the Doctor was telling Vega. 'Any earlier and we risk breaking one of the prime laws of time.' He snagged one of the surviving *Cirrandaria* security men who had accompanied them. 'Go ahead and warn the crew we have Nimosian guests on board, otherwise they might think it's a boarding party. Then get these people to sickbay and make sure Mr Delray's body is taken care of properly.'

'Yes, sir,' said the still dazed man meekly.

'But can your machine take us back to the *Indomitable*?' Vega asked.

'Yes, but not right now. One focus of the time loop is the alien ship, the other the *Cirrandaria*. If I'm to do anything to alter it then it has to be from here.'

'Doctor, after what I've seen I want to stop this as much as anyone. If the war that led to... that abomination we saw, started here, then I must warn my people before it's too late.'

The Doctor nodded. 'Of course, you must have the chance to try. Who knows? You may succeed. Let's go and find the Captain.'

'And I've got to take Dan back to his parents,' said Sam.

* * *

Lanchard was amazed to see the Doctor and Vega appear on the bridge, and doubly surprised by the curiously intent look Vega gave her.

'How did you get here? We didn't see the shuttle.'

'We took a short cut,' the Doctor said. 'I'm sure the Commander will be pleased to explain it all later. We had to give him a lift back as his own craft was lost.'

'Did you... find the passengers?'

'We recovered those we could. They're in sickbay being checked over now.'

'Where is Councillor Rexton... and Bendix?'

'They abandoned us,' Vega said bluntly.

'Let's say the councillor felt he had more pressing business to attend to,' the Doctor said. 'They're still over there, but we may not have seen the last of them just yet. Meanwhile, what's been happening while we've been gone?'

'Nothing good. A passenger stole a lifeboat...' She glanced at Vega. 'And your flagship destroyed it.'

'You'd better explain quickly,' said the Doctor. 'I think we're running out of time.'

Down in the sickbay, the joy of the Engers family in being reunited was one of the most uplifting things Sam had seen. Their tearful expressions of gratitude for bringing Dan Junior back were sincere and heartfelt, but she could not accept them without thinking of their doubles on the other side of the space-time bridge. Was that how it was perpetually fated to be: joy crushed by remorseless fate? She left them clustered round the bed where Dan Senior was still having treatment for the injuries to his leg, listening to his son trying to explain his adventures. She wondered if they would have time to listen – and to believe – it all.

She found Evan Arcovian resting in a bed a few along from Engers. Lyset Wynter, wrapped in a thermal blanket, was sitting by him.

'He had a breakdown,' Lyset told her. 'Some sort of shock. But they won't tell me what. They just looked at me very oddly.'

And now Arcovian had to face the loss of Delray. Would it make any difference to the little man's grotesque destiny? Sam wondered. But what were the staff hiding from Lyset?

Sam searched out somebody senior, and found Dr Gilliam finishing the task of applying dermaform bandaging to a woman with a badly damaged face. As soon as she was free, Sam flashed her Moderator's badge and asked about Arcovian.

'It's a fairly severe mental breakdown,' Gilliam admitted. 'He's been here since we found what we thought was, well, a ghostly form of Ms Wynter's corpse.'

'What?' Sam exclaimed. 'Show me. It could be important.'

Gilliam took her to the cold locker, opened the heavy insulated door and pulled out the long tray within.

There was nothing on it but a white sheet.

Rexton's head ached and his eyes felt raw from reading hundreds of annotated controls and trying make sense of them. The wording was precise, and yet still hard to interpret. What did COMPENSATOR FOR INTERNAL FIELD POTENTIAL VARIANCE mean in practice?

He hesitated, turning the phrase over in his mind. Maybe… He cautiously turned the large heavy dial to the right. The shimmering curtain of the interface drifted towards their end of the control room, causing Bendix to step hastily out of its way. Rexton twisted the dial left and the interface retreated out through the main entrance and into the central vertical shaft of the tower, where it halted. Apparently they could not be rid of it entirely.

'Well at least we can get to all the controls now,' Bendix said. 'If only we could understand them.'

'We will,' Rexton said. 'We must move fully into our space so we can leave with the data. This ship can't just be a tunnel between different parts of space. It must be able to move itself somehow. They have controls for everything.'

The sign, SELF-REPAIR: HULL COMPOSITE MATERIAL SYNTHESIS UNIT caught his eye as he spoke. Interesting. As soon as they learned about that back at the research base they could replace the patches they had fitted over the old ship and make it as good as new. For a moment his thoughts faltered as the possible implication struck him, but he firmly rejected it.

'It could be this bank here,' Bendix was saying, leading him across to another panel. 'Now the interface has gone I can see all of it clearly. Yes, look.'

SPATIAL AND TEMPORAL TRANSLOCATION, ran the heading of a large bank of controls. Various subsections read, UNIT CALIBRATION, FIELD EXTENSION PARAMETERS, POWER RESERVE, TARGET CO-ORDINATES, NODE EQUALISATION…

'This is promising,' Rexton agreed.

'As long as those creatures leave us alone,' Bendix said.

'If they were going to try to operate it themselves they'd have been here already,' Rexton pointed out. 'There's no reason why they should come in here as long as we don't draw attention to ourselves.'

Bendix started. 'But we have. You just moved the interface several metres…'

Rexton turned and activated his normaliser just in time to stop the wraith that was gliding through the main entrance.

Only insistent demands by both Lanchard and Vega got Commodore Sternby and Admiral Mokai into a split-screen three-way conference. Vega then related to the two fleet commanders, in clipped concise tones, what they had discovered at the other end of the hyperspatial corridor.

Lanchard listened incredulously. The ghosts were themselves, reaching back to them from some post-apocalyptic future where Emindar was lifeless? But Vega sounded frighteningly sincere, and the Doctor's steady presence lent further credence to the fantastic, macabre tale. She found herself believing. When Vega had finished, the Doctor faced the two military men.

'Everything Commander Vega has told you is true. If you want my advice I would say get as far away from here as possible and forget all about the alien ship.' He saw the expression on their faces and added sadly, 'But I don't suppose you'll do it.'

'Until we have craft modified for exploration of the alien vessel, we 'cannot verify your… most unusual report, Commander Vega,' Mokai said. 'I will send a shuttle over to collect you and your men for debriefing aboard the *Starfire*.'

'I was hoping to return to my ship, sir,' Vega said.

'Your own ship is under the command of one of my officers,' Mokai admitted gravely. 'I had to relieve your second, Fayle.' Noting Vega's mystified expression, Mokai moved stiffly on. 'I won't discuss the matter over an open link. Just hold yourself ready for retrieval.'

'You will not land a military shuttle on the *Cirrandaria* without my permission,' Sternby said.

'These are our men,' Mokai retorted angrily. 'On what grounds would you hold them there against their will?'

'They have made an unauthorised landing on our ship in mysterious circumstances. I want to see this travel device they used.' He looked at the Doctor. 'Perhaps if you could demonstrate it, that might give some credence to this fantastic story.'

'I'm afraid it cannot be moved at present,' the Doctor said.

'How inconvenient,' Sternby said, clearly disbelieving.

'It doesn't matter how they got there,' Mokai said. 'We are taking our men off immediately –'

'As Captain of the *Cirrandaria*,' Lanchard shouted over them, 'may I remind you that Commander Vega is my guest, and that I am obliged to him for his part in rescuing our lost passengers. He and his men may leave whenever and however they please.

'Captain,' Sternby said, 'in the current situation I am placing your ship under martial law –'

'That's outrageous!' Lanchard shouted.

Sam entered the bridge amid the babble of crossed words. The Doctor saw her and drew back a little way from the arguing group.

'Doctor,' she said urgently, 'while we were away they found Lyset Wynter's body in Delray's cabin – looking like a ghost. But now it's vanished.'

The Doctor stroked his chin thoughtfully. 'Now that is very interesting, Sam. It proves the nexus isn't totally closed.'

260

'The what?'

'The probability nexus: a zone of twisted time and space. The loop containing the alien ship is only part of it. These people are all trapped within it. We may be ourselves, if we're not careful.'

Sam looked across at Lanchard, Vega and the soldiers on the screen. 'Can't you explain that to them?'

'Do you think they'd believe me? Vega has already told them the truth. Now it's up to them to decide their fate.'

'But you said you'd try to help.'

'I can't change the big picture, Sam, because we've seen how it ends – perhaps how this little piece of history has always ended. There are terribly powerful forces at play here: pride, honour, fear, distrust.' He sighed. 'The four horsemen in new guises. It is their destiny.'

A terrible look of melancholia enveloped him – a weariness beyond her understanding.

'But you haven't really given up? Come on, you never give up!'

The Doctor said nothing.

As Rexton held back the wraiths at the door he shouted over his shoulder, 'Do it now!'

Bendix stared helplessly at the strange controls. 'But I can't be sure –'

'Then guess! Or haven't you the guts to make a decision?'

Bendix took a deep breath. Concentrate, he told himself. Activate the whole TRANSLOCATION panel. Boost power. Set field within parameters. If NODES meant the two ends of the ship, and he moved this one towards the other that opened into their own space…

The whole ship trembled. From the depths came the rising pulse of raw energy. He felt the deck tilt under him as concentrated megatonnes of mass flowed through the vast structure, warping gravity to their needs. On the external viewscreen lightning played about the great horns of the distant hull rim, earthing into the rocks about them with shattering blasts and illuminating the whole cavern. For a moment he felt like a god riding the power he had unleashed.

But then he saw a more incredible sight.

From out of the tunnel-pocked far wall of the cavern a pale luminous shape was emerging, flowing slowly out of the solid rock towards them. It was the *Cirrandaria*.

What were they doing bringing it here? What had happened to the rest of the rescue party?

A cloud of ghost creatures, some winged, some no more than drifting blobs, were emerging from the tunnels and swarming into the *Cirrandaria*'s hatches. There seemed to be hundreds of them. Why were the humanoid crew allowing it? What had happened back in the port cavern?

Then he understood, with cold horror, that the insane had taken over.

But did they realise in their madness what they were doing? Was this their final effort, drawn by what common instinct he could not guess, to travel back to find the people they had been? To feed again on warmth and life?

The warning alarms cut through the intership argument, as all craft detected the change in the alien vessel.

'Gravity shift!' a bridge monitor called out. 'Massive energy discharge... strong field fluctuations.'

On the screens they saw lightning play about the twin collars of spires. Sam peered closer and said, 'Doctor, I *can't* see through the other half of that ship any more. It's quite solid now.'

The Doctor nodded solemnly. 'This is it, Sam. We're entering the core of the probability nexus.'

Chapter Thirty-Five
Nexus

Rexton recovered from the stomach-wrenching sensation of the transition to find the wraiths he had been holding at bay had vanished. The central well of the tower shaft was empty of them and also any sign of the interface. Shakily he crossed over to where Bendix was resting against the edge of a control panel. The external screen showed no sign of the cavern, only stars. There were bright, irregular, moving points among them that could only be ships. He clapped him on the back.

'Well done, Bendix. Now, we must get the film away safely.'

Bendix was cautiously checking the external views. 'There are a lot of ships out there. Must be the Nimosians as well as our fleet. How are we going to get the film to them if they can't pick us up?'

'I anticipated that possibility,' Rexton assured him, unslinging his backpack, 'and took the precaution of bringing this from your ship's stores.'

He pulled out three short sections of tubing which he snapped together to form a device resembling a military hand-held rocket launcher.

'An emergency homing rocket,' Bendix said. 'Of course.'

'I have arranged that our forces should be on the alert for one,' Rexton explained, removing the precious film cartridge from his pocket and fitting it into the chamber in the body of the small missile. 'They will also be ready to develop the film, scan and transmit it at top speed. Always think ahead, Bendix.'

He fitted the rocket into the firing chamber and slung the launcher over his shoulder. 'Now, down through the central shaft and along to the nearest external hatchway...' His eye caught a control marked HATCH CENTRAL LOCKING. He pressed the relevant button, opening them. 'That'll save time.'

Bendix suddenly looked anxious. 'What about the ghosts?'

'They disappeared as we made the transition.'

'I suppose they went back to the *Cirrandaria*.' He looked at the external screens, but there was no sign of the ghost craft.

'Come on,' said Rexton impatiently.

The two opposing fleets went to maximum alert. Neither had modified shuttles ready to land on the alien ship and tow beams still failed to lock on to it, so the only option each had was to deny it to the other side. The *Cirrandaria* was also a problematical piece in the game and it too had to be taken into account. As both sides jockeyed for the most favourable tactical position, shuttles from the *Korgon* were launched towards the crippled liner.

'Two Emindian landing craft are outside demanding entry to the shuttle bay, Captain.'

Lanchard sighed. 'Without the main engines we can't outrun them. Better let them in before they blow the doors.'

'Sorry,' said Vega. 'Our presence here hasn't helped.'

'I think they were going to do this anyway.' She hesitated, then asked, 'Was it really as bad as you said over there?'

'Yes, it was.'

'And we were both there… as ghosts?'

'Yes. I know it must seem unbelievable.'

'The trouble is… I do believe it. I felt there was something wrong when we first set eyes on the derelict.' She took a deep breath. 'Excuse me, I have to tell everybody what's going on.'

She opened the general address system.

'This is the Captain speaking to all passengers and crew. The situation outside is getting pretty tense as you may have seen for yourself. This ship has been placed under military control and we are about to be boarded by Emindian soldiers. For your own safety, put on your emergency suits and stay in your cabins or any inner compartments of the ship.'

'May I?' Vega asked, and took over the microphone. 'Vega to all Nimosian personnel on the *Cirrandaria*. Do not engage the Emindian troops. We do not want to start a war on this ship.'

He finished and looked at Doctor and Sam. 'This is when it begins, isn't it?'

'I think so,' the Doctor admitted.

Lanchard said. 'I was considering asking you to evacuate as many of the passengers as you could, but it looks like we've run out of time. Thanks for what you've done, but this isn't your concern any more. You might as well leave in that machine of yours before our troops try to stop you.'

'We're going down to the TARDIS but we're not leaving,' the Doctor said. 'There may be something we can do to stop the very worst happening. We'll see it through with you. Come on, Sam.'

Sam looked desperately at Vega and Lanchard. Any words would be inadequate, but she couldn't just leave in silence. 'Good luck,' she said quickly, and hurried after the Doctor.

Standing on the hull of the alien ship, Rexton scanned the two groups of twinkling dots on opposite sides of the sky with binoculars.

'There's the *Korgon*,' he said.

Bendix handed him the launcher. He shouldered it, took aim at the distant target and fired. A simple, solid-fuel first stage propelled the small rocket clear of the alien ship's gravitational field. Five kilometres up, the homing system would cut in and direct it towards the nearest Emindian ship. Rexton watched the flare of its tail jet vanish into the darkness, then threw the empty launcher tube aside. 'Now, back to the control room.'

'Shouldn't we wait out here for recovery?'

'No, Bendix, we take advantage of circumstances. The film is only a safeguard. Now we can try for the real prize.'

'Sorry?'

'We have a ship that can quite literally go anywhere.' Rexton smiled grimly. 'We're going to see if we can take it home.'

Emindian marines spread efficiently through the *Cirrandaria*, taking stations at key points and firmly shepherding frightened passengers out of their way. A young lieutenant took possession of the bridge. To his surprise he found Lanchard sharing a drink with Vega in her day cabin.

'Since you've taken over my ship you might as well sit down,' Lanchard said with careless amicability.

'Commander, you are my prisoner,' the lieutenant told Vega.

The Nimosian did not appear in the least concerned. 'No, we're all prisoners,' he replied tonelessly. He gave the lieutenant a very disconcerting appraisal. 'I wonder: have you ever used a net and trident?'

They reached the TARDIS just ahead of the tramp of heavy boots. Sam felt it was like running away, but it was reassuring to be safe inside its walls again. The Doctor crossed to the console.

'Good, the capacitors are almost fully charged,' he said.

'What are you going to do – use the normaliser effect?'

'No, that only temporarily disrupts their bodily patterns. We need to do something more fundamental. Did you notice, during the fight in the starport, that none of the ghosts entered the TARDIS, even though they were swarming around it?'

'Yes. The Engerses wouldn't come in either.'

'The interior of the TARDIS is shielded from normal space, so it must sever the ghosts' link with their intradimensional phase band. They lose their individual patterns. With the power boost, I'm going to try to duplicate that effect outside the TARDIS across as large a volume of space as possible. It should completely disrupt the plane in which the ghosts exist.' He glanced at her as though appealing for understanding. 'They'll die.'

Sam just stood there, taking it all in. 'It'll be a mercy,' she said finally. 'That's what they want.' She remembered Vega's disintegrating face. 'Believe me.'

The Doctor nodded slowly and returned to his controls and the monitor which he had linked to *Cirrandaria*'s systems.

Sam frowned. 'Will we have to go back… I mean forward, to the spaceport to find the ghosts?'

'No. I think they'll come to us,' the Doctor said. 'The probability nexus is evidently unstable and that may have something to do with the nature and origin of the ghosts. It's also why I dare not restore them to full reality even if I could. Only their phase-shifted state has allowed them to interact with their former selves to the degree they have for this long. But if they became more real, or enough of them come together at the same time, it could be disastrous.'

Sam stared at him, eyes wide in realisation. 'And if you *did* fully restore them...' The Doctor nodded. 'Double occupancy of the same part of space-time...'

He clapped his hands together violently as if by way of demonstration. 'Yes. It would take a tremendous release of energy to dimensionally shift an entire starship so far out of phase with reality as the *Cirrandaria* was. One of the few possible sources would be the energy released when two identical bodies meet.'

The full implication struck Sam. 'You mean... they did it to themselves all along?'

'I think so, Sam. And very shortly, they're going to do it again.'

The message rocket sped into the heart of the Emindian fleet, cut its power and activated its beacon. It was swiftly drawn into one of the *Korgon*'s ports, where the film cartridge was extracted and rushed to the imaging laboratory.

Mokai received a call from the hangar deck.

'The two modified landers are now crewed and ready to launch, Admiral.'

'Well done,' Mokai acknowledged. 'Communications, code signal to fleet: Insertion Plan Delta. Launch landing craft on confirmation.' He stared at the image of the alien vessel on the screen. 'We're going to take that ship for Nimos.'

Sternby watched the launch of the landing craft and manoeuvring of the Nimosian fleet grimly.

'They're going into assault formation, sir.'

'Are our craft ready yet?' Sternby demanded.

'Another hour, sir.'

'Not good enough! We can't let them get down there. Open a line to the *Starfire*.'

Mokai's face appeared on the screen.

'There are still two Emindian citizens on the alien vessel,' Sternby told him. 'I state for the record that they are a prize crew, making that vessel Emindian territory. You have no right to land on her.'

'You have no proof whatsoever that they are on board,' Mokai retorted. 'However, I assure you that, should our landing party encounter them, they will be properly treated and returned to your care promptly and unharmed. Unless you care to suggest that the ship is crewed by these "ghosts", it is still a derelict and open to salvage by any who can take possession of her. Mokai out.'

Sternby stared at the blank screen for a moment, then opened a channel to the imaging laboratory.

'Has the film data from the message rocket been processed?'

'Yes, sir. We are encoding and transmitting on the ultra channel now.'

'Any personal communication from General Rexton with the film?'

'No, sir.'

That was typical of the man, thought Sternby – his only concern was the mission. Well, now his own orders left him only one option. On no account were the Nimosians to be allowed to take possession of the alien vessel. He thought Rexton would understand.

'Missile control, target the alien ship. Main batteries, one salvo each, set warheads to maximum yield. Fire when ready.'

The missiles streaked towards the great bulk of the alien ship, to be met by a wave of antimissile interceptors from the Nimosian fleet. Only two got through, and the interference field caused them both to detonate short of their target. A hundred metre circle of hull skin was fused and warped, while a blast wave of vaporised missile casing shook the ship's central tower.

The landing craft and their escort broke off their first run and circled clear of their target. Counterstrike missiles leapt from the Nimosian ship's launch tubes towards the Emindian fleet, while waves of darting fighters dived out of the night to engage their opposite numbers. Incandescent beams and pulses of multigigawatt magnitude stabbed across the intervening space as the two fleets' heaviest projector turrets exchanged fire. Another missile salvo sped away from the *Korgon* towards the alien ship.

The first battle of the war had begun.

Rexton and Bendix clung to the edges of the control panels for support as the ship trembled under the onslaught, but they kept on with their task.

There was no need to state the obvious. They had very little time left.

Sam turned aside from the monitor image, feeling hot tears of rage and despair pricking her eyes.

'What can we do?'

'Nothing,' said the Doctor. 'Our warning and the actions of the ghosts have all become part of what we sought to avoid. It was inevitable... but we had to try. All we can do now is limit the suffering.'

Three black-hulled Nimosian assault craft, having flown a long evasive arc around the conflict zone, intercepted the *Cirrandaria*, which lay a little back from the cluster of Emindian ships. They clamped on to its hull and cutting beams rapidly and efficiently sliced through external service hatches, opening the way for the marines themselves. They poured in, dividing up to take specific sections of the ship. They were met by fierce resistance from the occupying Emindian soldiers and the advance faltered, degenerating into a corridor-by-corridor struggle, then finally a bloody hand-to-hand combat. At the head of one of these infiltration parties was Corporal Talek Chen.

* * *

In his cabin on the *Indomitable*, Fayle felt the surges of power as the ship manoeuvred, and the concussion as it discharged its guns or took hits against its shields. But he noted all this with a curious detachment.

His encounter with the thing in Chen's cabin had, in a few seconds, turned his certainties upside down. He had tried to report the incident objectively and had been relieved of his command for his trouble. And now, even though they were fighting the Emindians, it no longer seemed to matter. Perhaps it was just the effect of shock, but he appreciated for the first time that there were greater mysteries and possibilities out there than he had ever dreamed of. It put mundane life, with all its fears and hatreds, into perspective. Now he waited, slightly impatiently, to find out what would come next.

In his own cabin Rask Chen listened to the pounding as the spirit of his brother said, 'Sorry, Rask. I tried...'

The next concussion threw Chen to the floor.

'I think I have Emindar on the target screen,' Bendix said. 'It's locked in, correcting for space-time distortion.'

'Offset by one million kilometres. We don't want to arrive on the surface.'

'Done... I think.'

'Now set temporal displacement back one year,' said Rexton.

'What? But we can't risk –'

'Our forces did not have time to finish the repairs and master the full functions of the other ship. We will give them time, so they will be ready. Do it!'

'But I'm not sure about the calibration –'

The ship trembled again.

'We have no time, Bendix. We'll take the risk for Emindar.'

'It'll take a couple of minutes – if we have that long.'

Rexton looked desperately over the controls. There were still so many they hadn't examined. The panel they'd used earlier had only negated the space-time separation between the ends of the ship. Now they needed to move just a few kilometres through space alone to get clear of the battle. Then he saw the sign that read NODES: REAL-TIME PHYSICAL DISPLACEMENT EFFECT.

Did that mean what he thought? There was only one way to find out. 'We're going to take evasive action,' he said.

Space contorted around the ship as the gravimetric potential grew between the ends of its main hull, then started to flow past it. To maintain an equilibrium the ship moved forward with the main control module leading, steadily gaining speed. It ploughed its way through the heart of the battle, ships of all sizes scattering before its huge bulk.

'Delray's ghost proved that the nexus is not yet in perfect equilibrium,' the Doctor said, as they watched and waited for the *Cirrandaria*'s doppelgänger. 'The ghosts' timeline at least can change. Delray remembered a different sequence of events in which Lyset Wynter had died through what he felt was his cowardice. So he influenced his former self to behave differently, and in effect swapped his life for hers. A tiny change, on the cosmic scale of things, but significant.'

'But if the ghosts are going to annihilate their former selves to start the whole cycle off again, won't they be finished anyway?' Sam wondered.

'I can't be certain of that, in their altered state. That's why I'll release the energy pulse just after they've made contact. At least we can be sure they'll be at rest then. It's just a matter of timing.'

'Doctor,' Sam said slowly. 'What if you did it early? Stopped them from turning themselves into ghosts in the first place? Then they won't be there to send the alien ship back, so the Emindians and Nimosians won't be here to fight over it...' She saw the look in his eyes. 'You *are* thinking about it!'

She saw that familiar dangerous smile play about his lips, defying the terrible sense of inevitability and doom that Sam had felt lying heavy upon them.

'It would be a terrible risk, Sam,' he said quickly. 'I wouldn't dare consider it, except we know space and time are mutable at this point. Yes, it might just work. There'll be some other confrontation and the war will happen anyway – that can't be changed. But at least these people might escape. But it could be dangerous for us too.'

'Go for it!' Sam said without hesitation.

In the *Cirrandaria*'s sickbay, which had become an emergency centre for the treatment of wounded from both sides, Dr Gilliam was sealing the stump of corporal Talek Chen's left arm, which had been blown completely off by an Emindian blaster bolt.

On the bridge, Lanchard saw the war-torn sky clear almost magically in front of them. And out of the void came the alien ship. Head on. They were looking straight down into its gaping mouth. The marine lieutenant was too distracted by the battle inside to notice.

Lanchard ordered, 'Hard to port!'

Nothing happened.

'Thrusters are inoperative, Captain,' the helmsman said.

'Engine room, we need thruster control!' Lanchard shouted over the comlink. Only the sound of gunfire came back to her.

She looked helplessly at Vega, then at the screens. The perfect circle of darkness was swelling by the second. But deep within it was a pale glowing form. Vega realised what it was even as he felt time closing in. The acceptance of destiny enfolded them in a strange calm.

'I just wish I could have been on my own ship at the end,' Vega said. 'At least you will keep yours, Captain.'

'You'll always be welcome on the *Cirrandaria*, Commander Vega,' said Lanchard.

Sam pointed at the monitor. 'The ghosts are inside the alien ship! Won't its interference mess things up?'

'Not as long as we don't try to dematerialise,' the Doctor said. 'Get ready.'

His finger was hovering over the switch that would release the vast reserve of power stored within the TARDIS.

* * *

Rexton saw the *Cirrandaria* lying immobile directly in their path. They were going to collide and he could do nothing about it.

He didn't know how to steer.

'Now, Bendix, now!' he roared.

Desperately Bendix hit the last of the buttons, just as the viewscreen was obliterated as though they had been enveloped by a firestorm.

Whether it had been a Nimosian or Emindian ship was now impossible to tell. The blazing mass of wreckage crossed the path of the derelict, grazed the forward end of its pipe-encrusted hull and broke up into a dozen lesser fragments and a cloud of smaller debris.

The fringe of this silent avalanche struck the central tower.

Rexton and Bendix dived through the main entrance of the control module as a ball of fire rolled into the central shaft after them, filling the air with fluttering fragments of burning labels blasted loose by the shockwave. A wind picked up as air began to escape through the damaged tower modules. They scrambled down the ramps towards the lower levels as the complex assembly of waveguides and energy grids began to collapse. Sparks showered over them from shorted contacts. Pulses of energy danced wildly. On the second level the silver mesh conduit leading to the temporal laboratory filled with flickering green fire.

As they ducked under it the structure collapsed, knocking them to the ground. Primary polarised temporal energy washed over them and sparks crackled between them, their bodies acting like shorted electrical terminals.

Bendix felt his suit shred and disintegrate about him, the metal corroding, the plastic cracking and flaking. His joints stiffened, his skin wrinkled. His cry of terror became a choking feeble whimper. Rexton thrashed wildly as his own clothing turned to powder and dirt, then rolled out of the beam and under the guard railing. As another fireball blasted what was left of Bendix to ash, Rexton fell kicking and screaming down the central well of the shaft.

273

In the space-time corridor directly under him hung the ghostly form of the *Cirrandaria*.

On the TARDIS's monitor they saw the *Cirrandaria* enveloped by the alien ship and its doppelgänger appear to hurl itself towards them. An instant before they met the Doctor pressed the switch.

The TARDIS's lights dimmed.

At that same moment the continuum twisted about them according to Bendix's last command.

The units of measurement stored in the uncalibrated targeting system of the alien ship were neither standard years nor kilometres. The ship would never reach its intended objective. But as it fell through hyperspace a vortex beam, actuated by its damaged systems, did flicker briefly into life, reaching out to touch a point in time and space beyond and before the co-ordinates set.

Then it faded and was gone.

Chapter Thirty-Six
To Begin Again

Pale stars burned in a grey void about the *Cirrandaria*, which itself was now a pallid insubstantial thing. After an interval the ghost ship's main drive was activated, and it began its timeless journey towards home and inescapable destiny.

Sam and the Doctor watched it depart from the TARDIS, which was hanging invisibly on the fringe of hyperspace. The Doctor's face was pale and pinched with regret.

'We failed,' he said. 'It's all starting again.'

'Well,' Sam said, feeling the weight of his sorrow, 'at least we tried.'

'I know.' He looked at the console displays. 'There was a huge surge of energy along the space-time corridor. Rexton must have tried to move the whole ship.'

'Where are we now?'

'The energy surge interacted with the field we emitted. We've been projected a little over a year forward in time and several light years closer to Emindar.'

'What about the real *Cirrandaria*? And the fleets?'

The Doctor operated the controls and the TARDIS dematerialised. Seconds later they appeared amid a thinning cloud of tumbling debris. A piece of hull plate drifted past with some lettering still legible: INDOMITABLE. A bloated corpse came into view and Sam turned her head away.

'Not a single ship survived,' the Doctor said tonelessly. 'They fought to the last, even though the prize they were fighting for was gone. In a year it will be the end for both their worlds. The phase-shifted *Cirrandaria* will arrive at Emindar to find a dead port and the repaired derelict. They'll use it to try to change the past and it will all begin again.'

'All because of one alien ship,' Sam said. Then she frowned. 'We never found out where it came from. Who built it? Something that size didn't just pop out of nowhere.'

'In a way it did,' the Doctor said. 'You see, the universe's accounts are only audited, so to speak, at the beginning and the end. Sometimes a little can be borrowed in between and returned again without upsetting things too much. The alien ship is never created or destroyed, just repaired by the Emindians with the information Rexton sent them, which he got from the labels they put on the instruments in the control room, which they made from his data... and so on. His final efforts must have sent it back, damaged and with its power depleted, to where the Emindians first found it. And so the cycle continues.'

'But it must have a beginning.'

'Pick any point you want. The ship was shaped within the nexus by the hopes and fears of the people who would later fight over it in response to its potential. An endless cycle of feedback making distorted wishes tangible. That was why it was so full of contradictions: the lock code and the nonsensical inscriptions, the way certain equipment would or wouldn't work, the interior being suggestive of alien origins yet so accessible to humans.'

'It's still hard to take in.'

'The TARDIS has recorded its time path through the nexus. You can see how it interacted with everything else,' he said absently, touching a few controls. A graphical image appeared on the vast, holographic display in the ceiling above them.

It resembled a sloppily tied multicoloured bow with three loops of different lengths, Sam thought. A dark-blue band ran across the display, sloping up from left to right, and was crossed in the middle by a rising curve of dark green. Both of these ran off the hazy edges of the projection. From the point they crossed, a small loop of pale green rose upward, a larger loop of red rose to the same height, then dropped well down, while a thin loop of yellow hung to the very bottom of the image. Arching along the vast display was a graduated timescale with an arrow pointing upward.

Sam realised the Doctor was staring at the image with an

expression of wonder and delight spreading across his face.

'We haven't totally failed after all, Sam,' he said.

'How? What's it all mean?'

'The blue line is the TARDIS's time track and the dark green is the *Cirrandaria*'s. The red loop is the alien ship, while the pale-green loop is the phase-shifted *Cirrandaria* – the ghost ship, if you will. But look closely where all the lines cross: the heart of the nexus itself…' He zoomed in until the knot at the centre of the image dominated their view and pointed dramatically. 'See: the timeline for the ghost ship curves up, merges with that of the alien ship but ends just as it crosses ours. It doesn't join itself. It isn't actually a closed loop. The pulse we radiated did disperse the ghosts *we met*. The ship we have just seen must have been created afresh by the energy surge from the alien ship, not by mutual annihilation with its doppelgänger. I was wrong – but the cycle has been broken anyway.'

Sam was trying to understand while peering intently at the screen. 'It looks like the ghost *Cirrandaria*'s track branches off from the real *Cirrandaria*'s as it crosses ours.'

'Reality divided about the TARDIS inside the space-time corridor,' the Doctor said. 'Apparently, that was our predestined role in the nexus: to help create faint *copies* of the *Cirrandaria* and its crew – and then to destroy them. The ghosts were never their future-selves doubled back in time. Their duplicated pattern must have reacted against some smaller object inside the corridor, so they became less substantial themselves. Then it was simply a matter of action and reaction throwing them forward in time.'

Sam felt confused relief. 'Well as long as they're at rest now.' She looked at the diagram again. 'Wait a minute. The real *Cirrandaria*'s time track runs off the top of the display.'

The Doctor was beaming broadly. 'I was wondering when you'd notice that. Obviously it reacted against the alien ship itself, which has been projected back thirty years or so from 3123 when we encountered it. Therefore, being of lesser mass, the *Cirrandaria* has been thrown quite a lot further forward…'

* * *

The *Cirrandaria* was in orbit about Emindar. Lanchard and Vega stood side by side on the bridge as the scanner data came in. The commanders of the assault forces were with them, but they were no longer fighting. There seemed little point now.

'The remains of cities… a few pockets of low-level radiation… but the air and sea are clean,' Lanchard said. She turned to communications. 'Still nothing on radio or hyperwave?'

'Some very faint signals on hyperwave, Captain. Can't quite make them out.'

'And nothing on the Nimosian channels?' Vega asked.

'No, sir.'

Lanchard looked at Vega. 'So, where are we?'

Before he could answer a distant rhythmic whirring sound became audible, growing into a harsh groaning. With a dull booming thud, a familiar tall blue box materialised in the middle of the room. A door in the side opened and the Doctor and Sam stepped out.

'We had to say goodbye properly,' the Doctor said brightly.

Vega recovered his voice first. 'What happened to you? Where are we?'

'According to our instruments,' Sam said with a grin, 'it's the fifth millennium. You've travelled a little over a thousand years into the future. The Doctor says time has been more forgiving than usual.'

The Doctor indicated the blue and white world on the screens. 'Emindar has not been resettled. In fact this whole sector has been more or less forgotten by the rest of the galaxy since the war. Let's say you've had a second chance. Not many people get that. It won't be easy, of course, but you've got the resources of this ship and what you can find down there. And your own courage, of course.' He consulted his pocket watch. 'But we have to go – and you've got a lot of work to do. Good luck.'

'Goodbye,' said Sam. 'Make sure Dan has a good world to grow up in.'

'I…' Lanchard began, still sounding dazed. Then she seemed to pull herself together. 'Yes,' she said. 'Yes. I promise.'

With a wave Sam stepped back inside the TARDIS. The Doctor paused on the threshold.

'Incidentally, the history books say that long after the war Emindar was rebuilt by settlers of unknown origins.' He smiled. 'I think we know who they were now.'

The TARDIS was back in its natural element, riding the dimension winds of deep hyperspace. The Doctor's eyes had that faraway look in them again. 'Vanderdeken,' he murmured to himself.

'Who?' Sam asked.

'The mythical Flying Dutchman. The captain of a ghost ship, doomed to sail the seas eternally attempting to double about the Cape of Good Hope. A bit like the *Cirrandaria*'s ghostly twin.'

'But at least it isn't for ever for them. Thanks to you.'

'I suppose so, Sam.'

'And the real passengers and crew of the *Cirrandaria* still have a chance to make good. It's better than nothing.' She frowned at the nexus graphic still glowing on the monitor. 'You never explained what the yellow loop represents. It goes even further back into the past than the derelict.'

'That must be whatever balanced the ghostly version of the *Cirrandaria* being projected forward.'

'Oh, what?'

'Something of equivalent temporal mass. The ghosts weren't very substantial, so it could have been quite a small object.'

'And will it cycle around for ever like the alien ship?'

'Yes, that's a closed loop.' A quizzical expression came over the Doctor's face. 'Without a beginning... or an end.'

Epilogue/Prologue

POLICE HEADQUARTERS, MELCONVILLE, NORTH BERRON, EMINDAR

EXCERPT FROM NIGHT PATROL LOG: 17th to 18th JUNIS, 3072

01.23 : Responding to call from residents in 104th Street Lower West District with Officer Sabinus. Unidentified lights and sound reported. Concerns over possible explosion. Investigated locality. In service way at rear of apart. block 3 found male child approx 7 or 8 years of age. Child was dressed in rags so poor they disintegrated to the touch. He appeared physically unharmed but confused. Did not respond coherently to questioning. Could not give name or explanation for his presence.

Extensive inquiries made among local residents but nobody could identify child. Accompanied child to Melcon Central Hospital where he was examined and pronounced physically fit, though still unresponsive. DNA test did not match with any family group on register. Communicated with Social Care Department and was advised to take child direct to local juvenile facility. Handed child into care of supervisor of Rexton Hall at 07.48.

End of duty period.
(signed)
Officer John Kale, MPD.